gay the pray away

natalie naudus

little mountain media

To everyone who was served hatred and told it was love:
We deserve better.

a note

Dear Reader,

When I started narrating audiobooks, I was drawn to queer stories, and I didn't know why. I came to realize that I saw myself reflected in these books, and that's how I came out to myself. As I deconstructed my strict religious childhood, I imagined what might have happened if I'd encountered a single queer book earlier in life, and how impactful that would have been. Then I dreamed up this story, set in the austere religious cult of my youth, where a bisexual girl finds a book that helps her find herself.

This book contains depictions of religious trauma, Christian nationalism, child abuse, and homophobia; but I've tried very hard, in this book as in life, to move through the darkness toward healing and love.

Natalie

gay the pray away

By Natalie Naudus

one

. . .

I cannot be trusted. It's one of the rules I've learned in this world I live in. My parents do not trust me, and I cannot trust myself. Even my *feelings* are lying to me. No matter how wrong something seems, I must ignore my feelings and trust only the Word of God as it is taught to me. Every question that is asked of me has a predetermined answer. I must always, *always* give the right answer.

I am always lying. I'm lying right now, with my face, during this prayer meeting. Mom prays, long and loud, and I keep my face still. Calm. Blank, through years of practice. Make the right shape, I tell myself, look devout. Draw your brows down, look like you are concentrating. You can *do* this, Valerie.

I try to focus on the prayers, but they just keep droning on. I wonder how many times my mom can say "Lord God" in one prayer. I stop counting after twenty. Cracking one eye open, I peek across the circle at Hannah. She's staring blankly at the carpet, but I catch her eye and she immediately looks away. Squeezes her eyes shut. Come on, Valerie, get your head in the game. Inhaling deeply, I carefully arrange my face into the shape of calm contemplation. I start to exhale but stop the breath. Slow down, don't sigh. Don't do anything that could be considered disrespect. Just a slow, gentle exhale.

"And, Lord God, we pray for our sister Donna's daughter, Lord God. May she, Lord God, find you, Lord God, and follow your ways, Lord God," Mom goes on.

I'm tight inside. I don't like prayer time. I might even *hate* prayer time. But prayer is important. Obviously. Prayer is talking to God and only a heathen would hate talking to God, and I am definitely not that. *Definitely* not. I breathe deep again and squeeze my feelings tighter, smaller; I mold the shape of my face stiller, calmer. Mom elbows me. Oh, she's stopped praying. Crap, it's my turn. *Say something.* I give myself a desperate pep talk. What prayer can I pray that will glide by the scrutiny? What prayer will make them nod thoughtfully in agreement but not attract any probing questions later? I huff out a silent laugh at the hilarity of planning a prayer addressed to God but performed to impress the people listening.

"Heavenly Father," I start. I clear my throat. A solid start, but not passionate enough. Come on, Valerie. Sound devout. "Thank you for bringing us here today." I lean into it. That sounds better. "We thank you for the gift of fellowship with one another. We ask that you bless us and keep us close to you always." A bit short, but I'm out of things to say. For Pete's sake, we've been kneeling here for an hour already. "In your precious son's name we pray, amen."

A collective sigh escapes the group. Not relief, obviously—who would be relieved to be done with prayer time?—but there is a definite sigh released around the prayer circle. The women look around, blinking in the harsh light after so long with their eyes closed, rising from their knees and discreetly stretching. I get up from my knees and am heading toward my friend

Hannah when her brother Andrew rushes in front of me. His lanky form is all angles and awkwardness.

"Hey, Valerie," he mutters, eyes down, body slumping in on itself.

"Oh . . . hey, Andrew." I try to continue toward Hannah, but he doesn't move. "How are you?" I ask, trying to be polite, even though I'm not feeling very friendly. But it's fine, because guys aren't really supposed to talk to girls around here anyway. No dating and little interaction, except with the intention of marriage. Courtship, we call it.

"Good," he mumbles.

"Um, I'm gonna go talk to Hannah now—"

He turns and rushes away as I'm still talking. Alright then. That was . . . something.

"Hey, Hannah!"

"Valerie!" Hannah beams at me. "How was your week?"

"Good, how about you?"

"Absolutely wonderful!" Hannah chirps. Looking into Hannah's smile is a bit like looking into the sun. It's blindingly bright, and a little ragey.

"Did you write your paper yet?" I ask.

"Yup! Thirty pages on the Ark of the Covenant and its message for our daily lives! You?"

"Not quite; I need to go to the library to do some research. I have a few things I want to look up."

"Oh really? I just used our Bible Encyclopedia!"

"Oh yeah, yeah I guess I could, I just wanted to do some more research."

Hannah grabs me by the arm and pulls me in closer. Her eyes quiver with excitement as she leans in and whispers urgently, "The Zellers scheduled a meeting with my parents!"

I wince and lean away at her squealing. My mind flashes to

the Zeller family. Ten children, fifteen-passenger van, kind of cute son named Seth . . . oh. *Oh.*

"You mean . . ."

"Yup!" Hannah shrills.

"You don't think . . . ?"

"*I think so!*" Hannah whisper-shouts, in a state of glee a few steps above her normal blinding cheer.

"But Hannah," I tilt my head, trying to put this gently. "You're only sixteen."

"Almost seventeen," she says defensively. "So by the time we finish our courtship—"

"I mean, yeah, I guess."

"I am *dying* of excitement. I mean, our families have so much in common! The Zellers have ten children, we have nine; we drive the same fifteen-passenger vans; we both even have the same kind of chicken! White leghorns! I mean, it's just so . . ." Hannah runs out of breath. Refills her lungs. "It just feels so right. Like the Lord has been planning this and is bringing us together in His perfect timing."

"Are you sure you want to? Getting married, I mean, it just seems . . ."

Hannah's bright smile drops so suddenly, I feel the mental whiplash. Gone is the bright cheerful countenance. The face beneath is suspicious and disapproving.

"Marriage is God's plan for women, Valerie." She leans into my name. A warning.

"Well, I'm happy for you," I backpedal. "Keep me posted."

"I will!" Hannah replaces her smile swiftly and securely. It's so strong, I wonder if I imagined the shadowy moment before.

"Alright." Hannah turns to leave. "I've got to get these littles to the bathroom and get the babies changed before we head out. I'll call you!"

4

I watch her skip across the room, vibrating with excitement, as she heads off to collect her many younger siblings. At sixteen years old, Hannah is as competent as any adult. She cooks meals, washes laundry, watches her siblings, spanks them with a wooden spoon as efficiently as any parent, teaches them to read and write. She seems mature enough to be married, sure, but I can't help thinking about how young she still is. I'm only seventeen myself, and certainly not ready to start courting anyone.

But that is what we've been taught. That courtship and marriage are the correct path for women of God. Men are raised to provide for their families, to lead and protect, and us women are to care for them and bear their children. To fill our husband's quivers with arrows for the Lord. I know this. I've heard it in sermons and devotionals and lectures again and again. And even though it sometimes stings to hear that I am not my own, that I belong to my dad and God and my future husband, that's my own sinful nature letting doubt creep into my mind. And so, I'm trying to pray. To hear the voice of God and believe what I've been taught with all my heart. And I hope that with enough faith, things will finally feel right, and I will feel the joy and peace that God gives to those who trust Him.

It's Thursday morning, and I'm sitting at the kitchen table for our family's morning devotional, staring blearily at the steam rising from my mug of tea. We go around the table and each read a verse from a chapter of Proverbs, taking turns until we've read the whole chapter aloud. I try to stay focused, but my mind drifts, my eyes glazing over as the drone of Scripture washes over me.

"Alright, take a minute and pick your verse," Dad says, and we all study the open pages of our Bibles intently. I begin to sigh, but stop, straightening my posture and letting the air out slowly. It's too early to give my parents something to lecture me about.

"A wise son heareth his father's instruction: but a scorner heareth not rebuke." Dad leans back, rests his hands on his belly. I can tell he's getting ready for one of his mini sermons.

"You children, David and Valerie"—he glances at each of us —"have a duty to this family. To listen to my instruction and obey always. To bring *honor* to our family. You know, honor is so important in Chinese culture." Inwardly, I groan and roll my eyes. Outwardly, I keep my face still. It's weird how Mom is the one who is actually Asian—she's from Taiwan—but my dad is the one always lecturing us on Asian culture. I joke to Hannah sometimes that my dad is more Asian than my mom, what with his lectures on honor and respect and familial duty. Honestly, it bothers me for reasons I can't quite explain, but when I've mentioned it to Mom, she tells me that we need to make sure Dad feels respected. And that means never contradicting him. So I sit and I nod, even if my thoughts are elsewhere.

Mom goes next with her favorite verse, and then it's David's turn. He's slouching sullenly in his chair, a dark hoodie pulled over his head. He's the physical embodiment of my feelings about morning devotionals, but I know I could never get away with looking that uninterested. The standards for me, the girl, are totally different.

"Sit up straight, David," Mom fusses at him. Ah, so he's actually getting a taste of the parental disapproval today. About time.

David slouches deeper. Well *someone* is feeling brave today.

"David," Dad says sternly. He sits up immediately.

"Take off your hood," Mom insists. David throws his head back in annoyance then reaches up and pulls his hood down, releasing a poof of coarse black hair that stands nearly straight up from his head.

"Aiya, you need to brush your hair before morning devotionals!" Mom chides him, but she stops when my dad gives her a look that says he wants to handle it. I shift in my seat. I was planning to ask for a trip to the library today, but if David screws things up for me by putting our parents in a bad mood . . .

"Go ahead," Dad prompts. We wait.

"Um, yeah, I guess the same one as you, Dad." David shrugs.

"And *why* did you pick that one?" Mom probes. David sits up straighter, and I see the moment his mask descends. The veneer of calm that I know so well. Don't show your feelings, don't admit you aren't enjoying the Bible study, just say the words they want to hear so we can all move on.

"Because, like you said, we have to bring honor to the family," David parrots.

"Great!" Mom beams. "Valerie? Your verse?"

I am prepared. I've been studying the chapter for the shortest verse: one that I can say the least about while still satisfying the unspoken but very real word quota of how much I'm expected to say. It's roughly two to four sentences per theoretical spiritual brownie point.

"Yeah, um, verse ten. 'Only by pride cometh contention: but with the well-advised is wisdom.'" I pause, take a nervous sip of my tea.

"Go on," Dad says.

"Well, I know I've been argumentative lately. With you." I nod at Mom and Dad. "And I'm going to try to listen better."

My parents beam. They love nothing more than when I

examine myself and come to the conclusion that I'm in the wrong and they are right. I can't always stomach acting this grossly submissive, but I need something from them today, so I can't take any chances. They may think they are the masters of me, but I'm always finding ways to manipulate them. When you've lived your life being as controlled as I have, you learn to quietly turn things around.

Prayers are prayed, and we all head out. Dad to work, David to his room to do his schoolwork. He stays up there all day, headphones on, hood up; no one knows exactly what he does, but as long as he says he is "studying," my parents don't seem to question much. I am not privy to such faith. Everything I do is under scrutiny. Taking a deep breath, I get ready to make my move.

"Hey, Mom, I need to go to the library. To do some research for my paper, for co-op. It's due tomorrow. Could we go?"

"Valerie! Why are you so late finishing it? I thought you wrote it already!"

"Oh yeah, it's mostly done, really, I just wanted to check out some more books for reference."

"We bought all those Bible encyclopedias, what else could you need?"

"Well, I wanted to relate it to current affairs a bit more? I heard on the radio about a new Sean Hannity book that sounded really good . . ." The bait is set. I see Mom consider the idea, happy that I've been listening to conservative talk radio instead of complaining about our strict music rules. I'm basically only allowed to listen to two radio stations: conservative talk radio, and the classical music station. The Christian radio station is acceptable only during sermons, but when a praise song comes on I have to switch it off. Praise music is "rock music," and rock music is sinful, of the devil, and not allowed. But I've been so good lately, and I kissed up especially hard this morning. I can see Mom bending. Victory. I can already smell the warm woody essence of an unread book.

"You know I really don't like you spending so much time in your fantasy worlds. I know you are hoping to get some new books to read for fun." She sighs as she gathers the mugs of tea from the table. "Alright, sure, we can go. Let's go now so you have time to finish writing it tonight. Only three fun books though, understand? David?" she calls up the stairs. "Do you need anything from the library?"

The library is a haven. On a Thursday morning, it's pretty quiet since most kids are, you know, in school. Mom sets up at a table close to the Young Adult section with her Bible, a devotional book, and her weekly planner. I want nothing more than to dive into the YA section and read absolutely everything, but my cover is that I'm here to research.

Many of my friends aren't allowed to read library books at all, unless it's a book recommended by a fellow homeschooling parent, and even then, their parents usually read the book first to check for "harmful liberal ideology." My parents tried to follow those rules, but I read so much and ask for new books so often, they've relaxed the rules. As long as the cover looks nice, I'm well behaved, and I suck up enough, I can read books for fun after school. I've gotten really good at figuring out which covers look acceptable to my parents and which covers will invite unwelcome scrutiny. Castles, flowy dresses without cleavage, and abstract art are good. Witches, wizards, and romance are bad.

There was a scandal a few years back when my mom organized a protest outside the library. I held a sign that read "Don't sexualize children" along with my mom and other church families for a few days, protesting a "sinful" book that had been placed in the YA section. But we won, the book was removed, and my mom's faith in the library seems restored.

The truth is, I live to read. Every chance I get, I'm tucked in my closet, devouring anything I can get my hands on. My life and world feel so small and strict and cold. I see the same people all the time who believe the same things, dress the same, talk the same, look the same. But books? Books are my escape.

Passing the YA section with longing, I first head over to the adult nonfiction section and pull the books I said I came for. As I pass from one stack to the next, a light-pink cover on the reshelving cart catches my eye. I lean down to read the title. *One Last Stop* by Casey McQuiston. I glance discreetly toward my mom. Still at the table. Snatching up the book, I crouch down behind the stack and flip through the book with curiosity, and then intensity, as I realize what I'm holding.

This is the most forbidden of books. A gay book. A liberal agenda, gay agenda, gay book. But it doesn't look evil and harmful; it looks pretty and joyful, and the pages smell faintly, impossibly of peaches. I know I should replace it and move on, never give it a second thought, but I'm mesmerized. I speed-read the first chapter and then lean out of the stack to check on my mom—she's still at the table. My breath is quivering, my fingers trembling, and I know time is running out. I should put the book back, walk away, forget about it, but something is fizzing inside me. I've never seen a book like this, and I don't know that I'll ever see one again. My eyeballs are *vibrating*. I'm zooming through the pages, and on page thirty-six as two girls are flirting with each other, I see the word *bisexual*. I have never, never seen this word before, and the room is spinning with the importance of it.

I lean out again—Mom is packing up her stuff, looking around for me. I know I cannot check out this book. There is no way that I can be seen with this book, and yet I *must* read it. I don't have a phone, and our internet has "family safety" censors with parental alerts. If this moment passes, it passes for eternity. Suddenly, impulsively, I reach under my shirt and tuck the book into the waistband of my denim skirt. My modest, baggy homeschooler blouse covers the bump. If I can just—

A crash. A librarian is standing at the end of the stack, staring at me, his mouth hanging open, the cart he was pushing having slammed into the shelf. I freeze. He's staring at me, his glasses askew, his hands still gripping the wheeled book cart, and I am sure I look as guilty as any guilty criminal has ever guilted. I have no idea how to explain the book in my waistband, the Gay Book that I am so obviously stealing. I slowly pick up my stack of nonfiction, back out of the aisle, and, heart pounding, head back to my mom.

Mom says she'll meet me in the car. I use the self-checkout for the nonfiction books, head toward the exit, walk through the lane dividers . . . oh crap! The alarm is going off—these aren't lane dividers, they are freaking security devices! I have never even *thought* of stealing anything *ever*. The functionality of things designed to catch *thieves* has never been of any concern to me, and now what, are the police going to come and arrest me?

"Miss?" I turn slowly to face the desk, and there is the cart-crashing librarian. I draw my eyes up his corduroy pants, past his sweater-vest to his bespectacled face. The whine of the alarm turns off. He smiles at me, a wide tense smile, full of meaning. "Our system is so buggy today, you're good!"

I stare. He gives me a look. I keep staring. I've been caught. Is he really going to let me go?

"Have a nice day!" he says with a get-out-already glance at the door and, in a daze, I turn and walk away. Picking up speed, I push through the door into the bathroom by the exit. I'm shaking. I'm a freaking *criminal* and, good grief, I have never felt so alive. I shove the books into my backpack—The Book on the very bottom—and run out of the bathroom, out the front doors, and throw myself into the car.

"My goodness, Valerie, calm down!" my mom says in exasperation. "Move slower, more ladylike!"

I nod wordlessly.

"Did you get what you needed?"

"Hah!" I bark, something between a cough and a laugh. "Yeah, I think I did."

two

. . .

When I get home, I deposit my backpack safely in my room, in the back of the closet, under an old coat. It should be safe. For now. I wish I could ditch everything and read. My fingers are itching to run along the dimpled spine while I lose myself in the pages, but it's just too risky. Appearances must be maintained. My best chance of preserving the secrecy of my contraband is, as always, a lying face. Slow movements. Outward obedience. I do a lot of schoolwork on my own, but I never know when Mom will pop in to check on me. I need to stick to my homeschooling routine.

Here's the thing. There are homeschoolers, and there are *homeschoolers*. My family is the italicized version. We are part of a homeschooling program called GTA, the God's Training Academy, which is an offshoot of IGBP, the Institute of God's Basic Principles. These people really love acronyms. We usually just call it the Institute. It's a Southern Baptist–themed homeschooling curriculum headed by a charismatic man named Ben Goddard and endorsed by some pretty big conservative pastors and politicians. The core teaching is that every-thing—and they do mean *everything*—that children need to learn is found in the holy book. The Bible. The B.I.B.L.E.

But, to expand on that boundless resource, they've made these Virtue Booklets. Each one breaks down a single Bible verse into different study areas: linguistics, history, science, law, and medicine. The homeschooling families in our circle study *only* these books, one Virtue Booklet per month. They read them, they memorize them, they transcribe them, they write papers on them.

My dad takes a slightly more lax view. He thinks we need some supplementary subjects like math and science. Mom disagrees and is concerned about the "worldly influence" of these subjects, so I know I'm lucky to have math and science books at all. But of course, the math and science curriculum we use is carefully vetted and biblically based; there are no mentions of leftist lies like evolution or global warming to be found in these books.

I wasn't always homeschooled. I was in public school through third grade, which would probably shock Hannah and the other members of the Institute, so I keep it to myself. It's funny how my family never *decided* to bury the fact that we used to be evil Public Schoolers, but the understanding that we needed to appear as devout as our friends just sort of washed over us, and we silently agreed to play the part of dedicated, lifelong members of the Institute.

I don't have a really clear memory of Springwood Elemen-tary, just vague recollections of smiling teachers, plastic lunch trays of square pizza and canned peaches, another girl in my class named Valerie with perfect dimples. But that last year in public school, my parents got super into Ben Goddard. We spent weekends traveling to his conferences in neighboring states, eating cold sandwiches in parking lots so we could hurry back into the church to catch the next sermon. After the first day of the conference, we'd rent a room at a cheap hotel and, after fighting with David for the blankets, I'd sleep in an angry heap on the floor, wedged between the air conditioning unit and the bed frame. We'd wake up early, eat a bleary-eyed hotel breakfast of a glazed donut and orange juice, and head back to the church for another full day of sermons.

At some point, after endless hours of droning talks about God's Plan for Families and the Biblical Roles of Men and Women, I'd beg my mom to let me lie down on the floor. Most churches had these sturdy sanctuary chairs, and I'd crawl under them, fitting myself snugly between the legs, tucked into the dark, the sound of Ben Goddard's voice slightly muffled by the cushions and clothing. I'd lie there with the cold metal gripping my shoulders, staring up at the underside of the square blue cushion, wondering when this family obsession was going to end.

I missed weekends spent picnicking at parks. I missed heading to the Millers' house next door on Saturdays to eat cold pop tarts and watch cartoons with their twins, Mari and Jamie. I didn't like the shift I felt, the new Religious Adult I was expected to be, my parents' expectations of me growing more rigid with every sermon on Raising Obedient Children and Taming the Wild Heart.

In the van on the way home from these conferences, my parents would enthusiastically recount what they'd learned, excited to "apply it to our lives." And bit by bit, we became Goddardites. Mom and Dad pulled us out of school and subscribed to the curriculum from the Institute. I was told not to prepare myself for a career, but to look forward to being a godly wife and mother. David was to grow into a man, a leader, and a provider. College was now "secular education" and forbidden. Ben Goddard's rules on modesty were implemented in our home. I was no longer allowed to wear pants, only loose skirts and dresses. I had to hide my figure and "avoid the gaze of men." My parents took the "cause not thy brother to stumble" bit literally and would ask David to look at me to decide if my outfit was in any way inspiring lustful thoughts. And over time, it all just became the new normal.

At this point, I've been a part of it so long, I'm so isolated from "the world," it's hard to know what I believe. Where I fall into all this. Some of it feels wrong to me, but all my friends now are obedient members of the Institute, and they accept these teachings implicitly. So there must be something wrong with *me*? My attitude and perception? I used to whine and complain about the Ben Goddard teachings and the endless sermons and Bible study, but I've been told the problem is me so often, I guess I believe it.

I catch glimpses of another world out there, kids playing sports or hanging with friends, but it's mostly through the windows of the van on the way to and from church. I stopped seeing my school friends. I stopped being allowed to watch cartoons. I only see my cousins twice a year, and they seem so unlike me. I'm technically not yet an adult, I guess, but I've been spanked and disciplined and molded into a submissive biblical mannequin. My relatives comment on how mature and well behaved we are, and my parents beam and credit Ben Goddard's teachings. To be honest, I'm lonely and frustrated, struggling to accept what I'm told is my place in the world. But when I fail to conceal my thoughts, when I disagree and raise concerns, I'm told to examine my own sinful self. To pray and strive to be more joyful and more content. So I'm trying.

I make myself a quick sandwich for lunch and hurry

through my math lesson. Mom, David, and I sit at the kitchen table and read out loud through a few pages of a Virtue Booklet. There are only so many Virtue Booklets in existence, and it's the second time we've studied this one. Mom dismisses me from schoolwork for the day with a reminder to check the homework for my online chemistry class and then, finally, I'm free. I do a little skip on the way to the stairs, stop myself, and climb oh so calmly and ladylike to my room. I close but don't lock the door; locking my door is not allowed, as it could help "hide sin"—exactly what, I've never figured out, but I guess I'm up to no good today so perhaps the rule makes sense.

I climb into my closet and shut the closet door.

My closet is dark and warm, smelling of wool and dust. It's the only place in all the world where I feel safe. Blessedly unseen. I feel around and plug in the white string of Christmas lights, and they warm the small dark space with their soft, kind glow. I crawl over shoes, a textbook, a crumpled sweater—and there, in the very back, with the hangers of clothes pushed forward to make a small pocket of air, I pull *One Last Stop* out of my bag and get to work.

I don't start reading right away, oh no. I must be smarter than that. More cautious. I worry the corner of the cover back and forth with my thumb until the layers start splitting. Carefully, I begin to peel off the beautiful pastel cover, whispering a prayer for forgiveness. I choke on a laugh—who am I praying to? To *God*, to forgive me for peeling the cover off an "evil" book? Maybe I'm praying to the book itself? I really don't know. I feel reckless. Impulsive. Feelings so unfamiliar, I thought they had left me entirely.

Shred by shred, the picture disappears until all that's left is a fluffy pink bird's nest of paper. Filling the pockets of my long denim skirt, I head to the bathroom and carefully flush the scraps. After washing my hands, I check and see that there's one tiny sliver of pink clinging to the side of the toilet bowl. I flush again and watch it disappear in the swirl of water. I head back to my room, close the door, dive into the closet, and finally take up the book again.

I laugh briefly at the absurdity of what I'm doing. I know I'm acting paranoid, like a freaking prisoner, but if my parents realize what I want and why, they will never ever stop praying at me. They'll isolate me further, which feels impossible, but there are still things they can take away. Tiny pockets of joy they can extract and crush. My brother was into some "sinful ungodly things" on the internet—I was never told what, exactly—and my parents got rid of the wi-fi. They removed his bedroom door, took him to the men's group where I'm guessing they laid hands on him to pray the sin away, and then made him wake up early for an extra daily devotional with Dad for a year—so no, I don't think I'm overreacting.

I steady my breathing, take up a pad of sticky notes, and print carefully, clearly: "Found after Prayer Group—take to church lost and found?" I affix this to the front of the mangled cover. Now, in case Mom or Dad or David finds it, I can explain that it was left by accident by a family who came over for Prayer Group at some point, and how I plan to return it to church but keep forgetting. And no, of *course* I haven't read it.

Mom tends to tear through my closet and drawers on occasion, sometimes looking for something specific, other times just looking. I'm told that it's my parents' responsibility to keep me accountable. To make sure I'm not hiding anything. Not "falling into sin." Until now, I've never known what I could possibly be hiding besides a library book with a swear word in it, but now I have something I know is forbidden and I am terrified. Finally, with my nervously chewed short nails, I carefully back the screws out of the air vent cover, place the book as far inside as I can reach, and replace the cover.

I start to leave the closet but hesitate. If it's found, it'll be obvious that I hid it. But what could possibly cause someone to look in my air vent? Air vent cleaners? I can't take the chance. I vaguely recall reading some mystery where a woman hid something in plain sight.

"Valerie?" I start violently at Mom's voice from downstairs. "Time to make dinner!"

"Be there in a minute!" I call, hoping my voice sounds steadier than it feels.

My heart is pounding, my brain stuttering with the immensity of my sin. I throw myself to the floor and back the screws out again. Remove the book and replace the vent cover. Then I put the book on my bookshelf. Flat against the back. I slide the Bible and a few Elsie Dinsmore books back into place, blocking the book from view. I hope it's enough.

I lie in bed listening for hours, watching the shadows crawl across the ceiling whenever a car drives by outside. Around eleven, I hear the indistinct sounds of Mom and Dad talking quietly in their bedroom. And then finally, silence. As quietly as I can, I crack my door open and peek into the hallway. Their light is off. David's light is off. All is quiet.

Just as I'm turning back into my room, I see David's light pop on and hear him shuffling around. He must've been waiting for our parents to go to bed too, some late night entertainment planned. We kind of have an unspoken agreement, David and me, that we don't tattle on each other. This place is strict enough, with our parents constantly searching for reasons to punish us, that we generally let the little things slide. Sometimes we even feel sorry for each other and try to divert attention if we can, when we know a parent is in an especially bad mood, when something minor is likely to get a severe punishment.

I know David is on his computer late at night, has hacked the neighbor's wi-fi so he can surf the web and watch pirated anime. Mom and Dad think he has no internet access since they changed the password and hardwired the office computer. They think it's the sole source of internet in the house. They think David is always studying and learning programming languages, and I've kept his secret. He knows I check out stacks of books that aren't parentally approved from the library and like to stay up late reading. It's a quiet truce among prisoners.

Slipping the stolen book up and out of its hiding place on the shelf, I head into my closet, close the door, and grope around in the darkness for the plug. I scrape the prongs around on the wall, feeling for the moment they slip into the socket, and the soft gentle glow of the white string of lights illuminates the space. I breathe deeply of the close, dusty air. I like to imagine it's a fairy cave in here. A magical little alcove all my own, glimmering softly with the secrets of the books I've read in here, the stories I've dreamed but don't dare write down. Mom likes to ask me why I spend so much time in my imagination, why I can't just read more nonfiction books about being a godly woman and preparing myself for motherhood, but honestly? I hate those books. This sacred space all my own is for beautiful dreams. This is my escape from the gross, unwanted hug of reality.

Tucking myself into the back corner, I cover my lap with an old blanket. It's cool in here. I know it'll quickly grow hot and stuffy with my own body heat, but I don't care. I love the feeling of curling up with a blanket and a book. I wish I could light a candle to set the mood, feel the awe of beginning this new, stolen book properly, but I know that would be stupid in a closet. Still, I squint and look around at the lights, seeing them blur and sparkle and flicker. I imagine them as candles, each one a tiny sacred flame. The tone set, I squirm a bit, sigh happily at the quiet bliss of the moment, open the book on my lap, and begin to read.

three

. . .

I jerk awake. A long string of drool clings wetly to my chin, and I smear it away with my hand as I sit up blearily. I feel a book tumble off my lap, and start violently. Oh no. I'm still in the closet. I fell asleep and now Dad is blaring the morning hymns from the downstairs speakers and Mom will be coming in at any moment to make sure I'm awake.

Heaving myself to my feet, I smack my head on the clothing rod. Gosh *darn* it! Blinking to clear the spots in my vision, I throw myself out of the closet. The cool air of my room hits my face, making me realize how stuffy that closet was, as I hear Mom coming down the hallway, calling out.

"Ten minutes, David," I hear her say as the handle of my door begins to turn. I snatch my Bible desperately from the shelf, launch it at my bed, and throw myself to my knees. The fabric of my nightgown digs into my skin as I clasp my hands in pretend supplication, elbows propped up on the bed.

"Rise and shine and give God the glory! Oh!" Mom switches to a whisper. "See you downstairs in ten minutes, sweetie. Remember we have Bible group today." She shuts the door quietly.

Collapsing face-first into the mattress in a moment of pure relief, I allow myself a deep, comforting sniff of my faded floral comforter. And then I get to work. Book fetched from the closet and concealed. Modest, parent-approved clothing donned. Hair brushed, face splashed with water. I run downstairs and am just sliding into my seat at the round table in the kitchen as Dad takes his seat opposite me.

"Late night *studying*, huh?" David whispers.

"Late night studying, *huh?*" I mutter back at him. We share a secret smirk, but then Dad clears his throat and begins yet another family devotional.

Dad prays first, and I try desperately to pay attention, but my mind keeps wandering to the book I spent all night reading. Then, as we move on to Psalms, Dad's voice a steady droning cadence, I finally have a moment to reflect.

I've perfected the art of a soft gaze. I look at the page of the Bible but unfocus my eyes and let my brain go where it wants. It's a fun trick I've learned after years of endless devotionals, lectures, Bible studies, and sermons. Eyes unfocused but pointed toward the page of my Bible, I let my mind drift back to the book I'd stayed up almost all night reading. Reviewing phrases, ideas; replaying scenes in my head. I'd never seen or heard the words *bisexual* or *queer* before, but my mind leaps around. Filling in the blanks. I've heard sermons and lectures and devotionals and gossip about gay people. Homosexuals. It all seemed very binary. Simple. Obvious. I've been told that being gay is a "poor choice" that some people make, and obviously I'm too smart and obedient to make a poor choice like that.

But as I'd lost myself in the book last night, I'd felt myself spinning through an absolute tangled galaxy of possibilities.

This world of gay and queer people in the book seems so joyful. It seems warm and fun and . . . relaxing? I know that's a ridiculous way to put it, but the characters in the book were just living life. Experiencing new things. They did of course think and reflect and have internal conflict, but none of it is the microscope of spiritual anguish that is my every waking moment. Friends and lovers in this book world *embrace* each other's individuality. They don't seem repulsed by differences. Most of all, there is an absence of fear.

I've heard the verse "perfect love casteth out fear" a million times, but I don't think I've ever seen it until I looked in this book. Acceptance. Friendship. Love. Love that transcends time and boundaries and all reason. A life of living, rather than hiding. Of sharing rather than shunning. I wish with all my heart that I knew how to get from this never-ending spiritual monotony to there.

"Valerie."

I jerk back to the table with a start. Dad is stern, frowning at me. Mom's gaze is probing. David looks quietly delighted that it isn't *his* turn in the hot seat today.

"It's your turn to read," Mom repeats with impatience. They've moved on to Proverbs, and my Bible is still open to Psalms. Crap.

"Oh, oops, um, what chapter are we on?"

David leans toward me and whispers, "Fourteen," but it's too late. My parents have already noticed my inattention.

"Come on, Valerie. Stop daydreaming and focus on the Word," Mom chides.

"Valerie," Dad starts, "we need to talk"—my heart constricts at his warning, the word *talk* triggers a squeezing in my lungs that I associate with lectures and prayers and the nightmare my parents call family meetings—"about your passion for the Word. If you can't focus during devotionals, if you aren't giving the respect and attention that the Word of God deserves . . ." He pauses for effect. I lower my head, trying to hide the annoyance I feel rising and quickly turning to anger as it thrums through my blood.

"Look at me!" Dad commands. So I look. I stare straight into his eyes, and I let a tiny flicker of the fire I feel burn there. The hot coal of hatred for every humiliation and degradation. Every spanking and scolding and lecture, every demand for respect from those who treat me with nothing but *disrespect*.

"Valerie!" Mom gasps. "Look down. Do not look your father in the eye with rebellion."

Slowly, savoring the rush of this tiniest sliver of autonomy, I push my eyes down to my Bible. Shuffle the crispy, fragile pages to the right place. I read aloud: "The simple believeth every word: but the prudent man looketh well to his going."

For one crystal moment, my mind is completely focused on the Bible. This verse, is it a . . . a sign? I've been believing every word. I've been following the rules. I've been squeezing and tucking and shrinking myself into the image of the perfect daughter of Christ. I am always failing and hating myself for failing day after day. Year after year. But now my eyes are open. And I. Am. Looking.

four

. . .

"Aren't you going to help carry these?" Mom calls after me, irritation lining her voice. I pause on my way into Hannah's house, groan quietly, and turn back to the van to help her with the bags.

"Did you pack everything you need for tonight?" Mom frets. "I didn't have time to check."

"I think I'm old enough to pack for myself, Mom." I pat my backpack before slinging it onto my back. "It's just one night."

"Make sure you two actually focus and have a productive evening. I know how chatty you and Hannah get."

"Why didn't David carry something?" I complain, ignoring her jab about my level of productivity.

"He has friends to talk to, you can handle this. Move quickly, class is starting soon."

Hannah's family is hosting our weekly Bible class at their big house about an hour from us. We're the only family in our circle to live in a suburban neighborhood; most families have sprawling property in the country. Isolation is an implied tenet of the Institute's doctrine. I'm staying tonight to pack blessing

Gay the Pray Away

bags for the local crisis pregnancy center. My parents said
something about it counting as a school activity because it's
community service. Whatever. The homeschool parents I know
will justify anything as educational.

As I climb the steps to the front door, paper grocery bags
crinkling in my hands, I see Hannah waving frantically from an
upstairs window. As I enter, I hear her flying down the stairs,
skirt swishing, socked feet thumping. She rushes into the foyer
and drags me to the study.

"Oh my *goodness* do I have news," she gushes breathlessly.

"Where should I put these?"

"Oh, here. Just put them in the corner." She grabs a bag
from me and tosses it carelessly. There's a pile of boxes and
bags in the corner, overflowing with diapers, blankets, and cans
of formula.

"Should I put my backpack in your room?"

"Valerie, just put it down. I have *news!*"

"About Seth?"

"Oh. Yes. But also—" Hannah lets it hang there, eyes
gleaming with the thrill of it. As much as we are admonished
not to gossip, gossip might be Hannah's entire personality. She
easily passes it off as a prayer request or concern, just like her
mom does. Actually, all the parents use this trick, now that I
think about it. "Remember how your mom prayed for Miss
Donna's daughter last week?"

"I . . . guess?" I vaguely remember hearing Mom pray about
that, but honestly, I tend to zone out during prayer time. And
sermons. And devotionals. I zone out a lot.

"Well, word is that she got kicked out of the private school
they were sending her to and they joined the Institute. She's
coming *today!*"

"What?"

"An honest-to-goodness *troubled youth* is going to be here!

Can you *believe* it?!" Hannah is whisper-shouting so urgently, I'm being blasted with her warm oatmeal breath.

"I'm only telling you this because"—ah, here comes the justification for the gossip— "Mom told me we need to be extra friendly to her, and minister to her. It's a great chance for us to show her Christ's love." She finishes rationalizing, but I don't care. There's something refreshing about Hannah's enthusiasm. Everyone else pretends not to enjoy gossiping so much, with solemn nods and promises to "lift the issue up in prayer" and "bring it before the Lord." Hannah clearly gossips for the thrill of it, and honestly, I enjoy it.

"She's the only child in her family, can you *imagine?* They must be new to the faith to have stopped at only one!" Hannah pauses and seems to realize what she's saying. My family is very small by Institute standards, and we stick out. The Pattersons have nine children, and they aren't even the largest family I know. It's weird how she just assumes people are less devout when they have fewer children, but most people I know would agree and find that thinking normal. I feel like such a weirdo, but I try to keep my thoughts to myself. No need to step into the path of my parents' wrath today.

"Anyways, *yes* I also have exciting Seth news to share with you, but we can chat toniiiiight," she sings, grinning at me. "I can't believe my parents agreed to a sleepover. I've never had a friend over before! But of course it's all about the blessing bags and being of service . . . Oops class is about to start, let's go!" She grabs my wrist and pulls me toward the family room. I almost trip over her brother Andrew as we go through the doorway.

"Andrew, *move*," Hannah says as we pass. He raises his hand to wave at me shyly and I try to raise mine back, but Hannah pulls me away.

Kitchen chairs and couches are arranged in rows and Mr.

Patterson, Hannah's dad, is getting ready to start. He's a local real estate agent who seems to make a good living selling houses to and from other church members. He also teaches a Bible class to the three—well, now four—Institute families. Between the Virtue Booklets, devotionals, Bible classes, and church services, it all adds up to . . . well, a *lot* of Bible.

"Welcome, everyone! Come on in, take a seat, it's time to get started! Let's open in prayer!"

As he begins praying, I slide onto the couch next to Mom, and Hannah picks up one of her fussing baby siblings from the floor. I tune out the prayer, feeling the excitement of a new family joining our group. It's so rare to meet someone new—and that's usually at church. And this new girl has been to *private school?* Which is, according to the adults, only slightly better than public school. "They aren't really Christians" is something I hear said about less conservative denominations. Catholics, Unitarians . . . I once heard an adult say *Episcopalians* with such venom, they got spit on me. I feel a quiet buzz of excitement at meeting someone from the world. From the outside.

"Amen," everyone murmurs, clueing me in to the end of the prayer.

"Amen," I echo.

"Before we begin," Mr. Patterson says with a smile, "we'd like to welcome Donna and her daughter Riley."

Everyone turns to look to the back of the room. There, in the kitchen with Mrs. Patterson, is the most beautiful girl I've ever seen. The light from the bay window streams across Riley's light-brown skin, illuminating the soft dark curls of her pixie-cut hair. She's wearing a white T-shirt and jeans —*jeans*—and looking like the coolest person I have ever, *ever* seen.

"Riley, why don't you take a seat next to . . ." Mr. Patterson scans the room for an empty seat. "Valerie? She'll help you learn the ropes. Alright, let's get started!"

Riley slips wordlessly onto the sofa, the old cushions sagging, gravity drawing us closer together. My thigh is touching Riley's, and the warmth between us makes my heart feel very funny in my chest. Riley smells faintly of shampoo and grapefruit, and I've never paid less attention to what Mr. Patterson is saying.

My mind spins. She is too cool to be here. She's wearing *jeans*! She must not have gotten the memo that jeans aren't considered modest attire around here, that boys will look too long . . . good grief, *I* am looking too long. Oh my god. Wait, did I just swear? Oh. My GOD.

"Hey," Riley whispers, drawing me from my thoughts. I turn my head to her and we lock eyes, and if I swore, I would swear that I've never seen eyes this brown before. "Do you have an extra pencil?" she asks. "I think I'm supposed to take notes or something."

Riley's voice has a gentle rasp, and her face has the most perfect smirk, like she's here to play the game too. Like she already sees through the bullcrap.

"Oh. Um, yes, yeah, sure." I hand her my own pencil and pull an extra one from my bag.

"Thanks." Riley leans toward me and bumps shoulders with me. My mind is sparking. I drop my pencil. It is consumed by the depths of the sofa and I do not care.

I know I will think of nothing but this shoulder bump, this grapefruit-scented moment, for the rest of my lonely life.

After Bible class, we eat lunch. I'm sitting at a table with Hannah and four of the Patterson littles, but then the baby poops and Hannah rushes off to change her, and I'm left alone. Well, not exactly alone—just me and a few tiny kids munching on their food. The moms are chatting in the kitchen, and the rest of the kids have headed outside or to the basement.

"Hey, mind if I sit here?" Riley gestures toward an empty seat.

"Oh yeah. I mean no. I mean . . . yeah, go ahead." Wow. Really smooth, Valerie.

Riley sits and takes a bite of her sandwich. Her fingers are long and slender, her forearms muscular. I can't stop staring at them, and I've literally never noticed *anyone's* forearms before. Why the heck am I still looking at her arms? Get a grip on yourself, Valerie.

I'm trying my best to think of something friendly to say while also trying very hard not to stare at Riley, when she says, "So, how long have you been doing the homeschooling thing?"

"Oh um, a long time. I went to public school for a little bit, but homeschooling is pretty much all I remember."

"Oh yeah? You like it?"

"Yeah, of course. I mean, I guess."

"Cool." She eats a chip off her plate and I peel my eyes away. Take a sip of my water. Drain the whole glass. Is it hot in here? I should say something, probably. Anything.

"So you . . . went to private school?"

"Yeah, Coleville Christian since kindergarten. Mom thought it was time for a change though. Kind of sucks to leave for senior year, but I didn't love it there anyways. Looking forward to graduation and college."

"Oh wow, you plan to go to college?" Our homeschool group is strictly anti-college, especially for girls.

"Yeah, I'm big into art. I'm pretty good, too," she says casually. I'm stunned at how easily she said she's *good* at something. When I was younger I used to say things like that, but it's been trained out of me. *Don't boast, Valerie,* my mom would chide me, or Dad would quote the Bible: "Pride goeth before destruction, and a haughty spirit before a fall."

"Oh really?" I say. "I'd love to see your work sometime." Ugh, that probably sounded so *dumb.*

"Oh yeah? Cool!" Riley grins, then leans in conspiratorially. "So are you like, super horny for Jesus like everyone else or . . ."

I'm stunned. My heartbeat quickens as a dozen thoughts run through my mind. How can she tell I've been questioning? Is my internet search history written on my face? *Am* I still a firm believer? And then, instead of answering, I choke on my potato salad.

"Woah there, you okay?" She reaches out and pats my back. Her hand is warm and strong. "Take it easy there. Aw, shit." She glances at the little kids at the table. "I mean, shoot, you're out of water. Here, take mine."

She hands me her water and watches me take a sip.

"I'm . . ." I cough. "I'm fine now. Sorry about that."

"Sorry for choking? Hah. No worries. I didn't mean to make you uncomfortable."

"Oh no, you didn't, I just . . . well, maybe a little bit."

"Listen, I'm not here to cause any trouble. Just put in my time, graduate, and get out of here." I'm stunned at her frankness. And I realize as she says it, maybe that's what I want. Somehow. Girls don't really leave home around here without getting married, but the idea of actually getting out of here feels like the most irresistible, illicit fruit.

"It's a bit weird for me," I start. "I mean, I've been here most of my life." I pause. Why am I telling her this? I don't know if it's the isolation of this toddler table or how emotional I've been feeling lately or my secret stolen book, but I want to tell her everything. I want her to be my friend.

"I guess . . ." I lower my voice, glancing around. "I'm still figuring things out."

"Cool," Riley says, taking another bite of her sandwich.

"Cool?" I repeat. I've got to stop doing that. I'm just not used to having my words accepted. Refuted, contested, dissected—yes. Accepted? Never.

"Yeah, cool. You know, your feelings are your own."

"My feelings are my own," I repeat again. Ugh, *stop* that, Valerie.

"Yeah." She smiles. And she has dimples.

five

. . .

Hannah and I are packing blessing bags in the basement of her house. Well, we *plan* to, but first we are spending some time lying on our backs, staring at the ceiling. Mom went home with David, and the other families have left too. We track the gentle thump of feet above us as the Patterson children run back and forth. Hannah told them we were doing important work down here and they needed to stay away, and so far it's working. I imagine it's hard to get a minute to herself in a house this full.

Hannah is talking about something, but my mind is on Riley. *Riley.* I've never met anyone like her before. I can still feel the spot on my shoulder where she bumped me. When she smiled at me in the kitchen a few hours ago, those dimples paralyzed me. I wanted to reach out and poke my finger into their center so badly, my fingers twitched. And her *eyes.* The shades and veins of brown sparkling there. The warmth of her hand on my back.

"I just feel in the middle of it, you know? Like obviously I'm on my mom's side but Miriam and I used to be close, so it's all so weird." Hannah whacks me in the face with a stack of diapers. "Are you even *listening*?"

"Oh, um . . ." I start. "I guess I zoned out there, what were you saying? Sorry. What about your sister? I know you don't see her often."

"*Ever!*" Hannah sighs heavily. "We used to be pretty close, until she left, and I know Mom and Dad are really disappointed in her and her choices. I mean, the last time I saw her she was wearing *pants*! And had cut her hair *short*! You know what the Bible says about that."

I nod while searching my brain for the verse. Did the Bible say something specifically about women dressing feminine all the time? I know the rules of the Institute say so, but I can't seem to remember if or where the Bible specifically said that.

"Where is she living now?" I ask, to show I'm listening.

"With my grandparents! Have you even been paying attention?" Whoops. I must have missed more than I thought.

"And your parents are upset about that?"

"Obviously!" Hannah huffs. "She's rejecting the values we live by. I mean, she has a *job*, for Pete's sake! Women aren't supposed to work outside the home!"

I nod knowingly. I've heard this all many, many times. I think back to when I met Miriam years ago, vaguely recalling a thoughtful girl with long brown hair, always dressed in our uniform of a long skirt and baggy shirt. She's a few years older than me—a gap that seemed enormous back then. I haven't seen or thought about her in years.

"Are your grandparents Christians?" I sit up, idly stacking cans of formula.

"Well, they go to church, but I don't think they are saved. They don't follow any of the principles we follow."

"Can't they still be Christians and believe *some* things differently?"

"I don't think so. Dad and them have tense conversations whenever we see them. They go to a liberal church. They even ordain gay people, I think? Women can be pastors too? Sounds like fake Christians to me."

Hannah sits up abruptly. Reaches for the plastic bags. "I probably shouldn't be talking about it. It's just, hearing Mom arguing on the phone with Miriam the other day got me thinking about her again, that's all. It's all fine, it'll all work out!" she says with false cheer. "We should get to packing these."

When I reach for a stack of diapers, Hannah looks at my chest. She bristles.

"Valerie, I can see your *cleavage* when you lean over, keep it covered. *Honestly.*" I flush, readjusting my shirt. My neckline is high, but it's hard to keep it from gapping when I lean over. We get to work filling the bags, packing each one with an infant diaper, pro-life literature, a granola bar, a tiny pair of baby socks, and a small can of formula.

"Isn't it early to give them diapers and formula if they are just pregnant?" I remark idly, sliding a pamphlet into the bag, angling it so the smiling baby face is clearly visible.

"It's supposed to help trigger their maternal instinct, you know? Seeing the baby stuff will make them sentimental and delay getting an abortion or whatever." Hannah is filling bags twice as fast as I am.

"Doesn't that seem a little . . . I dunno, manipulative?"

"Valerie, stop talking and fill faster. You are so slow." Her tone is harsh. Parental. The tone I hear her take with her younger siblings.

I work in silence. Hannah gets snippy sometimes. I mean, she's basically a parent to her siblings on top of being a kid herself. It seems like a lot. Hannah works even faster and I realize, with growing horror, that there are tears in her eyes. I don't know what to do. I've never seen her cry before, and her face is forcefully stony. But there they are: tell-tale tears brimming, one escaping to run down her cheek. She brushes it away angrily.

"Are you . . . okay?" I ask carefully.

"I'm *great*," she says harshly. Her mouth twists a bit, but she forces it back. I'm honestly shocked that tear left her eye. I'd expect her to order that salty drop to march back up her face and never dare appear again. Hannah is the most violently cheerful person I know. Her mask *never* cracks. My parents hold her up repeatedly as the kind of virtuous young woman I should aspire to be. Seeing her lose her cool is like biting into a donut and finding it filled with mustard instead of cream. It's just *unthinkable*.

"Is it something I said?"

"Oh just *stop*, Valerie," she says angrily. Then she composes herself. "Everything is great. Absolutely wonderful." She smiles at me, but it's more of a grimace. I've never seen her this out of control. I want to hug her but I'm also afraid she's going to snap. I guess, maybe, I'm not the only one with a fragile, faded mask.

"Is it . . . about Miriam?" I venture. Hannah's face crumples, desperate and ugly, and the tears begin to fall in earnest. I'm weirdly terrified by the display of genuine emotion, but she seems less angry now, so I reach over and rub her back gently. She cries—weeps, really—hot angry tears running down her face, gathering in her mouth, bursting around her teeth. I can't really understand what she's saying around her sobs. Something about . . . missing Miriam, and her parents being angry, and trying to keep everyone's secrets. She clenches her fists and starts beating her own head with startling force.

"Hey. *Hey!*" I gently push her hands down. She stops crying abruptly, shaking me off her. Then she stands, wipes her face, and smooths her skirt. I can see so clearly that her mask has been replaced. She cracked for a minute, but she is newly resolved to never let it happen again. I know the feeling well.

"Hannah, it's okay to . . . feel." I'm stumbling over my words. This is unfamiliar territory. I remember Riley telling me "your feelings are your own" earlier. What a new concept. It feels weird, but not *bad* weird. Good weird maybe? Maybe that idea could help Hannah?

"I suppose all of us in the Institute feel like we have to . . . you know, be perfect all the time, but maybe it's okay to . . . feel things sometimes?"

"I'm *fine*, Valerie. You are so slow, honestly. Finish your half, I'm going to go make dinner." If I hadn't just seen her lose it, I wouldn't believe it had happened. That, and the fresh redness around the edges of her eyes.

"Hannah, I just—"

"*No*, Valerie." That warning tone is back in her voice. She turns and runs up the stairs, leaving me alone.

"Andrew is studying to get his real estate license as soon as he graduates. Father and son together in business, is there anything more wonderful?" Mrs. Patterson beams at me across the dinner table. I nod and smile as I twirl spaghetti around my fork. I glance toward Andrew, who is very carefully *not* looking at me.

"Why don't you tell Valerie more about it, son?" Mr. Patterson prods.

Andrew swallows. "Oh, yeah. It's going well."

"Ezekiel." The warning in Mrs. Patterson's voice is jarring. I see where Hannah gets it from.

"Stop playing with your spinach and eat it," Mr. Patterson backs her up. Little Ezekiel looks up from his salad bowl.

"It makes me feel siiiick," he whines.

"I got this." Mr. Patterson stands from the table, walks toward the stairs. "Let's go, son."

Ezekiel's face pales, but he obediently gets up and walks slowly toward the stairs, his posture sagging, his eyes filling with tears. The seven other children around the table focus intensely on their food. The ones who haven't yet finished their salad stuff it into their face. We listen to the thump of Mr. Patterson climbing the stairs behind Ezekiel and then closing a bedroom door. A few seconds later, Ezekiel starts crying.

"Hannah, turn on some music!" Mrs. Patterson cuts in brightly. "No need to listen to that. Eat up, children! Andrew, what were you telling Valerie?"

"Oh, nothing," he mutters.

"No, go on, son! Tell her!"

"Oh, well, it's interesting. When I turn eighteen, I can take the exam . . ." He trails off as Ezekiel and Mr. Patterson return to the table. Ezekiel is crying, tears streaming down his little face. He sits back down, still sniffling, and reaches for his fork. I can't help but watch in horror as he shoves a piece of spinach in his mouth and chews, tears streaming down his face, and then he retches and vomits onto the table.

"Ezekiel!" Mr. Patterson bellows. "Back upstairs."

Ezekiel throws his fork on the floor and flies up the stairs. I hear a door slam. Hannah jumps up and runs to the kitchen for a rag. The kids around the table are quietly, urgently shoveling food into their mouths, but I can barely eat. Hannah returns and begins wiping the puke from the table onto Ezekiel's plate of unfinished spaghetti. Mr. Patterson stomps back up the stairs, and Mrs. Patterson turns the music up higher in anticipation of Ezekiel's cries. A church choir in four-part harmony blares from the speakers, and through it, I hear someone knocking at the door.

"I'll get it!" Hannah heads toward the door, plate and puke rag in hand.

"Wait!" Mrs. Patterson calls in panic, but Hannah doesn't hear her. The music is too loud. She shuts off the music and rushes around the table toward the door, but there are so many chairs and children in the way. In the jarring quiet I hear the door open, and a plate shatter.

"Hi, Hannah," a voice says.

"Miriam?"

six

. . .

"Well, Miriam . . ." Mr. Patterson says.

"It's Mira now."

"*Miriam,*" Mr. Patterson says pointedly, "go ahead."

"What? I thought *you* had something to say to *me.*"

I rub the soapy sponge over the plate as silently as I can. Hannah has herded all the children upstairs, probably to get ready for bed, and Mr. and Mrs. Patterson are with Mira in the living room. I feel guilty for hearing everything as clearly as I do; maybe I should go upstairs with everyone? But I'd told Hannah I'd take care of the dishes, and I'd hate to leave her with yet another chore to do.

"Me? I was told you were coming to repent and apologize—"

Mr. Patterson stops short in confusion, and it's like I can hear their heads swivel to stare at Mrs. Patterson.

"I wanted you two to talk things out," Mrs. Patterson says defensively. "I thought if you two could just talk . . ."

"I can't believe this," huffs Mira. I gently turn on the faucet and start rinsing the plates, gingerly stacking them in the drying rack. I can feel the intensity of the conversation growing, and my skin is pricking with unease.

"You told her I was going to apologize?" Mr. Patterson is indignant.

"I should have known better, known you would never apologize for anything."

"Why should I apologize? You are the one who has strayed from the *Word* of the *Lord*—"

"Can you not take your head out of your ass long enough to take a look around?"

"Be not wise in thy own eyes."

"Oh really, so you *are* gonna doubt yourself for a second?"

"Fear the Lord. And depart from evil."

"I can't with you."

"Don't come back until you are ready to repent," Mr. Patterson yells as I hear the front door slam again. The window in front of the sink shudders with the change in pressure, and I wince.

Mrs. Patterson comes into the kitchen, her eyes brimming with tears. She starts when she sees me, then struggles to compose herself.

"Valerie, would you mind taking this bucket of scraps out to the chickens? You can just toss it over the fence to them. I'll finish in here."

"Oh sure, Mrs. Patterson," I say, taking the handle, glad for a reason to leave this shaken-soda-bottle house.

"And I don't know what you heard, but it's just a little misunderstanding. Nothing serious." Her voice is bright and thin.

"Yeah, sure," I say, and slip quickly out the front door. Mira is standing there in the driveway, puffing on a vape. I don't know that I've seen anyone vape before, except in passing outside a store or gas station. I walk slowly down the steps.

"Hey, um . . . Valerie, right?" Mira gives me a half wave. "So, I'm an idiot and left my keys in there." She runs a hand through her short hair. "Just tossed them on the credenza. Old habits or something. Figured I'd wait for things to cool off before I . . ."

"Oh, I can get them for you—here, just a sec." I put the bucket on the ground and head back up the steps. When I open the door, I hear Mr. and Mrs. Patterson arguing in the kitchen, but they pause when they hear me. I'd thought it would be nice to get out of *my* house for the night, but the tension here is so thick it's hard to breathe.

"Just forgot my sweater, it's chilly!" I call, snatching the keys and my sweater and slipping back outside, making sure to close the door loudly so they hear I've left. I head down the steps and hand Mira her keys.

"Thank you. So much," she says, releasing a juddering breath. "I just couldn't go back in there."

"Yeah." I look at my shoes. "I didn't mean to listen, but things seemed pretty intense."

Mira snorts a sad laugh. "Yeah. Yeah, you could say that. I don't even know why I let Mom convince me to come back. I should have known things never change around here."

Mira is wearing jeans and a hoodie, looking so effortlessly normal and . . . not from *here*. I'm burning with equal parts curiosity and disdain. I feel the superiority I've been taught to feel—like I'm somehow better for living in approval while Mira is so shunned. But I can't help wanting to know how she did it. How she got out. What life is like on the outside.

"Hannah said you are living with your grandparents?" I ask tentatively.

"Yeah. Yeah, they're great. They are putting me through college. They love me. Unlike these people." She scoffs and jerks her chin toward the house.

"I mean, I know your parents love you."

"This, Valerie?" She gestures toward her parents again. Her voice is trembling with conviction. "I know it's hard, even impossible to see when you are inside, but the way they *love?*" She throws up disdainful air quotes around the word. "It isn't *love*. It's control. It's abuse."

My lips turn down at the word *abuse*. It seems so harsh. So ugly. "I mean, calling it *abuse* seems like a lot . . ."

"'Abuse' can mean a lot of things, kid. Emotional. But physical, too. Kids aren't supposed to be hit! They aren't supposed to be told they are terrible and sinful just for being who they are! Just because people *say* 'I love you' to their kids doesn't mean they *treat* them with love."

I'm stunned. I've never heard the parenting methods I see all around me criticized so harshly before. I've sat through sermon after sermon about how parents must use their God-given authority to raise obedient children. I can't even wrap my mind around the word *abuse* the way Mira is using it.

"I mean . . . we *are* sinful," I try. "We probably, like, deserve it, you know?"

"No. No you don't, Valerie. You probably aren't ready to hear or understand this now, but you? You are *good*. You don't need to be fixed or molded or whatever they say. It's everything about the Institute and these people that is wrong."

She's just casually tossing off blasphemies, and I can't decide if I'm horrified or impressed.

"Listen, like I said, you probably aren't ready to hear this. But if you ever are and you want to talk, email me or message me on Insta or something. I've been through everything you've been through and worse. Trust me." And with that, she slides into her car and backs it down the driveway, her headlights sliding across me as she turns the car and drives away.

I pick up the bucket of scraps and walk very slowly to the

fence. The chickens run toward me and mill around in antici-pation, their cooing gentle in the still night.

I'm stunned at how this night has gone. I saw Mira, the prodigal child, and she didn't seem as insane and sinful as everyone says she is. But what she said was obviously extreme. I hear the parents say often that, sure, the Institute and Ben Goddard's teachings aren't perfect, but we shouldn't "throw the baby out with the bathwater." Like, there is still good and truth in there, right? There must be. But Mira's words keep turning over in my head. About love, and acceptance. There are things we shouldn't accept, though, right? Sin? But what if I'm too far inside to see clearly? What if women wearing pants isn't sinful? What if women having jobs is okay? If that weight of sin was somehow lifted off me, what would I do? Who would I be?

As I dump the scraps over the fencing, my mind returns to Riley. She didn't look or talk like I've been told good women do, but she seems good? Like, *so* good and beautiful and perfect? I'm confused, and tired, and I'm not sure how I should feel.

Later, I crawl into my sleeping bag beside Hannah's bed. It's mostly quiet, but a house this full is never truly silent. I hear someone murmuring down the hall, and the distant sound of a toilet flushing.

"Is Ezekiel okay?" I ask quietly.

"Oh yeah, he's fine. He does this all the time."

"Oh. Okay." Tonight must be a pretty regular occurrence. I think back to what Mira said, about abuse. I hear a door some-where open and close. I want to unpack some of what happened tonight, but my guard is up around Hannah. She's so warm sometimes that she feels like a friend; but then she turns angry and cold so fast, it's disorienting. Like earlier, in the basement. I guess we are all living under a lot of pressure.

"So that was Mira, huh?"

"Miriam."

"Huh?"

"Her name is Miriam."

"But she said she goes by Mira now."

"Honestly, Valerie, she's not your sister. It's *Miriam*," Hannah snaps.

I don't answer. I just stare at the dark ceiling and wait for Hannah's anger to pass. I'm used to being snapped at, and I find the best way to avoid worsening the situation is to freeze and wait. I've seen rabbits do it: just hold motionless and hope that people will look away and move on.

Hannah sighs, and continues. "I just wish she would repent, you know? Ask for forgiveness and return to the faith. She used to be so obedient, you know? But she got lured away by the world. Mom and Dad would forgive her if she'd just repent and turn her life around."

She pauses, but I don't interject. I don't want to say the wrong thing again. I close my eyes and let her words wash over me. I'm kind of a pro at half-listening.

"My grandparents are being so unreasonable, too. Why would they shelter Miriam when she's being so disobedient? They are just . . . ugh, awfully liberal, you know? Like they aren't *crazy* liberals, but they don't believe everything we do, and they think it's okay to usurp Dad's authority like that? To help Miriam with her rebelliousness and plans for college? And independence? Women are supposed to be helpers. Mothers. Not breadwinners. It's indecent. Like, we know—*we know* it's a lie of the world to think that women can be independent. We need to be under authority at all times. Like, look at Riley, that new girl today—good grief, what a rebellious, worldly girl."

My eyes snap open, and I tune back in to Hannah's mono-logue. "Riley?"

"Yes, Riley," her voice drips with condescension. "With her tight jeans and her short hair, honestly she looks almost like a boy. It's disgusting. People need to just look like they are. Some-times you can't even tell these days if people are a boy or a girl, it's so upsetting to Mom and Dad." The words just pour from Hannah, ideas she's heard a thousand times, ideas that are now an effortless part of her own thinking.

I know I should keep quiet, but . . . "I think she's nice." I avoid commenting on her appearance because I do not trust myself to discuss how long her legs looked in that denim, the curl of her hair, the way the corner of her collarbone peeked out of her shirt . . . and those *forearms*. Nope. I do not trust myself at all.

"Ugh, Valerie, you are ridiculous. Appearances matter. Anyways, I have to get up early to make breakfast. Goodnight."

Hannah turns away from me in her bed with a huff, the springs beneath her creaking as she settles.

I put my hands behind my head and stare at the ceiling, wide awake again. I think about Hannah and the times we've been close. We spent a day last summer hiking through the woods and ended up at this creek where we found the most beautiful red clay that we dug from the banks with our hands and laughingly smeared on each other's arms. It was silly and whimsical; flecks of clay dotted Hannah's face, her hair drenched in sun and wind, and there was a moment when I had the thought maybe she was going to kiss me. She didn't, of course, and it's not like I usually feel like that with Hannah, especially when she's tense and ready to snap at me half the time. But I remember thinking, if she were a boy, I'd really want her to kiss me. It was like, that was the only way my brain could translate that thought—through the barrier of all I'd been taught.

But reading that book, seeing love so tender and real played out on its pages, somehow ordered a jumble of feelings in my chest. And I don't know what to do with any of it, except to acknowledge that I feel things that I know are forbidden. Feelings I've explained away in the deepest, most private corners of my mind. Feelings that somehow persist, despite all the effort I've put into crushing them. And if there is any chance at all that I'm *not* broken? That I'm maybe okay, or even good the way I am? I need to follow that thread.

seven

. . .

When I walk into the church lobby on Sunday, there she is. Riley, gorgeous, standing next to her mother. Mrs. Patterson is smiling her brightest Sunday smile, welcoming them and explaining the layout of the church; and when Riley turns and notices me, I nearly drop the box and bags I'm holding.

"Hey, Valerie!" she says, coming toward me. "Need any help? Here, let me take that." She reaches out to take the box from me, and I let her. I guess it makes sense that she'd come to our church now, I just hadn't expected or prepared myself to see her here. In my church lobby. Looking impossibly stunning in a simple skirt and blouse, her curls glossy and her freckles scattered like stars across her cheeks.

"Where are we taking these?" Riley asks. I realize, with great embarrassment, that I've been staring. Saying nothing. Like an absolute idiot.

"Oh, hey! I did not expect to see you here! Kind of, you know, caught me off guard," I ramble, shifting the grocery bags from my elbows to my hands.

"Yup, new school situation, new church, it's . . . a thing. Where are we taking this?"

"Oh, yeah, sorry, this way." I gesture with my chin down the hallway.

"I'll meet you in the sanctuary, Mom!" she calls as we head to the kitchen. I push through the swinging door, Riley following me, and we unload the refreshments into the big industrial refrigerator.

"Wow, do you usually bring so much"—she hands me a ziplock bag and I lay it on the shelf—"cubed cheese to church?"

"Oh, no not usually. We are providing refreshments for the visitors' reception after the service," I say.

"Ah, that explains it."

I'm trying desperately to focus on the task at hand, but Riley's presence has me completely off balance. It's hard to know where to look when I'm facing her; I don't want her to think I'm staring at her, but maybe I am? Or just trying not to? Is it hot in here?

"You can actually come! Since you and your mom are new here, you know?" I try to play it cool, taking the bags of sliced meat from the box and placing them next to the cheese. "Here, we can leave the rest in the box, I'll take that from you." I slide my arms under the cardboard, and our hands touch as I pull it away, my fingers kissing hers for the briefest of moments. Every synapse in my brain is firing in Technicolor and I spin to place the box on the back counter, hoping desperately that my face isn't as flushed as it feels. When I turn back, she's leaning on the stainless steel counter, drumming her fingers carelessly on the surface. Her hands are tan and strong, the tendons flexing. Why is my mouth so dry?

"Should we, you know . . . ?"

"Oh, yeah! Yes. We should." I turn distractedly toward the

fridge, then toward the back counter, and complete the circle, facing the door and Riley again.

"Yup, uh-huh, looks like things are"—I try desperately not to look at her—"squared away in here, we should just . . ." I try to step around her, but trip on her foot. She reaches out quickly to steady me by the shoulders, her hands strong and firm and scorching through the thin weave of my shirt.

"Woah there."

"Ugh, I'm such a klutz, I'm so sorry."

"Hey, no problem. You okay?"

"Oh yeah, I'm great! I trip like, all the time. We should probably just head to the sanctuary, I'll see you later!" I choke out and throw myself through the door and down the hallway.

What the heck is wrong with me? I wonder all through the sermon, robotically standing and sitting and kneeling and mumbling at the right times. Is Riley behind me in the sanctuary? I don't see her in front of me and can't come up with a reason to look behind me. I wonder if she's looking at the back of my head. I reach up to smooth my hair at the thought, and then yank my hands back down. Then I sit on them.

"Sit still, *honestly*," Mom whispers harshly at me. Toward the end of the sermon she taps me, and we slip out of our row to prep the food for the visitors reception. And there she is: Riley, sitting in the back row next to her mom. She smiles at me as I walk by, and I smile at her, and the exchange leaves me warm and tingly.

As I wash my hands in the kitchen, I wonder if she'll come to the reception after the service. As I slice apples and oranges and lay the fruit on a tray, I wonder if she'll keep coming to church here. As I carry the trays to the reception room, I wonder what her hands feel like, and if she's thinking about me too, and if I'm totally imagining everything. I probably am, aren't I? So what if she's the coolest girl I've ever met, so what if her face is so smart and interesting and she smells like citrus. I'm just *noticing* those things. That's all. Just observing facts, things about her that exist. It would be ridiculous *not* to notice that when she grins it's slightly crooked, or that her freckles look like specks of chocolate.

By the time we've finished setting up the reception and the service has let out, I've completely talked myself back to level footing. Riley is beautiful, and I have noticed. That's it, that's all there is to it. What a relief to have arrived at this most sensible conclusion. Now I can proceed with our friendship and feel calm and reasonable in her presence.

As people begin trickling into the room, I busy myself with meticulously fanning the cocktail napkins by the drinks.

"Hey," someone says behind me. I turn, and there is Riley— looking stunning, I notice absolutely clinically. She snatches a coffee cup from the stack, reaches into her pocket, and starts unwrapping an Andes Mint. I watch in fascination as she breaks it into pieces and drops them in the cup, repeats the process with a second one, and then pumps in some hot water from the dispenser.

"Nice service!" she remarks as she stirs the melting bits of candy.

"Where did you get those?" I ask, trying to understand what I'm seeing.

"Oh, they had them in a bowl outside the office—here, I got a handful." She hands me a few and I take them, confused but fascinated. She peels the lid off the jumbo can of hot chocolate mix and starts adding scoops of it to her cup, stopping at inter- vals to stir the powdery sludge.

"Peppermint hot chocolate!" she says as she stirs, then takes an appraising sip. "Hmm, needs cream." She pours in some vanilla coffee creamer. Tastes it again. "Oh hell yes, that's delicious. Here, you try." She holds the cup out to me. I hardly know this girl, and I'm pretty sure I'm not supposed to share a drink with someone who says *hell* outside of a sermon, but I take the cup and put my mouth where her mouth was. And holy crap, it tastes delicious.

I don't go many places, but the places I do go become sparkling occasions to see Riley. Riley at church. Riley at Prayer Group. Riley at Bible class.

I don't know how to process my own electric feelings. At first I tell myself I'm just jealous. Jealous of Riley's dreamy curls and adorable smirk and effortless cool. But as time goes on, I'm having a hard time making sense of the unhinged kaleidoscope of color in my mind whenever Riley is close. I hear the parents whispering among themselves, in hallways and on the phone, about Riley's broken family and plans to minister to them, and I stifle a laugh in my chest every time I hear it. If anyone is *unbroken*, if anyone is confident and collected and unshakeable under whispers and gossip and scrutiny, it's Riley. I want to be her. Be around her. I want to be where she is, and somehow, some way, absorb some of whatever magic flows from her.

I finish reading, rereading, and re-rereading *One Last Stop*. I smile and beg and manipulate until I get permission to ride my bike to the library by myself. And there, in the furthest corner, in the cubicle with the computer facing the wall and my seat facing the entrance, I get on the internet. With one eye on the entrance in case someone I know comes in, I start with L and read my way through articles on the GBTQIA and the +. I read articles by Episcopalians (worse than heathens, according to our pastor) about homosexuality and the Bible, and how the conservative ideology I've been taught is *not* universally accepted.

I head home, I smile and submit, I pray out loud, I pick a favorite verse during family devotionals, and then I'm back at the library. I google every "dangerous liberal doctrine" I can remember being trashed in sermons and lectures. I'm high on spite, amazed that the things I've heard reviled from the pulpit have become my guidebook to learning about the world. I read about feminism, intersectional feminism, Kimberlé Crenshaw, and critical race theory.

My world until now has been a vacuum. A sterile, carefully curated sedative of rhetoric designed to keep me in line, too scared of God to ask questions. But now, I am un-scared, I am asking question after question, and Google Almighty keeps answering.

I laugh when I think of my parents censoring our home internet, reviewing David's and my search history every week, questioning us on why we were on this website or that. I feel drunk with the sheer power of the knowledge I am absorbing in the unregulated wilds of the public library.

I'm finishing up a research session, the sunlight through the tall windows in the back of the library growing golden and long. I log out of the computer, gather my pile of books, and head to the front desk. I have second thoughts about a book in my pile and stop next to a returns cart to decide. The cute illustration on the cover looks innocent; the two girls aren't even touching or looking at each other. Mom doesn't usually go through my pile, but it is possible that she'd go through my library account online to see what books I checked out, and see the cover, maybe read the description. I sigh regretfully and place it on the cart. Better to play it safe. I already read the first few chapters; hopefully it will be here on a future visit and I can finish reading it. I'm deep in my thoughts as I place my stack on the desk, and I'm startled when I look up into the face of the kindly sweater-vested librarian who helped me steal that book that one time.

"Oh!" I say in surprise.

"Find everything you need?" he asks cheerfully. His sweater-vest today is a soft baby-blue, his glasses round on his kind face.

"Oh, um, yeah," I reply awkwardly. I tense up for a confrontation, for him to mention the day I stole that book, but it doesn't come.

"Library card?"

"Oh, sorry." I fumble for it in the pocket of my backpack. "Here you go."

"Excellent." He scans it and starts scanning my books. "That book you were considering is great, by the way. You should definitely check it out another time!"

"Oh, yeah?"

"Yeah, it's one of my favorites this year."

I'm torn. He's so nice and I want to tell him things, but I don't know who I can trust. But I guess he helped me commit a crime, so maybe he's, like, in this with me at this point? "I started reading it, but I don't think my mom would be happy if she, you know . . . saw I checked it out."

"Ah." He continues scanning my books, piling them in front of me. I place them gently into my backpack. "You know, this was just returned." He reaches over and pulls a book off the cart, then shows the cover to me. It's two birds, one blue and one red—completely innocent looking. "It's queer but, you know, super discreet cover. Do you want to check it out?"

I consider.

"Sure!" I say, confused by his kindness, but grateful. "Thank you!"

"Valerie, honey?" Mom asks me on a Tuesday. "Would you mind if Riley came to Knoxville with us?"

The Institute's yearly convention that we attend takes place in Knoxville every year.

"Oh, sure!" I agree immediately. Then I worry, was that too eager? Should I dial it down a bit? "I mean, yeah, I guess that would be fine."

"We'd have to get another hotel room. Five people in a room is too many, and of *course* we can't have her in the same room with your brother. Would you mind sharing a room with her?"

"A room with her?" I repeat stupidly.

"Yes, your father and me and David in one room, you and Riley in the other. Her mom is a single mother." Mom tilts her head and pulls her lips down in a pitying kind of judgment. "She works from home and has been able to homeschool her while working, but she can't take the time off to come to Knoxville. I think it's a great chance for us to minister to them. And you'd be a great influence on Riley, after all the time she's spent in the world."

I can't decide where to start—whether I should say that Riley's mom seems just fine to me, or that Riley doesn't seem worse for having grown up outside of the Institute; whether I should say that Christian school isn't exactly "the world." But I'm also a bit lightheaded at the thought of sleeping in the same room with Riley of the sinuous forearms and the slender fingers and the dimples.

"You know how busy the conference is," Mom continues. "We'll only be at the hotel in the evenings."

"Oh yeah, yeah, okay," I agree, somehow miraculously faking calm. "That's . . ." I take an unsteady breath and force a shrug. "That's fine with me."

eight

. . .

"So Riley, where did you go to school before joining the Institute?"

We are all packed into the minivan for the day-long drive to Knoxville. Mom keeps twisting around in the front passenger seat, peering into our faces to analyze our expressions, trying to make conversation with Riley, but her questions are a weird, hyper-cheerful kind of nosy.

"I was at Coleville Christian," Riley answers politely, sitting straight in the bucket seat next to me. Her ankles are crossed easily over the coolest sneakers I've ever seen.

"Ah, I see," Mom tuts remorsefully, like Riley has just admitted to punting a kitten into the ever-after. "Well, we are so glad that you're in the Institute with us now."

"Thanks, Mrs. Danners." Riley is perfectly behaved but unreadable.

I wonder if she likes me. Not *likes*-likes me, obviously, just like, normal-like. I just can't tell. I mean, I don't think she *doesn't* like me. She did bump her shoulder with my shoulder that time, and she gives me that quiet, secret sort of smirk on occasion.

"Well, Riley, we are just so glad you could come with us," Dad starts. I groan silently, knowing the usual trajectory of this speech.

"Thanks, Mr. Danners."

"So glad you could join," Dad repeats, warming up his spiel.

"Thanks!"

"A real joy to have you here. We just hope you feel really, really welcome."

"Thanks…?" A crack appears in Riley's perfect cool. She looks at me with a question on her face, and I smile back apologetically. Dad always does this. Says things that sound right in a way that makes you feel like he means the opposite. Like when he tears me down constantly, makes me feel like I'm a horrible, sinful person but then says he's so proud of me, like that should smooth it all over.

"Can you turn on the audiobook?" David whines from the backseat. We've been making our way through The Chronicles of Narnia.

"Oh sure, honey!" Mom reaches toward the stereo, then pulls her hand back. "Well, we didn't have time for our family devotional before leaving this morning, so let's listen to a sermon first."

"Moooom! Really?" David and I groan, but Mom ignores us and puts on a recorded sermon from a Southern Baptist pastor.

"That's quite enough," she chides us sternly, and we quiet immediately. "The Word of God is more important than stories."

"Amen," Dad agrees, nodding emphatically, his hands on the wheel.

I tamp down the positively heretical thought that the Bible

itself is a collection of stories, and lean my head against the window, trying to tune it out. But the emphatic delivery of the pastor, the slow formulaic build toward angry yelling over his congregation, seems designed to needle into my calm.

I glance over at Riley, who is looking out the window, immovably chill as always. Suddenly bold, without thinking it through, I reach my boot across the van and gently kick Riley's shoe. She looks up in surprise, her face breaking into that perfect smirk when she understands my friendly nudge. We share a secret, silent almost–eye roll, then turn to look out our own windows again.

I bet normal families don't have to listen to sermons on road trips. I glance over at Riley, my eyes catching on the short buzzed hair above her neck. I turn away and rest my forehead against the window, the cool glass blissful against my suddenly too hot face.

When we finally arrive at the hotel, everyone is tired and road-worn. My parents typically argue a lot on road trips, and the strain of keeping cheerful for our guest has their smiles looking very thin. Riley and I drag our small suitcases into our room, followed by Mom, followed by Dad.

"Girls, as we said, no watching TV. It's all dangerous secular propaganda," Mom says.

"Yeah, Mom, we heard you."

"Well, we thought we'd just remove the temptation for you entirely. Doing you a favor really," Dad says as he strides to the dresser, unplugs the TV, and picks it up, his arms stretched awkwardly around its bulk.

"Oh, we can't watch, like, anything?" Riley asks, and Dad pauses in his path out of the room. "Like, we could keep it on

Animal Planet? Or Food Network?" Riley continues helpfully.

"Best to avoid all chance of evil, girls. Of course we completely trust you, but this is for the best." Dad swings around to head for the door, his arms locked in a widescreen embrace.

Riley jumps back to avoid getting smacked with the swinging screen and steps right into me, her butt snug against my hips, and I panic and take two steps back, knocking over a lamp. I reach for it desperately to steady it, and Riley apologizes and gropes for it too, our hands meeting at its base. We pull apart and glance toward my dad who is, thankfully, still busy sidestepping, threading the screen through the narrow passage to the door.

"Goodnight, girls, sweet dreams!" Mom calls from the hallway and shuts the door, leaving a weird silence and the faded outline of the missing TV on the dresser.

"Okay then." Riley plops onto the king size bed, stretching excessively—really, why would anyone need to stretch quite that much—and finishes by lying on her back, hands behind her head. Her white T-shirt is so, *so* nicely fitted, and even though she's switched to the "modest" shapeless skirts required by the Institute, she wears them with a sort of ironic panache—like she's wearing the skirt, it is in no way wearing her. I notice with panic that her shirt is pulling up away from her skirt, and I catch a sliver of skin before I turn away and search for something, *anything* to say to keep my cool.

"Sorry about them." I apologize for my parents, staring at the popcorn ceiling and then the short hotel carpet. When I glance back, Riley has adjusted her shirt, and I'm distracted by the fact that I've never seen Riley as relaxed and unguarded as she is right now. I'm still searching for a side of Riley that I don't find completely irresistible.

"It's not your fault, it's fine. Totally fine." Riley lets out a big yawn.

I don't know what to do with myself. It took a minute, but it's finally dawned on me that there is only one bed, which shouldn't be a big deal. It's not a big deal. It's actually like, no deal at all. It's just a normal friends-sharing-a-bed type situation.

"Don't worry, I don't snore!" Riley laughs, which I realize is possibly—no *definitely*—the prettiest laugh I have ever heard.

"Oh yeah, no, I wasn't worried." I throw my hand up in a casual shrug, but knock into the lamp again. I lurch to steady it. "Wow, haha, this lamp is like, super wobbly."

"Yup, lamps do that," Riley says. Ugh, why can't I put words together around this girl? "Hey, did you want to use the bathroom first?"

"Oh, no, you go ahead."

While Riley heads off to do whatever it is super hot girls do in the bathroom, I spiral. Okay yes, I thought it. *Yes*, she's super hot. What the heck is happening to me? I've had crushes on boys before. Crushes that Mom noticed, and that we smashed into oblivion under the Word of God. I've always wondered how I'm supposed to keep my attraction completely *off*, but then presumably flip that switch on for marriage? Because my parents talk to me about marriage. A lot. And this feels an awful lot like a crush. Oh frick, can I call it a crush? I've never felt quite like this. It's not a great idea and I'm trying to tamp it down as hard as I can, but I am a teenager and my hormones are raging and Riley smells like grapefruit . . .

"Hey, all yours!' Riley flops back on the bed, and she's wearing a tank top and shorts, which puts my mind straight into an emotional blender, so I grab my stuff and dash into the bathroom.

While I brush my teeth, I give myself a pep talk. Get a grip, Valerie. It's just a sleepover, Valerie. You go out there and climb in your side of the bed and go *the FRICK TO SLEEP, Valerie.* I've never been allowed to swear, nor have I ever been around much swearing, but somehow I know some words and every moment is bringing me closer to using them. I don my pjs, which seem hopelessly frumpy compared to Riley's cool AF ensemble, but Mom won't let me wear anything immodest even in my room. I pull on my baggy nightgown. NIGHT. GOWN. Good grief, I look like a flipping granny. Why am I, the uncoolest person in the world, about to share a bed with the *coolest* person . . . ?

I compose myself. I leave the bathroom slowly, faking calm. I am a tall cool glass of chill. Unflappable as Mom and Dad when faced with evidence of their own mistakes. I head to my side of the bed, slip beneath the crisp white duvet, and turn toward the window. Outside, traffic whizzes by; in here, the air conditioning unit rattles and hums, and a lightbulb in the bathroom buzzes faintly. Next to me, Riley breathes deeply, and her breath pulls me with her in a gentle, relaxing movement of air. In and out. I feel the stress of holding myself together in front of my family begin to lessen.

"Val?" Riley's voice is gorgeous in the silence. "Oh, sorry, can I call you Val?"

I've never had anyone call me Val before, but I have never loved anything more than the way it sounds in Riley's Earl Grey voice.

"Yeah?" I whisper.

"Thanks for being nice to me. It's been kind of a rough year. And people around here are . . . you know. It's just nice having you around to even things out, I guess? Anyways, thanks."

I listen to the silence. I wonder who dared cause Riley to have a rough year, and what kind of vengeance I can wreak on her behalf. I struggle to stand up against the wall of my parents' wrath for myself, but I suddenly feel I would take a shovel and attack the ocean for Riley. I wonder what more there is to Riley's cool exterior, and whether I could possibly be lucky enough to earn her secrets.

"No problem," I whisper into the cool hotel air. And then, after a moment, "Thanks for being nice to me." I pull in a breath. "I've kind of been waiting for a real friend."

nine

. . .

"Here we go!" Mom practically squeals as we near the stadium. I glance awkwardly at Riley to see what she thinks, but she's staring calmly out her window. Mom is usually pretty serious, but events like this make her giddy. Through the windows of the minivan, we see large families on the sidewalks streaming toward the stadium, all in matching uniforms. White shirts and navy pants for the boys and fathers, white shirts and ankle-length navy skirts for the girls and mothers. No sensual ankles visible.

"What do you think, Riley?" Dad crows from the driver's seat.

"Um . . . wow," Riley says, looking out her window.

"You won't see more fifteen-passenger vans in one place anywhere else in the country!" Dad says proudly.

"Indeed," Mom agrees, freshening her lipstick in the flip-down visor and fluffing her curled bangs.

"Hey, it's the Zellers!" David yells, waving excitedly out the back window.

"Maybe we can walk over with them!" Dad says as he turns into the lot.

"Ooh, the Pattersons too!" Mom wrings her hands in excitement. "I'd hoped we'd meet up! They must have caravanned here!"

I squirm in my seat. My family is so excited, it's embarrassing. I guess I used to be all-in too, but the glow has faded for me lately. And with all my doubts and new thoughts, I'm not sure how I'm going to feel.

We pull into a parking space and pile out of the car. The Zellers and Pattersons are still unloading, getting kids ready, babies changed, Bibles collected and placed in each child's hands.

"Valerie!" Hannah squeals, crushing me in a hug.

"Hey!" I laugh as she shakes me. "Take it easy there."

"Oh my goodness, hi, Riley! I forgot you were riding with Valerie!"

"Hey, Hannah!" Riley gives a little wave.

"You look really . . . nice!" Hannah smiles aggressively.

"Oh yeah, thanks." Riley shifts on her feet. "My mom got the memo about the uniform. Not gonna lie, baggy clothes like these are pretty comfy."

"Well, they aren't baggy for no reason!" Hannah chides. "Modesty is the best policy!"

"Oh yeah, sure." Riley shrugs.

"Hey, Valerie," a soft voice mutters over my shoulder, hot breath assaulting my ear.

I jump away. Do my best to recover. "Hi, Andrew." I turn to face him, and then take a few discreet steps backward so we aren't quite so close.

"I gotta change the baby, back in a minute!" Hannah says, hurrying behind the van.

"How was your drive?" Andrew mutters, staring at the asphalt.

"It was great, you guys'?" I pause. He continues to stare at his feet. "Full van for you, huh?"

"Yeah," he says. "It was good." The silence stretches. Why does he always try to get my attention when he doesn't have anything to say?

Thankfully, David walks up to us, white shirt perfectly tucked, Bible under his arm. "Hey, Andrew! Ready for AWAKE Academy?"

"Oh yeah." Andrew turns to chat with him and I relax a bit.

"So," Riley says, "we aren't allowed to hang with the boys at this conference, right?"

"Yeah, it's a whole thing. They keep us separated and teach us different things." I lean in. "It's always felt a bit unfair, honestly? The boys do hikes and obstacle courses and rappelling, but us girls are kept in conference rooms—" I glance toward where Hannah disappeared. She hasn't returned yet. "And they lecture us on purity and preparing ourselves to be wives and mothers."

"Yikes," Riley says quietly. "Good times, good times."

"Alright, Pattersons!" Mr. Patterson booms. "Form up!"

The kids line up at the rear of the van, descending by height in their crisp navy and white.

Mr. Patterson seems to notice us for the first time. "Hi there, Danners clan! Lovely to see you! And Sarah!" He points finger guns at my mom. "Can't wait for you to make us some of that fried rice again!"

The Pattersons head out, and we follow them. Riley walks next to me, joining the growing stream of people on the sidewalk.

"Well, that was rude," Riley says quietly.

"What?"

"You know." She gives me a look. "That fried rice comment."

"Oh. Yeah." I reflect. "It's weird, but I guess I'm used to it? People say stuff like that to my mom all the time."

"I'm sure," Riley says. "Doesn't make it less weird though."

"I think they're trying to show how cool they are with my mom being Asian?" We slow down to distance ourselves from the group. "I tried to ask her about it once, but she insisted it doesn't bother her."

We walk in silence for a bit, our long skirts swishing and pulling at our ankles with each step. It's noisy and hot, exhaust fumes clouding the air.

"Being multiracial sure is a mindfuck," Riley says quietly. I glance at my parents, but they're busy in their own conversations.

I turn the word *multiracial* over in my head. I'm self-conscious that I haven't encountered it before, but it sounds right. "Is that the word for kids like us?"

"Yeah, or *biracial*, whatever works." Riley grins.

"I . . . I didn't even have a word for it."

"Huh?"

I pause, embarrassed. It's not often that I talk to someone from the outside, and whenever I do, I feel the weirdness of my upbringing keenly. I feel like I should hide my ignorance, but Riley waits patiently. "Well, it's a little weird because my dad is white, and he's the one who does the teaching about my heritage." I glance at Riley again, and her face is neutral. Patient. "He always says I'm half Asian." I pause. "Or, you know. That other thing."

"Oh god." Riley tosses off the profanity effortlessly. I'm jealous of how easily she does it. "Not the e-word," she says.

"Yup." I nod. "Ugh, I *hate* being called exotic. It took me a long time to realize it because . . ." I lean closer and lower my voice further. "It's my own family who calls me that. They think it's a compliment or something."

"I know the type," Riley says sympathetically. "And I thought I stuck out at Christian school. Ha. This home-schooling cult is almost completely white."

My head snaps toward her. "Cult?"

"What?" Riley looks uncomfortable for a second, and then backpedals. It's loud on the street, but we are pushing the boundaries as it is by talking here. "Oh never mind, we can talk later."

"Wait, I want to know what you mean."

"Stay close, girls!" Mom calls back to us, "Here we are!"

As I walk into the stadium with my family, the word *cult* keeps rattling around in my head. I wonder how Riley came to that conclusion. I mean, it's ridiculous, right? This is just a religious homeschooling organization, maybe a little extra in some ways, but there are so many of us. It can't be, can it?

We draw closer to the stadium, and I'm reminded of just how huge this event is. In all directions I see a tide of families, all dressed in navy and white. We wade through the swell of people, following Dad to our seats, squeezing past a family of at least a dozen children wearing matching T-shirts that read "Joneses for JESUS." Another family kneels around a man I assume is their dad, who is praying loudly over them, hands raised and trembling like a Baptist preacher.

Mom is glowing. She lives for this. Dad too. Their eyes take in the crowd around us hungrily, greedily, shining with admiration and excitement. As we find our seats, the lights are already dimming for the opening session, and the energy in the stadium is frenetic. The lights rise on the onstage orchestra and they begin to play, their suspenseful music building until a live announcer booms out over the PA system, his voice echoing through the stadium. A loud helicopter sound blares, and suddenly, young men in military uniforms rappel from high up in the ceiling onto the stage. The crowd around me jumps to their feet, screaming. The men are members of AWAKE, the Institute's paramilitary organization that has several military-style compounds around the country. As the music and noise and energy swell to a peak, Ben Goddard himself walks out to take the podium.

I've definitely been carried away by the hype before. I've screamed and waved and felt what I was sure was the pure spirit of God. I've stood in line with a hundred young girls just to have my Bible signed by Ben Goddard. A few years ago, when I was suffering from migraines, Mom somehow arranged a meeting with him, and he laid his actual hands on me and prayed. When I started crying from the immensity of being in his presence, he wiped the tears from my cheeks, his fingers uncomfortably thick and rough on my face. But this year feels different.

I'm hyper-aware of Riley standing next to me in bewilderment, of how zealous and frantic the crowd is, and I'm also keenly aware of how . . . *different* I feel this year. Maybe it's the "deconstruction" I've been doing secretly. I guess that's what they call it online. I glance toward Mom, who is crying tears of joy. I wonder if people can tell that I don't believe with my whole heart anymore. If they can see the doubt I feel written on my face. I feel so unanchored. The secret reading, the questioning I've done—I feel like I've been pulling apart pieces of my faith without any idea where I'll end up. I've always felt like an outsider in the secular world, but now I feel like an outsider here too.

I really don't know if I belong anywhere at all.

As Ben Goddard begins speaking—stopping frequently for rapturous applause—I feel like I'm seeing everything in a different light. I've heard so many sermons on *worldview* and how your fundamental beliefs color the way you see things, and it's actually true. Before, when I saw a mother with a dozen children, I thought she looked so devout and godly. Now, I wonder if that same mother is happy. The kids I thought were so perfect and obedient before now look rigid and stressed. I see a boy flinch when his dad raises a hand in worship, perhaps used to those same hands dealing out punishment. The fathers I've been told are strong leaders seem harsh and overbearing. The screaming crowd full of religious zeal now seems frenzied and blindly devoted.

Ben Goddard speaks for over an hour. He invents words, defines terms, and uses them to tell the crowd what God's plan is. He exhorts us to keep our families growing, for wives to submit to their husbands and bear more children, for husbands to protect their families, for young people to marry each other and birth many more children to be soldiers in God's army. He preaches that everyone in the household is under the authority of the man of the house—the father—and that children and wives must always submit themselves. He calls it an "umbrella of protection," and insists that no one should ever step out from under it. If families follow these rules, Goddard's rules, God will bless them. Health, wealth, wisdom—all these things wait in store for those who follow Goddard's teachings, who stay on the right path. Goddard explains how the Institute is growing nationally, internationally, and he insists that soon entire cities and even countries will be a part of this faith.

As he drones on, I can't help but think back to what Riley said on the walk here. A *cult*, she called this. I feel so stupid, but I've literally never thought of it as a cult before. Cults are a weird thing that happens to *other* people; we call other Christian denominations cults all the time. Because we have the *true* religion. But the more I turn it over in my mind, the more it fits.

And if it's true, if I am in a cult, how do I get out? How would I even begin to leave my faith, my family, everything I know?

I sneak a look at Riley. It's so hard to tell what she's thinking, but I might see a bit of confusion on her face? Maybe even a twitch of fear?

Our eyes meet and I reach out and take her hand.

I panic for half a second, wondering if I've done something dumb, and start to pull my hand away, but Riley grasps it firmly and smiles a little at me, seeming to relax. She takes a deep breath and squeezes firmly, her hand smooth and warm in mine. I see Mom notice, and I freeze. How am I going to explain this? My mind is racing, but she smiles warmly at us. She seems to think it's cute. Two girls holding hands in prayer is completely normal around here. I let out a shuddering breath. I may be thinking other thoughts, about how beautiful Riley's hand feels in mine, about the warmth I feel and the texture of her skin against my fingers, but no one knows.

Maybe there are people here who don't believe. Maybe there are others who quietly question and doubt. I don't see them—can't see them in the weird chaos of frenzied devotion. But with Riley's hand in mine, for the first time in forever, I feel a little less alone.

ten

. . .

"What was your favorite thing that you learned tonight?" Dad asks us later as we sit on the edge of the hotel room beds eating cold rotisserie chicken and baby carrots.

"I'll go first!" Mom says. She is positively glowing from the thrill of the evening. "I was really convicted by the idea of keeping our home Christ-centered. It's so easy to lose our focus and look to the world, when everything we could possibly need can be found in God's Word."

"Amen," Dad agrees prayerfully. Nodding, he turns to David. "How about you?"

David chews thoughtfully. Usually he seems to struggle to come up with parent-pleasing things to say, but tonight he seems genuinely interested.

"It was really cool seeing those AWAKE program guys rappelling onto the stage. I think it'd be really cool to attend the program when I'm old enough, maybe?"

I remember the guys marching around in paramilitary uniforms. Now that I think about it, why would the Institute need military-like facilities? Riley's cult comment from earlier keeps spinning in my mind.

"Wonderful!" Mom beams. "We would so love that. Oh, praise the Lord."

"Anything that keeps you close to God and in the community, we will support," Dad agrees. "I hate to see families torn apart by children who fall away, like Miriam and the Pattersons." Dad shakes his head gravely.

Don't cults try to keep people from leaving?

"I'll go next!" Riley pipes up. Dangit, I should have been ready sooner. Going last is a sure way to invite the most scrutiny.

"It was cool!' Riley says. "Cool seeing such a diverse group of people come together with a common goal!"

I choke on my carrot. Riley delivered that line with a straight face, and Mom and Dad are so passionate about this stuff, the sarcasm sails directly over their heads.

"Oh, for *sure*." Mom nods emphatically.

"Absolutely!" Dad agrees. "There's the Cole family. And that other family. What's their name?"

"The Lees!" Mom supplies. "Praise the Lord, the Institute brings *everyone* together!"

I'm about to lose it. I'm struggling to swallow the bits of carrot in my mouth while trying to tamp down the laugh I feel threatening to erupt. I angle myself away from Riley, because eye contact would be the end of me right now. It's hilarious that a group this large, thousands upon thousands of people, has exactly two families—well, two and a half, including us—who are not white. The glaring exceptions that prove the rule.

"Are you okay, sweetie?" Mom asks.

"Oh, yeah, I'm fine, I just . . . swallowed funny." I take a sip of water and snort-laugh into the cup again. Riley reaches over and pats me on the back, which does not help at *all*, but after a minute I have control of myself.

"Oh, I guess it's my turn." Mom and Dad have chiding looks on their faces.

I've sat through hundreds, maybe thousands of these family meetings/dinners/devotionals, and try as I might to come up with the right answer, sometimes I just can't. Sometimes my brain won't let me fabricate another perfect piece of shit to feed the eternally hungry God machine.

"I was just . . . um . . ." My mind is traitorously blank. Good grief, don't I have a backup plan for this? I scramble for an idea. "I was just convicted that I need to be a better listener. To you." I nod at my parents. "And be a more obedient child."

"You've said that same thing for the last few family devotionals." Mom frowns. "I mean, I don't disagree with you, but I hope you aren't failing to pay attention. You know we spent a lot of money to come here, and—"

"Your mother gave up her career to stay home and home-school you." Dad talks over her. "I hope you appreciate it and apply yourself this week. I don't want to see any of your rebellious spirit. You have such a willful, sinful spirit in you. You always have, despite all we've done to help you." He pauses for emphasis, picking up steam as he goes. "You've always been a willful child. Resistant to the rod of discipline, which you know I use as the authority of God in your life. You need to repent, seek God's grace, and turn your life around before you're in danger of straying from the faith. Do you understand?" He's growing increasingly stern, his anger so familiar, I marvel at how it can still hurt so much.

I nod wordlessly, dipping my head the minimum amount that my parents will accept as consent. I stare at the wall, squeezing my nails into my palms, anger building and building with nowhere to go. I wonder if other parents humiliate their kids in front of their friends. I wonder if other kids have to endlessly think of how to keep their parents from getting angry, if other kids are always trying to satisfy God or their parents, and whether the unhappy voice of God coming through my parents is maybe just . . . my parents.

"Valerie. Say something," Dad commands.

"What do you want me to say?" My voice is shaking despite my best efforts. We sit in tense silence, and Dad waits expectantly, like his lecture will have changed my heart. Like the guilt-slinging is going to make me bloom like a flower and weep with gratitude for everything they've given me. I stay silent. The best I can do is try not to crack and *scream* everything I'm feeling. Really, if they had the slightest *hint* of the thoughts that run free in my head . . . Riley's stomach gurgles loudly in the quiet and David laughs. Mom shoots him a look, and he hides his face behind a napkin.

Riley stands up, looking around awkwardly. "My bad, excuse me. If it's okay, I'm going to head back to our room. I'm feeling a little off." She shoots me a look, tilts her head slightly in invitation for me to leave with her. She's offering me an escape.

"Oh, of course." Mom unfreezes, returning to her cheerful church persona.

"Sweet dreams, girls—see you in the morning! In the lobby at 6:00 a.m., ready to serve the Lord!"

I hop up and follow Riley into the blissfully judgment-free hallway, and to our blissfully parent-free room.

"Hey, thanks for getting us out of there," I say as I shut the door behind me. "I'm sorry about that. My parents can be, like, really intense."

"Oh yeah, no problem!" Riley flops onto the bed. "And you don't have to apologize, it's totally not your fault," she says, kicking off her shoes.

I feel myself tearing up, and I'm not sure why. "I mean . . . I am the reason they were upset."

"I mean, that's what they believe, but they are grown-ass adults bullying their kid for no good reason."

"Well . . . I was being rebellious, I guess."

"Valerie!" Riley huffs. "You didn't say the magic thing they were thinking in their brains fast enough, and that makes you a bad person? Seems like a pretty fucked up guessing game to me."

I guess it makes sense, but I've never really thought about it like that. It's also never occurred to me, truly, that I'm *not* responsible for the actions of my parents? It's just that every time they are angry or disappointed it's always, *always* my fault, or David's fault. It's so hard not to believe that it's true.

"Hey, you okay?" Riley must see the tears in my eyes. I try to push them down. "You okay?" she repeats. "I didn't mean to . . ."

"It's not you." I sniff, trying desperately to squeeze my feelings back into their cage. "I'm just having a lot of feelings about everything. I'll be fine."

"You know," Riley says, sitting up in bed, "it's like, totally okay to have feelings."

And at that, I burst into tears. I just can't hold it back. It's so rare, so foreign to have someone care about me, care what I really think and feel. Someone who doesn't insist I squeeze myself into a cross-shaped cookie cutter of perfection every minute of every day.

"Hey." Riley grabs me by the hand and pulls me to sit on the bed. She wraps an arm around my shoulders as I sob. The sheer pressure and anger compressed inside me comes pouring out. My fists are clenched and I'm gasping, heaving. I'm so freaking *angry*. Riley gently rubs my back. "It's okay, hey, it's okay to let it out. I gotchu."

I pound my head with my fists. "I can't"—I gasp—"I just . . ."

"Breathe, Val, breathe with me. Geez. I don't think I've ever seen someone cry so angry before. Let it out. It's okay."

"Ugh, I just always . . . this is why I . . ."

Riley takes my face in her hands and looks me in the eyes. My heart aches at the kindness of her face. The warm, endless brown of her eyes. "I'm here. I'm gonna listen. But just try to breathe for a sec. I'm seriously worried you might pass out or something."

I pull back, trying to compose myself, and then throw my arms around her. We sit like that for a while, Riley rubbing gentle circles on my back while I weep. Slowly, the sobs slow and I'm no longer angry-crying, just crying. My eyes are swollen and red, snot is running down my face, and I laugh. A snotty chortle at my own ridiculousness.

"Hey, there you go. It's okay. Alright. Now that you're breathing again," Riley says, "you wanna talk?"

"Sorry. Ugh." I wipe the tears from my eyes, sniff the snot back into my nose. Swallow. "Ugh, gross." I laugh.

"Mm, emotional damage snot. Yummy," Riley deadpans, and I snort-laugh again. "Top shelf stuff," she continues. "Salty, smooth texture, a hint of—"

"Stop, so gross!" I cackle, and I don't know if these tears are from laughing or crying anymore. "Ugh. I'm sorry."

"Like I said, you don't need to apologize," Riley says gently, "for anything."

I take a gulp of air. Collect myself. "I'm like, a really bad crier."

"Ha. I'd say you're *excellent* at crying."

"I mean when I cry, it's just awful. I get the heaves and I can't breathe and it's always such a mess."

"Crying is normal, Val." I've never loved anything as much as the way Riley says my name. *Val.* "Maybe you need to cry more often? Not hold stuff in quite so hard?"

"Oh yeah, that's definitely true, but"—I laugh wetly—"have you met my family?"

"Oh yeah, I guess I do see where that tension comes from —" Riley jumps up from the bed and runs for the bathroom.

What did I do? I *knew* I shouldn't have cried, but I just couldn't keep it in anymore, and now I've totally freaked her out.

I hear retching from the bathroom.

"Oh fuck!" Riley moans.

"Riley? Are you okay?"

"No. Oh fuck no." The words end in a heave and the splash of vomit.

eleven

. . .

"Are you okay? Should I come in?" I'm standing outside the open bathroom door, unsure of what to do. Should I go in and hold her hair? Is that a thing? But her hair is pretty short, isn't it? Ugh, she sounds so miserable.

Riley retches again, and then I hear the toilet flush and the sink run.

"Riley?" I peer into the bathroom.

Riley comes out, her face pale and sweaty. She crawls into bed, and I bring her the empty ice bucket, just in case, and a cold wet washcloth.

"Can I get you anything else?"

"No."

"I'm so sorry, Riley."

"I'll be okay. Just dying a little."

"Was it the chicken?"

"I dunno. If it was, why aren't you sick too?"

"I don't know. I did go to Taiwan a few years ago to see relatives, and I was stupid and drank some tap water and got really

80

sick. But I haven't thrown up since then, so maybe I'm like, stronger from it?"

"I don't think it works like that."

"I don't know, maybe it does." I lie down in the bed beside her. Then I sit up, snatch the room phone from its cradle, and dial my parents' room.

"Hello?" Mom answers.

"Hi, Mom. Riley is sick."

"Oh no, what happened?"

"I don't know, she said she didn't feel well and just started throwing up." I glance at Riley. She's curled around a pillow, eyes squeezed shut.

"How are you feeling? Are you sick too?" Mom says.

"I'm okay right now, but if it's a stomach bug I'll probably get it too, won't I?"

"I'll send your dad to the vending machine for some Gatorade. What flavor does she prefer?"

"Um, let me ask her." I turn to Riley. "What flavor Gatorade do you like?"

"Blue," Riley says so, so sadly.

"She says blue, Mom."

"Alright, I'll have Dad leave it at your door. Let her know we are praying for her. Check in with me in the morning and let me know how you both are doing."

"Okay, thanks, Mom." I replace the phone and glance at Riley again. She's still curled up in a ball, bedding crumpled at her feet. I carefully pull the sheet and blanket up, tucking them gently around her.

"Thanks, Val," she says miserably.

"You gonna make it?" I place my hand on her shoulder and stroke her arm. My fingers itch to move a curl from her forehead but I stop myself.

"I think I'll live." Riley sighs. I try not to think about how very sad and still somehow very cute she is.

A knock sounds at the door.

"That'll be my dad." Opening the door, I find two blue Gatorades sitting on the carpet. I guess Dad wanted to keep his distance from the vomit. I pad softly back toward the bed.

"Riley? Do you want some now?"

"Noooo . . ." Riley moans, shifting uncomfortably. "Not now. Maybe in a little bit."

"Okay, let me know if you need anything. I'm gonna go brush my teeth, be right back."

When I climb back into bed a few minutes later, Riley is so still, I think she's asleep. I feel sorry for her, sick and far from home with near strangers. I wish I could help her. The window unit purrs. Traffic whooshes past. So many people headed so many places. I wish I knew where the heck I'm going. I watch the shadows and light crawl across the ceiling, keenly aware of the girl in bed beside me. It's nice to feel less alone.

"Val?" Riley croaks into the stillness.

"Oh hey," I whisper. "I thought you were asleep."

"Can you talk to me? I could use a distraction. I'd watch TV, but . . ."

"But my dad took it."

"That was weird, right?"

"That's my parents. My whole life, actually. It's all pretty weird." I stare at the ceiling. "Anyways, what can I tell you to take your mind off things?"

"Tell me something nice?" Riley pleads. "Like, something happy? What's something that makes you happy?"

I smile in the darkness. Riley seems so tough, so unflappably cool during the daytime, but seeing her like this, soft and needy, she's beautiful. And her needing me? It makes me feel beautiful too.

"Books," I breathe. "Words. Beautiful words. Sharp words. Every chance I get, I'm at the library. I love books. Getting lost in them. Smelling them."

"Smelling them?" Riley chuckles softly.

"What, you've never smelled a book before?"

"I guess I haven't. I do love the feel of paper when I'm sketching, so I guess it probably smells nice too."

"You draw?"

"Yeah. I'd love to draw more, and there's stuff my mom won't let me draw but . . . yeah. I love it."

"What do you want to draw that your mom won't let you?"

"Oh, well—"

"Oh it's okay," I interrupt. "I was just curious but . . . you really don't have to tell me." Goodness knows there are countless things I'm not allowed to do. Parents never seem to need a reason to slap down yet another rule.

"No, it's okay." Riley pauses. "I like to draw girls, and . . . boobs."

"Boobs?" I laugh but stop short when I see she's serious.

"You know what, never mind."

"Wait, no! I'm sorry. I didn't mean to laugh, I was just surprised. Seriously, it was just unexpected, no judgment. I promise."

I turn to face her, one arm folded under my head, the dim glow from the streetlights gentle on Riley's perfect face. "Why do you like to draw boobs?"

"You sure you aren't gonna be all judgy?"

I reach out and touch Riley's hand. I'm so sorry that I laughed, and I can't stand the thought of Riley thinking I'm condescending. "I know my family seems absolutely nuts, and you would be correct if you think my parents are the judgiest people on the planet. But I promise, I'm not like that." And maybe I can see why she likes to draw boobs, I think. Boobs *are* pretty cool. "No judgment. I swear."

"Wow, you swear? Aren't you rebellious." There's that perfect smirk again and those freaking dimples.

"Shut up and talk, Riley." I laugh, trying to tuck away this helpless, mushy feeling.

"Oooh, feisty Val. I like it." Riley chuckles weakly. "Okay. Well. I saw these boob mugs at a thrift store one time, and I couldn't stop looking at them. Just breasts made of clay on the side of the mugs, different sizes, different shapes. I loved them." She takes her hand out from under mine as she talks, begins to gently trace a finger over my knuckles. I do my best not to shiver. "I've always loved drawing. Art was always my favorite class, I was always doodling and sketching. But when my mom found my sketches of boobs, she kind of freaked out. Took away my art supplies. Told me to straighten up."

"Wow. I'm so sorry."

"Yeah." Riley removes her hand. Tucks it under the covers. "It really sucked."

"Is that why she joined the Institute?" Riley is silent, but I wait.

"Actually, it's a long story, and I thought you were supposed to be the one telling *me* things. I'm the sick one here."

"Hey, I *am* distracting you, aren't I?"

"Yeah, I guess so." Riley turns onto her back. I miss her face already.

"Okay, well," Riley begins, then hesitates. "You sure I can trust you? You seem cooler than the rest of the Institute people, but this is like, really personal."

"I'm cool, I promise," I assure her. "I'm not exactly sure who I am and who I'm going to be, but I'm not going to hold a God knife to anyone's throat."

"Heh, people really do use God as a weapon, don't they? Okay. Well, I got kicked out of Christian school."

"Really?" I say carefully. I'm not going to be caught off guard and laugh again.

"Yeah. For kissing a girl."

I don't know what to say, but I don't want to leave Riley hanging.

"Oh," I say carefully. I feel a twinge of disappointment. It can't be jealousy, can it? "Do you miss her?" I ask.

"The girl I kissed? Oh no, we didn't like each other like that. I mean, I do like girls, in general, but we were both miserable in the horror show that is Christian school, so we planned to do something that would get us both expelled. Honestly, I was sure my mom was going to give up on trying to reform me and let me go to public school."

"Wait." I sit up in shock. "You thought you were going to get sent to public school, and then she turned around and joined the *Institute*? You've got to be kidding me!"

"God, I wish I was. I really thought that once I was expelled I'd finally be able to breathe—but nope! Instead, I've gone from the frying pan into the fire."

"Into the freaking furnace."

"The flames of fucking Mordor." Riley chuckles. "It's hilarious. I'd be laughing my ass off if I wasn't so miserable."

"Yeah, it's pretty awful. I feel so tight and angry all the time and . . . well, you saw me lose it earlier."

"You really keep all that inside all the time?"

"Always. I know it's intense when it comes out, but most of the time I can just twist my feelings tighter. Push them deeper."

"I'm no therapist, but . . . that can't be healthy."

"Yeah, it's for sure not." I flop onto my back.

Riley rolls over, shifts uncomfortably.

"You okay? Can I get you anything?" I ask.

"I'm okay for now." She pauses. "You know what, Val? You're really nice."

"Oh, I'm not really. I mean I try, but I'm really very selfish."

"Val." Riley stops me. "That's the religious mindfuck talking. You're a good person. I'm a good person. Even if the adults around us don't see it, we have to believe it."

Tears well in my eyes again, and I take a quick gulp of air. I don't know why Riley's kindness connects directly to my feelings, but there she goes once again.

"You gonna cry more?" she asks.

"No," I say tearily.

"It's okay to cry, Val."

"No, it isn't. I mean yes, I guess it might be okay somewhere out there to just feel feelings, but I'm still *here*." I try to breathe past the tightness gripping my chest. When I speak again, my voice is quivering with coiled intensity. "I still have to sit at a table with my parents several times a day, every day, and examine myself and read the Bible, and convince them that I'm obedient, and submissive, and not . . . I don't know if I can even say it."

"Hey." Riley takes my hand in hers. "Is this okay?" I nod and grab on, squeezing her hand in mine. Riley's eyes are full of kindness and gentle strength.

"I don't think I can say it," I whisper. I'm so tired. I want to tell Riley how scared I am. How I think I might be queer or bi or pan or something, but I can't bring myself to say it out loud.

"It's okay," Riley says. "Tell me about it when you're ready."

I feel the grip of anxiety in my chest unspool as I lie there in bed with the kindest, most beautiful person I've ever known. Still holding hands, we drift into an exhausted sleep.

twelve

. . .

The rumble of a passing truck startles me awake. I look blearily toward the window. What? Oh. Hotel. Hotel room. I turn my head to glance the other way—and there is Riley.

At some point during the night, we let go of each other, and I curl my fingers around the remembrance of Riley's hand in mine. The closeness of our conversation last night, the bliss of being heard, of being seen. The morning light falls in gentle pools across Riley's face, and I can't help but watch her. She's so beautiful, relaxed and peaceful like this. Her chest rising and falling in an easy way.

She wakes slowly, eyes blinking and opening, and she looks at me looking at her, and that smirk creeps across her face.

"Watching me sleep, Val?"

"Maybe," I reply with a boldness I'm still trying to understand. This feeling is so new, but maybe I like it. Riley stretches luxuriously, hands above her head in fists, toes pointing down, peeking out from beneath the crisp white sheet and blanket. "How are you feeling?"

"Depends on who's asking."

"Hm?"

"Well," Riley says, that smirk growing, "what if I was struck with a horrible forty-eight-hour stomach bug? What then?"

I stare at her in awe. I consider myself quite excellent at manipulation, but I've never gone so big before. So bold. Riley might be an evil genius.

"You don't mean . . ."

"Yup! I do. I'd rather hang here with you for two days than sit in a conference room with the army from *The Clone Wars* singing the praises of Ben Goddard. So, I might not be feeling completely recovered."

"You absolute evil genius."

"Why, thank you." She looks so pleased, flushing at my compliment.

"I'll call my mom."

"And I'll go perform in the bathroom." I feel myself grinning with a giddiness I can't contain as Riley gets out of bed, looks back at me, winks, and heads into the bathroom. It takes me a moment to remember what the heck I was doing. I dial Mom.

"Good morning, honey! How is Riley?" I must still be dazed from that freaking wink, because I stammer, unprepared to spin the lie, until I hear Riley retching from the bathroom, and it all comes back to me.

"She's been sick all night." More sounds of retching and . . . is that splashing?

"Oh no," Mom frets. "I was worried about this, the poor thing. But these things are usually gone in twenty-four to forty-eight hours. Have you been sick?"

"Oh, well, I haven't thrown up, but . . ."

"But?"

I pause. Mom is not a complete idiot; I'm going to have to

sell this. I pitch my voice into the sad, sick zone and summon my best pathetic, obedient child energy.

"I've been feeling pretty queasy."

"Oh dear."

"Yeah, and I have really bad diarrhea." It's not true, but it *sounds* true. I mean, who the heck has ever lied about having diarrhea?

"Oh no, sweetie, I'm so sorry. What terrible timing. Is it really all that bad? You could probably still make it to some of your sessions."

Riley sticks her head out of the bathroom to check on my progress, and I gesture for her to keep going. She retches exaggeratedly, runs back into the bathroom, and the splashing picks up again.

"Oh dear, that sounds just awful. I guess you two had better stay put. We have to get going here, we've all got sessions to get to. I'll put some snacks by your door in case you're up for it later, and we'll check in with you tonight. It's going to be late, after ten. Are you sure you two will be okay?"

"Yeah," I say, sighing. "We'll make it."

"I guess I *could* skip today and stay with you two . . ."

"I'd hate for you to miss the conference, Mom—you go ahead. We'll be fine."

"All right, if you're sure."

"I'm sure, Mom. You go enjoy."

"We'll pray the Lord heals you quickly so you don't miss any more sessions. I'll let the Pattersons know so they can be praying too. Drink some fluids when you can, and I'll talk to you tonight!" She hangs up.

I am stunned. I cannot believe the power of a brave, bold lie in the face of parents who think I've been disciplined into submission. I can't help but wonder what else I could get away with.

Riley comes out of the bathroom. "How'd we do?"

"We did it!" I squeal.

"Um, *you* did it! That was some grade-A fake-out there, Val." Riley is looking at me with such pride, I blush.

"How about you? How did you manage the actual vomit splat?"

"I *may* have poured some water into the toilet at the right moments."

"Again, you are an absolute evil genius."

"You sounded pretty fantastically evil yourself."

There's a knock at the door. We wait a moment and open it to find some crackers and ramen cups. Whoever left them (probably Dad) did not wait around to see us. I retrieve our hoard, place it on the empty dresser where the TV once stood, and dive back into bed with the glee of a perfectly executed scheme. I sigh in ecstasy, stretching in the crisp sheets, enjoying the swish of the bedding against my bare legs—the unreal freedom of a whole day in a new place with no parental oversight.

Riley leaps onto the bed beside me, her weight nearly bouncing me off. "I don't mean to brag, but who just got us out of day two of cult camp?"

"You did." I beam at her.

"Now now, I can't take all the credit." Riley grins. "I did have help from a brilliant young actress."

"Brilliant, huh?"

"Brilliant and talented."

"Well then." I preen.

"And beautiful." We lock eyes for a moment, and I feel the moment stretch. I scramble to change the topic.

"Cult camp, huh?"

"Yes, it's a cult! Don't tell me you haven't been thinking this."

"Not exactly? I mean, I've heard people joke that it's *not* a cult, but . . ."

"That's exactly what someone in a cult would say! I mean, come on. Cult leader?"

"Check," I confirm.

"Is the leader a white man?"

"Check!"

"Does he have a set of essential teachings that will change your life?"

"Gigantic check!" I draw a huge check mark in the air.

"Does he need beautiful women around him to better serve God?"

"Woooah, woah woah, hold the phone," I say. Riley reaches over, grabs the phone and holds it. I giggle.

"Holding," Riley says solemnly.

"You adorable weirdo." I laugh. "Okay, but seriously, Ben Goddard does actually have kind of a harem."

"You're shitting me."

"He does! He meets pretty girls at conferences, and he asks their families to send them to the training centers to be his secretaries and assistants. They work in his office and accompany him everywhere. He specifies how they have to dress and wear their hair and even their makeup. Dude." My mind is spinning, connecting the dots.

"Hannah's older sister lives in Indiana at a training center and works really closely with him." The pieces are falling into place, and I can't believe I haven't seen it so clearly before. "He dictates what everyone wears," I say.

"Mega creepy." Riley grimaces.

"And I've heard rumors that the parents and pastors all strongly deny, but it sounds like he might be doing some shady stuff with his secretaries."

"Okay, well, gross," Riley says. "If I hadn't already barfed so much, I'd be barfing again, so thanks for that. But the cult label is looking pretty strong."

"Damn." I feel the profanity roll off my tongue, and after waiting a second for a lightning strike that doesn't come, I feel flush with the power of it.

"*Damn,*" I say again, with more strength, relishing the word. "It does fit!"

"Okay, other culty things. Do they try to keep people from leaving or shun them if they do?"

"Holy frick, they totally do!" I'm having revelation after revelation. My head is whirling with the simplicity of it all. I'm stunned at how all of this has been right here the whole time, and the people around me don't *see* it. Choose not to see it.

"When boys grow up and leave home, if they stop attending a parent-approved denomination of church—or, God forbid, stop attending church altogether—they're treated like outcasts."

"For real?" Riley asks.

"For real. The girls aren't supposed to leave home until they get married, and the fathers will only agree to a marriage if they approve of how Christian and conservative the guy is. Actually, Hannah's sister Miriam left home. She's living with her grandparents and going to college, and they treat her like an outcast! They whisper about how she's fallen away, and they try to keep the other kids away from her 'corrupting influence.' It's a whole thing. Damn. This is a lot."

Riley leans in. "This is a lot to take in. I mean, Christian school and Evangelical or fundie church feels pretty cultish by itself, but all of this?" She gestures vaguely toward my parents' room. "Is even more. You seem to be handling it pretty well for someone who just realized they were raised in a cult."

"A cult," I repeat. "A cult. I'm in a goddamn cult!"

I have never, ever said *goddamn* before, and I give it a

second, looking around in anticipation, waiting to see if something will happen.

And nothing does. No lightning bolt, no divine appearances, no swift consequences. I can't help but think about all the small, supposedly sinful things I've done lately. Reading a gay book, lying to my parents, reading about feminism on the internet, trying out some swear words, maybe feeling some feelings for this girl. Each time I try something new, something I've been told is forbidden, I brace myself for something to happen. And nothing has. Either my conscience is broken or I've been fed a lot of lies. In fact, I've only felt more *myself* the more I've left the path. I feel like I'm starting to see the world clearly for the first time.

"Whatcha thinking?" Riley breaks into my thoughts.

I wave my hands. "All of this? Lying to my parents? Swearing? Calling my faith a cult? It's new to me, and I've always been told the guilt of the sin would be crippling and God would punish me. But instead? It's all feeling pretty okay." I smile.

"Yeah?"

"Actually, more than okay. It feels good? Really good. Like I'm breathing deep for the first time in a long time."

Riley is smiling at me, and the day is ours. We are incredibly, deliciously alone. "Parents are gone until tonight, huh?" Riley grins. "What do you say we go explore?"

thirteen

. . .

We walk through the automatic sliding doors of the hotel and cross two parking lots, following the siren call of the sprawling Super Target. I've never been in a store unsupervised before, and at Riley's suggestion, we walk every single aisle, blissfully aimless, sniffing candles and sinking our fingers into plush towels. We discuss the merits of various shades of lipgloss and nail polish. In the hair products aisle, we select theoretical shades of hair dye for each other.

"I've never been allowed to even *think* of dyeing my hair before," I say.

"Oh really?" Riley replaces the box she was holding.

"Yeah, I'm supposed to be thankful for what the Lord gave me. Something about it being arrogant to think I know better than God, when he already picked a color for me?"

"Seriously?" Riley snort-laughs. "Pretty ironic considering Ben Goddard is like a hundred and dyes his hair jet black."

"I . . . never thought of that before."

"No man his age has jet-black hair. He obviously dyes it!"

"What the heck? I guess he does! What a hypocrite!"

"Classic cult. Telling the little people how to live while the men in charge do whatever they want."

"The more I think about it, the angrier I feel."

"Yeah. That happens a lot when you pay attention to what's going on in the world." Riley gestures to the shelf of dye. "Pick a color! Hypothetical, of course. I think your parents might notice if you suddenly had pink hair."

"You pick for me," I say.

She looks at me very seriously, holding up one box and then another next to my face. "Midnight Jade," she announces, handing me a box of dark-green dye.

"Green? Why?"

"Because you secretly want to be very loud." She smiles.

"I . . . kind of love it."

"Yeah?"

"Yeah, like, I feel like my thoughts and feelings are bigger than they're allowed to be, you know?"

"Yeah, that makes sense." She reaches out and gently fingers the ends of my hair. Pulls her hand away. "Okay, do me."

I look at the browns, but there is no shade of brown more perfect than Riley's own. I feel myself smiling as I look at the boxes of silver and gray. I wonder how she'll look when she's old, and know she'll be as perfect as she is now.

"What?" she asks.

"Oh . . . well, I don't know . . ."

"Just say it, Val! Anything for this imaginary hair dyeing adventure!"

"Okay, here. Silver Stiletto. Because you are gonna be so cool as an old lady."

"Old lady?" Riley laughs, taking the box. "I freaking love it."

In the detergent section, Riley slips in a small puddle of

lavender-scented detergent and falls on her butt, then sits there laughing. When I pull her up, she doesn't let go of my hand. She holds on as we walk the length of the aisle. In the pet aisle we discuss our pet preferences (me, cat—Riley, dog) and in the home goods section we touch wicker baskets and novelty mugs. Riley takes her time looking through the art supplies section, and I flip through the beautiful writing journals. Riley rolls down the kids' aisle on a tiny plastic fire truck and effortlessly juggles three rubber balls, tossing them back into their tall metal cage. She's so dazzling in every way, I can't seem to take my eyes off her. Can't stop marveling at every little thing she does to squeeze joy out of every moment.

"Wait!" I pull Riley into the juniors' clothing section. "I want to try on some clothes."

"Yeah? Anything in particular?"

"Just normal clothes. Stuff I'm not allowed to."

Riley's eyes light up, and she grabs my hand, pulling me close. "Oh my god, *please* let me pick some! I would love to style you!"

"Okay, okay!" I laugh, delighted by her enthusiasm. Riley walks through the racks and shelves gathering clothes. "Let's see here, do you like the threadbare distressed look?" She gestures to a pair of jeans on display.

"Um, maybe less tattered? I think my legs would get cold."

"Oh, I got you." She thumbs through a stack on a table. My eyes are drawn to her fingers. Beautiful and strong.

"You really don't get to pick out your own clothes?" she asks as she holds up a pair of jeans in front of me, then shakes her head and refolds them.

"I could, kind of, but the rules are pretty strict. And my dad always gets the final say."

"Your *dad*?" She turns to me, tossing me a pair of jeans.

"Yeah, and sometimes David."

"Wait what? I'm new to this level of cult, you're gonna need to explain." She turns to me, giving me her full attention.

"Well, when I get a new shirt or skirt, or especially a swim-suit, I have to try it on for Dad and David. And they say whether it causes them lustful thoughts."

"I'm sorry, *what*?!" Riley gapes at me.

"Like, to see if it makes them think any impure thoughts."

"Oh I heard you, I just can't even begin to unpack how deeply fucked up that is."

I stare at the worn carpet. "It always felt bad. I've never liked it, but the other Institute families do it too, so I thought it was normal? I guess it is kind of icky."

"*Kind* of icky? Val." Riley puts her hands on my shoulders. I meet her gaze. "You are not responsible for the thoughts of men."

"I'm not? I mean, I don't want to make their lives harder . . ."

"You aren't. Their issues are not your responsibility. And your own family—I can't believe I have to say this—your father and brother should not have lustful thoughts about you, period. I'm so sorry you've had to go through that. That is so . . ." She runs a hand through her hair in frustration. "It makes me so mad."

I take a shaky breath, lowering my eyes. I hear her, I want to believe her, but I feel the grossness and disgust that lives in my body. The shame.

"Val? What is it?"

"It's just so embarrassing, you know?"

"You have nothing to be embarrassed about, Val. All of that is on them. Not you."

I dash away a tear with the back of my hand. "Okay. I'll try to believe that."

She puts the pile of clothes in my arms and pushes me into

a dressing room. I'm a tiny bit disappointed she doesn't come in with me, but I'm sure she's just giving me space. I take off my long blue skirt and shapeless shirt. I pull on one pair of jeans and try to zip it—too tight. The next one is a looser fit that zips and buttons easily. Then, I put on a shirt.

I turn to look in the mirror. Reach out and gently touch my reflection. Ripped jeans and a simple tank top on an Asian American girl who looks so completely . . . *normal*. I could be anyone. I don't look like I'm not allowed to wear pants, or like I have to let my father inspect everything I wear to see if it's hiding my figure enough. I don't look like someone who has been taught that men are the authority in all things. I don't look like a girl who has been told that her purpose in life is to serve a husband and have a dozen children. I could go anywhere. I could do anything. I could be myself. No one can tell from looking at me how weird and awful my life is.

"How does it look, Val?" Riley calls from outside the door. I turn and swing the stall door open, and as I look at Riley looking at me, I feel warm and soft inside. Like I want to be seen by Riley, and being seen makes me braver. Stronger.

Riley grins. "You look perfect. I wish we could get these for you for real, but . . ."

"But my parents. It's fun just to look. And to know that . . . that I could be different."

Riley's mom sent her with some cash that my parents politely refused, so we pick out a picnic lunch together—a baguette, olives in oil, some cheese. I'm not sure I can tell myself exactly why I want this lunch to feel a bit fancy, but I do. I want it to be pretty and elegant and special. Riley selects a package of big soft cookies, and I grab a bottle of sparkling lemonade. "Haribo or Albanese gummy bears?" she asks me in the candy aisle.

I tap my chin thoughtfully. Out of the corner of my eye, I see her watching. I tilt my head to the side, letting the hair fall away from my neck, feeling her eyes on me. I don't know what I'm doing exactly, but I like feeling her gaze. It's a delicious new feeling, being admired by someone I like so much. "My favorite gummy candy is grapefruit, but no one ever has it." I glance at her. She swallows and looks back to the shelf. I should feel more self-conscious, flirting with this girl, but I don't. I feel brave and beautiful under her gaze.

"*You* smell like grapefruit," I say boldly, recklessly.

"Do I?" Riley asks, lowering her voice.

"I mean, not that I was sniffing or anything," I backpedal, suddenly shy.

"Well, that's hardly fair, I haven't gotten a good sniff of you yet."

"Go ahead then." I meet her gaze with challenge in my eyes, and she steps closer. Leans toward my neck with excruciating slowness, maintaining eye contact. I can see every freckle on her face, every dot of black in her brown irises. Her lips are parted, and if I just lean forward, I could kiss her.

Then she looks down, her lashes hiding her eyes as she leans closer and smells my neck, her breath and scent washing over me. She looks back up, reaches her hand toward my face... and grabs a bag of Haribo peaches from the shelf.

"These are my favorite," she says casually, with a smirk that shows she knows exactly what she's doing to me, as she turns away and heads down the aisle.

We pay for our groceries and wander toward a soccer field. Following a narrow asphalt path, we find a creek, and there on the bank, a gorgeous weeping willow tree. The branches spread in a draping canopy, wispy arms floating softly in the breeze. And under those green curtains, we sprawl on the mossy grass.

"Oh my *god*," Riley says through a mouthful of cheese and bread, "the simplest food really is the best sometimes."

"Yeah," I say, ripping off another piece of bread. "What's that Bible verse about better is a simple meal with love?"

"Than a fattened calf where there is hatred," Riley finishes. "Yeah."

I take a long drink from the bottle of lemonade.

"Now *this*," Riley says with a flourish, "is the perfect bite. One olive, with oil drizzled on the bread, and a piece of cheese. Here, you have to taste this."

"I'm eating the same food as you!" I laugh.

"Please?" she pleads, making big sad eyes at me, and I laugh and open my mouth. She feeds me the little stack of food, and I feel a flutter in my chest when her finger brushes my lip.

"Perfect, right?"

"Hmmm . . ." I chew slowly, trying to keep my face serious.

"Oh come on, that is the best bite you've had today and you know it."

"*Okay*, okay it's perfect!"

"Wait, is that . . ." Riley hops up and dashes to a nearby bush, examining a vine closely. "Val!"

"What is it?"

"It's honeysuckle! It's the right time of the year for it. Oh my *god*, it smells so good." She returns with a handful of delicate white and yellow blossoms. "You have to smell them," she insists, handing me a few. I do, and they smell sweet and pure. Like honey and happiness and sunshine.

"They grow in pairs of two. One always opposite the other. Like lovers," she says as she pinches the base of a flower with her fingers and pulls the stem through, coaxing out the honey.

"Here, taste it!" She holds the slender filament out to me, a drop of nectar clinging to the end of it, and I open my mouth obediently. I suck off the bead of syrup. It tastes like love.

I lie on my back, looking up at the perfect tangle of branches, the sky winking blue through the canopy, and Riley lies down too. We look at each other. I find myself looking at her lips and keep thinking about what it would be like to kiss her. Despite everything I've been taught, everything I thought I believed, the thought of kissing Riley feels like the most natural, right thing I could do right now.

"Riley?"

"Yeah, Val?"

"Well, I guess I was wondering if . . ."

"Yeah?"

I sit up. "Well. I was wondering, and if it's weird please just say so and we'll forget it ever happened, but. Could I . . . could we . . . do you want to kiss?"

Riley is so close, and she reaches a hand up so, so slowly and softly brushes my hair away from my face. Then she leans in, and I lean in too. Our lips meet. And we are kissing. Riley's lips are so warm and soft, and her hand is on the side of my face, her thumb gently tracing along my jaw. She pulls back.

"Is this okay?" she whispers.

"Yes." I lean in, and we kiss again. Deeper this time. I carefully reach a hand behind Riley's head, the soft spiky hair there tickling my fingertips. A million willow leaves shimmer in the breeze, echoing the shivery, zingy feelings in my chest, in my lips, in my fingers. We pull apart, smiling.

Riley pulls our foreheads together. "Val, I . . ."

"That was amazing!" I laugh, throwing myself back on the mossy ground, touching my lips in wonder.

"That good, huh?" Riley laughs, watching me.

"Riley. I've been taught that I shouldn't even kiss until my freaking wedding day, that anything before that is shallow and meaningless. But this, you, me . . . how could this be wrong? Kiss me again!"

"If you insist." Riley grins, pulls me toward her, and kisses me.

"What's this ring?" Riley asks me as we lie beside each other, watching the willow branches swaying in the breeze. Our hands are entwined, and she's rolling my ring around my finger absently.

"Oh this?" I hold my hand above us, wiggling my ring finger and the little silver circlet on it. "This is my purity ring."

"Yeah?" Riley reaches up to touch it. "I have one too, somewhere, but I stopped wearing it. I'm guessing if you didn't want to wear yours anymore, your parents would have something to say about it."

"Yup. I hate having to look at it though. Lots of bad memories."

"Well here, let's fix it! May I?" Riley holds out her hand, and I slide the ring off my finger. Place it in her palm.

"Let's see. This ring, Valerie." She stares at me very seriously.

"Yes?"

"It represents some new things now."

"Okay?"

Riley jumps up and leans down to the creek, dipping the ring in. I can't help noticing how nice her butt looks as she does so.

"Okay, bad vibes washed off." She takes her seat beside me again, shaking the water off. "Now, this ring stands for you being true to yourself." I feel those pesky tears creeping back into my eyes. "It stands for you being perfect the way you are, and not listening to those who tell you otherwise." I'm fully crying now, tears streaming down my cheeks. Riley is shimmering so brightly. "It stands for you being worthy and deserving of love and respect exactly the way you are. It stands for your absolute love and acceptance of yourself."

She takes my hand, sliding the ring onto my finger, and I take Riley's face in my hands and kiss her.

fourteen

. . .

We fall, laughing, through the door of the hotel room well in advance of my parents. My lips are swollen from kissing, my face aches from smiling, my tongue hurts from sucking the sugar off too many Haribo peaches. I have never, ever been happier. I feel a sickening dread when I think of my parents returning, of going back home to my isolated existence, but I push those thoughts away. I'll deal with them later. For now, I want to soak up every drop of joy that I can.

Mom calls our room and I complain about a day spent on the toilet. I tell her that I can't even imagine leaving this room tomorrow. Mom frets, says she'll leave more Gatorade and food outside our door, promises prayers, and that's that.

In some ways, deception feels novel and shocking, and in other ways it's the perfect culmination of a lifetime of lying in small ways. Of making the right shapes with my face, with my hands, with my body. Year upon year of kneeling and bowing and showing deference. It makes perfect sense to be lying in these harmless larger ways. I muse again about sin, and how doing these things called "sinful" doesn't feel bad. I wonder who—besides God, I suppose—is the victim of my kissing Riley. Who is the victim of skipping the cult conference? Of not forcing my thoughts to be the same as my parents'? I feel certain that the answer is no one. I am hovering above the ground with the bliss of our kisses, of seeing and being seen, and Riley seems so happy. How could this be wrong?

Riley makes us cups of noodles, brews water through the tiny coffee maker into the styrofoam cups. While the water steams and spits, Riley pulls something from her pocket.

"Is that . . . grass?" I ask.

"Guess again," she says, rinsing the green bunch in the sink. She pulls a pocketknife from her other pocket and flicks it open with a practiced flip of her wrist. It's honestly the hottest thing I've ever seen, and I still don't know what it is I'm seeing.

She lays the greens across the little tray next to the coffee maker and expertly slices them. As she works, the smell slowly reaches me.

"Onions!" I exclaim.

"Yup! It's either that or field garlic, I forget if there's a difference. It's completely safe to eat and completely delicious." I'm mesmerized. She removes the cup of noodles from under the coffeemaker's spout and sprinkles the onions over the top with the care of a chef. She prepares the other cup and brings them over to the tiny table, setting plastic forks beside each cup with a flourish.

"Voilà! Your dinner, milady!"

"Thank you, chef!" I dig my fork into the noodles, stirring gently. They come unspun, the threads of wild onions mingling with the blond noodles and sunset shreds of dried carrots.

Riley slurps noisily. "What are you waiting for, Val?" she asks, stirring her cup with enthusiasm. "Do you not like onions? Shit, I should have asked."

"Oh no, that's not it. I'm just used to praying before I eat."

"Oh, do you want to? We totally can."

"No." I smile. "I think I wanna skip." I shove a big forkful of noodles into my mouth—delicious, salty, slightly chewy. The onions add a fresh tang that reminds me of . . . "My mom always puts green onions in soup," I say.

"Yeah?" Riley wipes her mouth with a washcloth.

"Yeah." We finish eating, drinking as much of the salty broth as we can stand. I think about my mom. About my parents. About how weird it is to feel duty and love but also resentment and anger.

"Val, I want to talk about today," Riley says.

"What about?" I ask, carefully pulling shreds of carrot and onion from the bottom of the cup with my plastic fork.

"Well, you kissed me. We kissed."

"Yeah?" I smile at her, then reach my hand over and put it on hers. She lifts my hand from the table and folds it between hers.

"It just seems kind of fast, and like, I know I'm new to the Institute, but that seems pretty frowned upon around here and I just want to make sure you are okay with everything."

"Okay?!" I laugh. "I've never felt so happy and beautiful. Let's kiss more right now!"

Riley laughs, raising my hand. She unfolds my fingers and gently kisses the center of my palm. My whole body twitches from the sensation.

"Seriously though," Riley says, placing my hand on her thigh and covering it with hers. "I was surprised. And I would never want to make you uncomfortable. In fact, I've been trying *not* to make any moves and then you go ahead and start making them."

"Listen," I say, raising my hand to her beautiful face. She smiles gently at me, so warm and unguarded that I want to cry.

"I'm listening!" She laughs.

"Okay. So. I realized that I'm bisexual or pansexual a few months ago. I always thought I must be straight because I've liked boys before, but then I stole a book from the library, and then—"

"Val, you stole a book?"

"Hey, are you listening or not?" I tease.

"Listening, continue."

"Okay, so. I've been realizing some things about myself that make so much of my life make sense, and make all of the Institute and church parts make less sense. And I know this might seem ridiculously fast to you, from someone who has had so little . . . experience . . . but what I'm trying to say is: I've never felt as much myself as I feel around you. And I've never felt about anyone what I feel for you. And every time we touch, it feels so right and I'm not thinking about sin or rules or whatever, I just want more and more of that *rightness*. This wild goodness that I've never felt before." Riley's eyes are burning into mine, and I wish I could tell what she is thinking, but now that I've started, I need to finish.

"And I understand if this is too fast or I seem super silly and naive or whatever, but I'm not doing *this*"—I gesture between us—"out of a desire for anything but to follow my heart for once. And I just really want to keep going if you want to." I don't think my voice is as calm or steady as I'd like, but I hope Riley can hear the truth behind it.

"My turn?" Riley asks after a pause.

"Your turn."

"I've wanted to kiss you for a while now. And I didn't initiate because . . ." Riley looks down. Hurt flashes across her face so clearly, I feel it in my chest. "Well, I've been told a lot of awful things." She shakes her head, pushing whatever vile things she's been told aside. I can imagine what they are because I've heard sermon after sermon about these things. Angry misinformation spewed in the oily cloak of righteous authority. "And it's not that I believe those things. I know I can't change who I am. But those things still hurt, and I just never, ever want you to feel like I'm leading you, or pressuring you into something you don't want. So, as long as you promise to tell me or stop me if you are ever uncomfortable—"

"I promise," I interrupt.

"Can I kiss you now?" she asks, a hunger and dominance in her eyes that makes my insides shiver straight down my body into the worn woven fabric of the hotel chair.

"Yes," I breathe.

Riley grabs my face and kisses me. I tangle my hands in her curls, my nails scraping the soft spiky hair at the base of her neck, and she lets out a quiet moan. That sound does something to me, shakes loose a hunger in my soul, and I kiss her back with a fierceness I didn't know I possessed. She kisses my neck, bites my ear, sucks gently on my collarbone, and I am awash in sensations. Riley stands and pulls me by the hand into the bed, and we tangle together, kissing, tasting, exploring with our hands and lips and legs. A tiny bud of a thought forms in my mind, blooming into an idea, and I decide to keep being brave and reckless.

"Hey," I say breathlessly, pulling back, "maybe this is stupid, but I was gonna take a shower. Do you wanna take a shower together?"

"Really?" Riley asks. "You are full of surprises, Val." She laughs. "I'd love to, but I want to take things slow if you want to."

"But this might be our only day together, like this." My words hang in the space, and I know she understands. That today is special, that we are gloriously unsupervised. I know I'm being reckless, but I want to follow this caution-free joy for once.

"I don't know that I want to have sex, but I'd love to take a shower with you. Is that stupid? You can totally say no."

Riley stands and pulls her T-shirt off, and my mind loses all thought. She laughs and takes me by the hand, pulling me toward the bathroom. I toss my clothes to the floor while she turns on the water. I slip into the warm stream while she takes off her underwear and joins me.

We laugh at the delight of the hot water slicking our skins. We kiss. I reverently soap Riley's back and chest (how is this real?), and she soaps mine. I discover a tiny tattoo of a mushroom on her side, and she points out the constellation of freckles on my shoulder. I stand outside the stream as she rinses off and I get instantly chilly. She sees me shiver and pulls me under the steamy stream with her, wrapping her arms around me, strong and brown and beautiful.

Wrapped in fluffy white towels, we brush our teeth beside each other. I'm all smiles in the mirror, my hair black, slick, and straight. Riley's hangs in wet waves down her forehead. We are teasing, laughing. I didn't know anything in life could feel this easy. This simple and perfect. She laughs at the way I floss each tooth gap precisely three times and I watch the way she finger-styles her curls, fascinated. We kiss again, our mouths toothpaste-fresh. We put on panties and nothing else, tangling in bed, glorious beneath the white duvet.

"Let's spoon, Val." I feel Riley smile as she whispers against my lips.

"I don't know how to spoon," I say, feeling shy all of a sudden. There's so much I don't know.

"Of course not. Here, just turn." Riley gently angles me

toward the window then presses her body to my back. Her arm slides under my pillow, wrapping around to hug me while her other arm reaches over my shoulder, completing the circle. I'm cocooned in her warmth. I've never felt anything more exquisite.

"'Night, Val," she whispers sleepily into my ear.

fifteen

. . .

My mom wakes us up with a phone call telling us to make sure we rest plenty today (we were resting until you called, but thanks) and that they'll be back tonight. Knowing our luck is running out, I tell her we slept through the night and should be able to attend the conference tomorrow after a quiet day today.

When we are sure my family has left, we get dressed and head down to the complimentary hotel breakfast. We make waffles with little pre-made cups of batter, and I show Riley how I slather mine in yogurt. Riley makes a ridiculous sandwich with French toast, hot sauce, and sliced hard-boiled eggs, washing it down with apple juice. We stuff apples and oranges into our pockets and, back in the room, Riley fills the ice bucket and puts the fruit inside "so it'll be cold and tasty later."

Riley wants to draw me, so I lie on my stomach, chin in my hands, and she sketches me in the margins of her Bible. She picks Song of Solomon "because it's all about boobs anyways", but doesn't draw my face "so you don't get in trouble if someone finds it."

"Isn't that the rule with sending nudes?" she asks as she sketches thoughtfully. I'm utterly entranced by the way she bites her lower lip when she's concentrating.

"But I'm not nude. Also, how the heck would I know?"

"Okay yeah, but the principle is not to send your body and face in the same shot, so you can always say it wasn't you."

"Ooooh so like if your mom finds the sketch?"

"Bingo. Okay, you can look." She holds the sketch out to me and there I am, stretched across the top of the page. There are so few details, and yet somehow it feels dreamy. I can feel the comfy-sprawl, crisp-clean-sheet happiness of the moment.

"Wow, you're really good!"

"Stand by the window and let me do another one?"

"Okay." I stand and lean back on the wall, one heel crossed over the other, hands behind my back.

"I drew my mushroom tattoo you noticed last night."

"Oh really? It's beautiful!"

"Yeah! Thanks! I went with a friend from school and we lied about our age. An apprentice copied the design from my sketch. I have a lot of tattoo design ideas." She pauses, runs a hand through her curls. I feel the corners of my lips twitch upward as I watch her, so stunning as she focuses on her work.

"I'm hoping I can get an apprenticeship when I graduate," she continues. "If my mom doesn't loosen up when I graduate, I guess I'll move out."

"Woah," I breathe. I guess somehow I knew that graduating high school and turning eighteen is adulthood, but I've been so groomed by the Institute, I hadn't really understood. I explain as much.

"Girls in the Institute don't really leave home," I say with embarrassment. "We are supposed to stay under the protection of our fathers until we get married, and then our husbands are supposed to be in charge."

"What, so you never live on your own? Never have a job?" Riley looks up over her sketch.

"That's like, a major principle. Women can never be out from under the authority of men. It sounds so effed up as I'm saying it now, but yeah. No college, no job, no life. Just marriage and babies."

"Well that fucking sucks."

"Yeah. It does." I trace a foot over the ridges of the rough hotel carpet. "As much as I think that I think for myself, it's embarrassing how controlled my thoughts still are." I say, staring down at the floor, shame creeping over me.

"Hey, come here." Riley throws aside her Bible and pencil and pulls me into the bed. "I feel fucked up sometimes just growing up Evangelical. And I've at least been in private school, around other kids who question and push back. You've been in this cult your whole life?" She looks at me questioningly.

"Half my life?" I pause to think. "I guess we were just super churchy, but I've mostly been homeschooled. And we've been in the Institute for most of it."

"Well, I'd say you are doing amazing. Certainly thinking for yourself more than the other kids, like your friend Hannah."

"Ugh, Hannah!" I snort-laugh. "She'd die if I told her about any of this. Which I will not be doing," I'm quick to clarify. "She's been lecturing me on my lack of interest in marriage."

"Gross." Riley groans. "Can you even imagine having to look into the eyes of one of the Bible group guys? Like Andrew, Hannah's brother? I always feel like he's watching you weirdly."

"What? No, he's so shy, he just likes to say hi."

"Which means a lot from a shy guy!"

"What? No." I discard the idea. "Yeah, definitely not trying to follow 'the plan.'" I pause, hesitant to say my feeling aloud, but knowing it's true in my heart. "I would rather stick a fork in my eye than be married off to any of that crowd. I just couldn't do it."

I reach out and gently pull one of Riley's curls. It springs back into its perfect spiral, magic for someone with hair as straight as mine. "So like, what do normal kids do when they graduate high school?" I ask.

"College, or get jobs," she says, stretching out on her back. "Sometimes both. Some kids move out, some keep living at home. Everyone is different."

"Sounds nice," I say wistfully.

"You know, as much as your parents *say* they hold all authority over you forever, unless that authority passes to your theoretical husband, they can't actually, like, legally keep you home once you turn eighteen."

I stare at her. Processing.

"They can't?"

"No, they absolutely cannot. When you're an adult, they lose all legal authority over you. Paying for everything yourself might be hard, but they can't keep you locked up."

I stare at her.

"They can't?" I repeat, feeling like an absolute idiot.

"How did they keep this information from you?" Riley asks disbelievingly.

"I just heard so much about the stupid authority umbrella, God and father and then husband, I thought it was a real thing..." Processes have started in my brain and, good grief, they are picking up speed.

"Riley!" I shout. "I turn eighteen in May! I can leave! I can get out! I can't believe I haven't realized this before. I'm a complete idiot."

"Hey, cut yourself some slack. You've been doing some pretty big brain stretching lately."

"I can get out," I repeat slowly. Tasting it.

"You can get out!" Riley laughs. "Have you really not realized this before?"

"I guess not," I say, embarrassed again, but Riley is quick to calm my self-flagellation.

"Come here," she says. She tosses her sketch pad aside and I join her on the bed. We lie nose to nose. The intimacy of the moment takes my breath away. I can see every delicate freckle on her face, the warm endless brown of her eyes seeing into my very soul.

"Val?" Riley looks down. "I really like you."

"I like you," I reply, smiling, feeling warm in my chest.

"It's weird liking you so much, with how little time we've spent together alone."

"Right? It feels like we are never alone. This is a miracle!"

She meets my eyes, reaches out and palms my face softly, lovingly, then she leans forward and kisses me. I'm lost in the warmth of her lips, the taste of her, this perfect swirling moment.

It's weird to like someone this much. To love someone I don't know so well. But I feel like I've been waiting all my life to feel the way I'm feeling now. To know myself and be ready for a brave, beautiful moment. To think thoughts all my own, to feel my breath in my chest and know that it belongs to me. To know that I belong to myself, and that I can choose who— besides myself—I want to belong to. And I know, as I kiss Riley, that I want to belong to her. That we can belong to each other and everything else be damned, if we can live in this perfect snow globe moment, this feeling is worth giving up anything for.

Riley makes a small noise in her throat and my soul leaves my body. I slip my hand around the back of her neck, pulling her in, melting into this kiss, knowing how fragile everything is and how small I feel in the world, but that right here, right now, the world shrinks and we grow until everything is this moment.

sixteen

. . .

The next day, we attend the cult conference. We've missed so much, thank god, but what we do sit through is an endless parade of conservative rhetoric. Speaker after speaker exhorts us to keep ourselves pure for our future husbands. Riley snickers and whispers, "Husband? No thanks."

The heteronormativity really is quite stunning when I reflect. There is no scenario I could dream up in which my parents would allow me to spend two days unsupervised with a teenage boy. We don't even date—dating is forbidden. Instead, we "court," like old-timey castle people. *Courting* means heavily supervised dating with the intention of getting married, and there are established courting rules. Everyone is afraid of even the appearance of evil. But hanging with another teenage girl? A certain hot teenage girl who smells like grapefruit and whose skin tastes like heaven? No problem. I chuckle in my padded auditorium seat. My parents are so oblivious.

A beautiful young woman in navy and white talks to us about ways to modify clothing to make it more modest. She showcases her vintage skirt with a slit and a kick pleat that fills in the gap so that when she walks, we see only the swish of pleated fabric, and not the evil devil flash of her pale ankles. She shows a slide on the giant screen of creative ways to tie scarves to conceal "promiscuous" necklines. I salivate thinking of Riley's collarbone and . . . lower. The woman shows a slide of vintage hairstyles and how they "frame the face" and "draw attention to the eyes and away from the body," and I think of Riley's perfect short hair and how I want nothing more than to turn and stare at her. It's amazing how much time is devoted to teaching us how to avoid the attention of men.

"I hope they are spending this much time teaching the boys about consent and sexual harassment," Riley whispers in my ear.

"I seriously doubt it," I return quietly.

When we break for lunch, everyone lines up—thousands of young women in blue and white, picking up chicken sandwiches and cans of soda. Riley and I find a spot to eat together in the shade of a tree in the sprawling park area behind the conference center. Through the park, we can see the boys participating in their program. They wear khaki, with bandanas around their throats, and they are sweaty and muddy from obstacle courses and outdoorsy activities that look so much more fun than the chilly conference room purity lectures we've been sitting through.

For the first time, I don't particularly care. I've always been jealous of the boys' program, wished myself different, wished I could do the fun camp adventure-type activities, but now it doesn't matter. As long as I'm here with Riley, I'm happy. I wouldn't wish myself anywhere else. I glance around, worrying that someone I know will see us together, will somehow be able to tell that I've been kissing this beautiful girl, but there are so many thousands of students. I don't see Hannah, or anyone else I know.

Riley keeps examining the grass around us.

"What are you doing?" I ask.

"Oh, I recognize some of these!"

"Isn't it all just . . . grass?"

"Look closer." She holds a wide leaf in her fingers, stroking it with her thumb, and I feel my face heat.

"They each have their own shape, pattern, name."

I marvel at the wholesome wildness of her.

"Tell me the names?" I ask.

"What?"

"The names of the weeds!"

She grins at me, runs her fingers through her rowdy curls, then gestures to a clump of green. "This one is broadleaf plantain. If you ever get a bee sting, you can crush one up and put it on the sting as a poultice. Or, you know, chew it up and put it on that way."

"Spit and all?" I grimace.

"Spit and all!" She reaches out to finger another. "This is violet. The leaves are edible. You can make a really beautiful pesto with them. Actually, the flowers are edible too."

I'm barely seeing the plants—I'm watching her. The sparkle in her eyes, her strong fingers touching each leaf, the utter hotness of her sheer competence. My fingers itch to reach out and touch her, but there are too many eyes around. Every one a spy for White Republican Jesus.

"And somewhere there should be . . ." She casts her gaze around. "Ah-ha, here we have a lil baby burdock. These stalks are tasty, and the roots are edible too!" I giggle at the way she says "lil baby burdock." She's so strong and firm yet entirely soft and nurturing.

"I had no idea so many weeds were edible. Where did you learn all this?"

"Well"—she sighs deeply—"back when I had a phone, I was

obsessed with foraging TikTok. It's so dumb, my mom took it away because of 'the gay.'" She says the words mockingly. "But really, I was mostly there to learn about foraging for mushrooms and shit." She smirks. "And also the gay."

Our eyes lock, and we smile. The sun is slanting through the tree branches, a beam of light touching her eyes just right and illuminating the deep brown of her irises into sparkling multi-dimensional amber. I don't know what's happening to me, not really. All I know is that this, right here, feels right, and I want more and more of it.

Our last night before we head home, we shower together and then lie curled around each other in bed. I'm spooning Riley, and I've learned that I like spooning every which way. Big spoon, little spoon, all the spoons. Every way feels perfect as long as one of us is curled around the other.

"Val?" Riley asks into the quiet space of the room.

"Yeah?" I breathe, smelling the curve of her neck, kissing her gently behind her ear.

"How are we gonna talk? You know, when we go home."

I reflect in the silence.

"I don't know. I don't have a cell phone. I have an email account for online classes, but my mom checks it regularly to see what I'm up to. I guess we could pass notes at church?"

"We'll figure it out," Riley whispers into the linen-crisp quiet of the room. "Just keep an eye out. I don't know how, but I'll find a way."

seventeen

· · ·

The days after the conference pass in a blur. I write papers for Bible class, we study the Virtue Booklets. I endure sermons and lectures and devotionals. I ride my bike to the library and read every gay book I can find. I log in to the library computers and read more about critical race theory and abortion and my rights when I turn eighteen in a few months. At home I look down deferentially when my parents lecture me, I avoid eye contact so I appear submissive, I pick my favorite Bible verse during devotionals. Outwardly, I shrink and bow and submit while inside I grow and stretch and rebel.

I see Riley at church and we chat in corners, steal away to the grove behind the church for embraces and kisses, but we don't have the time and space that we had at the conference. The trains of our lives are on separate tracks and they converge only briefly. I miss her so much. I want to return to our magical days together, but the dark forest of my life closes in. I want kisses and glances and peach gummy afternoons, but I don't know how to get back there.

It's mid afternoon, and I'm standing in the kitchen, chatting on the phone with Hannah. I lean across the kitchen counter on my elbows until my mom walks by. She smacks me on the butt with the papers she's holding and whispers loudly, "Stop sticking your butt out, it's not ladylike. Two more minutes, I need my phone back." I straighten until she leaves the kitchen, and then I sprawl back out. It feels like every time I breathe, my mom is criticizing me. But here's the thing I've realized about her constant disapproval; if she's going to be mad at me no matter what I do, I might as well give up on trying to make her happy.

"The Zellers have been over for dinner at least once a week," Hannah is saying excitedly. "Seth seems to especially like my desserts, so I've been making fancier ones. I made a chocolate cheesecake with *gorgeous* chocolate shavings last night. He seemed super impressed."

I pop a grape into my mouth from the bowl of fruit on the counter. Having your almost-fiancée evaluate your cooking as part of deciding whether to marry you sounds pretty *medieval child bride* to me, but I can't say that to Hannah.

"We went on a walk after dinner, but stayed in full view of the house, of course, and no holding hands obviously," Hannah continues.

"What, no moonlight kisses?" I joke lazily.

"Valerie, of *course not!*" Hannah says, so scandalized it almost sounds like she's pretending, but I know she's not. "The Zellers had been bringing fresh bread from a local bakery, but they found out the owners were *gay*." She whispers the last word, like it's too dirty to say out loud. "So obviously they've had to find a different bakery. I made sure they know that I am an expert bread baker, so they won't have to worry about home-made bread ever again if things between me and Seth go well!"

I feel a twinge of fear at the word *gay*. I've never talked to Hannah about this before; honestly, I hardly ever hear the word *gay* outside of raging sermons about "the homosexuals." Ah yes, this is how I got to be seventeen years old before learning the word *bisexual.* Or *queer.* Or *LGBTQIA+.* Basically the only one I've heard whispered occasionally is *gay.*

"Oh yeah?" I say. "Was the gay bakery's bread bad or something?"

"Well yeah, I mean, no, it was really good, but obviously they can't keep shopping . . . hold on." I hear a child wail in the background. The cries sound more urgent than I'm used to hearing. Then a hymn plays through a speaker, the volume getting louder until it covers the sound of the child crying.

"Sorry about that!" Hannah comes back on the line. I hear a door open and close, and then the sounds of the sobbing child and the music grow fainter. "One of the littles is getting a paddling."

I don't know what to say. David and I don't really get spanked anymore, but I know other families spank their kids a lot. That poor kid sounded really upset.

"Are they okay?" I venture.

"Oh yeah, I mean you've seen how difficult Ezekiel can be."

I flash back to him vomiting on the table.

"Anyways, what was I saying?" she continues. "Oh yeah, obviously we can't shop there anymore."

"Why not?" I don't know why, but I want to hear her say it. I can control so little of what happens around me, sometimes a bruise I ask for feels better than one inflicted without my consent.

"You know why," Hannah says. "Because it's sin."

"Oh yeah," I reply noncommittally.

"My dad always says everyone has gay thoughts, you just have to choose not to act on them," Hannah continues. "Which makes sense. Like, everyone knows girls are more attractive than boys, but we can't *act* on it."

I almost choke on my grape. Hannah's dad, the prim Mr. Patterson, thinks everyone has same-sex attraction? And so does Hannah? If straight people are real and truly exist, it makes me wonder how many people in our community are queer but will never admit it. I wonder how much less angry and tightly wound our parents would be, how much less sexual misconduct and scandal there might be, if everyone was allowed to be themselves. If we were all free of these made up rules in this pretend world.

My mom comes back in the kitchen and holds out her hand, her face as impatient and disappointed as ever.

"Hey, Hannah, I gotta go. See you Sunday!"

Hanging up, I hand Mom her phone. "Thanks!"

"Sure, honey. Hey, Valerie?" Her tone changes, and her face is full of exaggerated kindness. She stops me from making my planned quick exit from the kitchen.

"Yeah, Mom?"

"I spoke with Mrs. Patterson the other day"—Hannah's mom? Why does this involve me?—"and she said that Andrew's been trying to be friendly toward you."

"Oh . . . I, um, okay?" Honestly I've barely noticed, but I guess he does seem to somehow stumble across me with a few awkward words when we are at church or Bible class. I'm not sure what Mom is getting at though.

"Well, has he been?"

"I guess so. He usually says hi."

"Okay, well, try to be nice. Ask him how his week has been, make conversation. You know you are a prickly person. Try to be more kind and inviting."

I bristle. I'm not trying to be "prickly," but I genuinely have no desire to be friends with Andrew. He's all awkward angles and weird vibes and like, that's fine, but I don't particularly want to hang around him.

"Well, I just don't think we have much in common, Mom." I try to answer diplomatically, but I hear annoyance creeping into my voice.

"Watch your tone, young lady," she warns. I sigh. I'm so good at groveling and tiptoeing around my parents' egos, but sometimes it feels impossible to make them happy and still maintain even a shred of myself.

"Just try to be friendlier to him. He's shy and could really use some encouragement. Talking to you could help him with his self-esteem."

I bristle. "I don't see how it's my job to make him feel better about himself."

"Maybe it's not your job, but it's a good thing you could do, so why wouldn't you?" my mom asks severely, the mask of friendliness completely dropped by now.

"Because I don't want to?" I raise my voice. "Because it's not my fault a teenage boy is hella awkward, and a chore to be around, and has the social skills of a paper bag!"

"Valerie. Watch yourself."

"I don't see why this is my problem!"

"You watch your tone! Go to your room and pray about this. I think God has some things to say to you about your attitude."

"You can't just put words in God's mouth, Mom!"

"Go to your room!" she snaps. She takes a breath and lowers her tone, but not her intensity. "Stay there, read your Bible, and pray. Your father will come discuss your behavior with you when he gets home."

Stomping to my room, I slam the door and throw myself into my closet. It's dark and quiet, the sounds of the world muffled. I plug in my Christmas lights and sag into the corner, landing on the hard corners of a few books, their spines digging in to my ribs and chest.

I scream into a fistful of blankets. I hate everything, but at the moment, I specifically hate *this*. Why is it *my* freaking fault that I don't find Andrew interesting? Why am I forever scolded and lectured and punished for having a freaking opinion?! In the books I read, in the fantasy worlds I try to live in, strong girls accomplish great things. They conquer kingdoms and worlds and hearts, they challenge rules and conventions, they disagree with crappy council, they fight friggin *dragons*, for fork's sake. But in my life, every time I disagree, I'm *rebellious*. I'm *difficult*. I need to talk to God and pray for help fixing my attitude. Maybe my attitude is fine. Maybe my attitude is *anger* because this whole setup, this whole parents-and-God-vs.-me scenario, is awful and stupid. I stare up at the water-stained ceiling.

As long as I can remember, I've had a recurring dream about a secret passage out of my closet. Sometimes it's a tiny spiral staircase; sometimes it's a ladder that leads to a hatch. But it always leads to a secret room at the peak of the house, where I keep the things I love, where I keep my secrets. I've had this dream enough times that sometimes I think it's really there, that secret happy room where my feelings can feel and my hopes can hope. But lying here, staring at the shadowy ceiling—the paint yellowed with age, the corners crowded with cobwebs—I feel the heavy, heavy weight of every impossible, beautiful dream that lives in my soft, hurting heart. And I realize that I will never be happy here. I will never be able to be myself or belong to myself in this house, with my parents pounding me down daily with the fist of God. I need to leave.

Walking into church on Sunday, I'm vibrating with excitement. I can't wait to see Riley. I'm walking briskly toward the sanctuary to look for her when Andrew intercepts me, standing in my way, his skinny form somehow imposing, blocking my path.

"Hi, Valerie," he mumbles.

"Oh, hey. Hi, Andrew!" I pull my face up into a smile. Why is he always trying to . . . I'd say "talk to me," but he doesn't talk so much as stand in my way and stare.

"How was your week?" he tries.

"It was good!" We stare awkwardly at each other's feet. "How was your week?" I did get a lecture about being *nice*, so I guess I'll give it some minimal effort.

"It was great!" He smiles. I guess he is nice, I should be nice. I'm just so genuinely annoyed by him on a cellular level. Every epithelial cell in my skin is leaning *away* from him.

"We've been splitting wood."

"Oh yeah?"

"Yeah, getting ready for the winter. You know."

"Cool."

We almost make eye contact but both swerve our eyes away from each other, him staring at my shoes and me peering behind him toward the sanctuary.

"Well, I guess I'd better . . ." I start.

"Oh yeah, of course. See you around, Valerie!"

"Bye, Andrew." I catch sight of my mom across the foyer. "Have a great week!" I add cheerfully, projecting it so she hears. Good grief, my life is such a pathetic performance, always. His face brightens like he thinks I mean it.

"I will! You too!"

I hurry past my mom with a quick "Hey Mom, I'll save us seats!" and into the sanctuary, looking around for Riley. There, off to the side, I see Riley and her mom already seated. Perfect. I slide in next to her with a quiet smile, laying my sweater out across the seats to save space for Mom, Dad, and David.

"Hey!" Riley grins at me. God, I missed her.

"Hey," I breathe. She leans forward and gives me a hug, and I remember that hugs are okay. No one will suspect anything from a hug. I throw my arms around her and squeeze.

Riley laughs. "You hug like a train wreck! Let a girl breathe!"

"Sorry!" I laugh. "I just missed you!"

"Yeah. Me too, Val."

My mom slides into the seat next to me, greeting Riley and her mom warmly, and the service starts. I don't hear a thing, my thigh pressed tight against Riley's the whole time. When the pastor launches into a lengthy prayer, Riley reaches her hand out, palm up, and I smile. Blessed be heteronormativity, I guess. I take her hand in mine—it's warm, her calluses are rough. Her thumb strokes over my hand, and it's all I can do to keep from moaning out loud in church.

I've never wished for a prayer to last *longer*, but I could happily sit here holding Riley's hand all freaking day. Sadly, the prayer draws to a close and Riley gives me a parting squeeze. We lock eyes as our hands slowly slide apart. I am so, *so* gone for this girl.

After the service, we steal away to the grove of trees behind the church. As the trees close around us and the church disappears, I launch myself into Riley's arms, showering her face with kisses.

"Hey!" She laughs. "I missed you too!"

"Riley," I groan. "I missed you so much. I don't know how I made it through the week without you."

"I missed you too, Val," she says, her hand on my cheek. I lean into her hand, closing my eyes as her thumb gently brushes my skin.

"Here, I brought you this." She pulls a carefully folded paper out of her pocket. On it are adorable sketches of a mushroom doing cute things. Actually, two mushrooms. A Riley-looking mushroom with a crooked grin, and another shorter mushroom that looks kind of like me. The mushrooms shower together with a tiny sponge and a scrub brush, they lie together spooning in bed with a blanket pulled over their stems. One mushroom dices a smaller mushroom on a cutting board, while the other looks in through the window in horror. I laugh at that one.

"Cannibal mushrooms? Mushroomibals? Cannishrooms?"

"They're dumb, you don't have to keep them."

"No!" I hold them out of her reach. "I love them. They are so you. So us. Thank you."

"Come here," she says, low in her chest, and pulls me toward her. Her lips are soft and her hands are strong. She tastes like green tea and toothpaste. We kiss briefly and both glance around anxiously as we pull away, but no one is around. I miss the perfect safety of our hotel kisses.

"Tell me about your week?" she asks, pulling me down beside her. We sit on a plush blanket of pine needles, branches reaching around us, shielding us from the sky.

"Ugh, it was alright, I guess. My online chemistry class has been tough. I've been studying a lot, but it's good."

"I'm jealous," she says. "I'm so fucking bored, with nothing but Virtue Booklets and Bible study. It gives me plenty of time to draw, though, so that's cool."

"I thought your mom didn't like you drawing?"

"Well she can't hide every pencil, pen, and piece of paper in the house." Riley shrugs. "Honestly, I think she's just waiting for me to graduate high school and get out of her hair. Like I said, the homeschool thing was just a last ditch effort to get me graduated after I got expelled." She reaches up and fingers my hair gently then squeezes my chin affectionately, her thumb pressing firmly into the almost-dimple on my chin.

"Oh, and I've been listening to that book you said you loved. *One Last Stop?*"

"Yeah?"

"The narrator is alright, but the book is just incredible. I love Myla and Niko and everyone so much, I can't wait to find that for myself."

"That's what I loved too! The freedom and the joy, it's so *good!*" I think about the freedom I felt while we were away. The magic of not only being with Riley, but being *myself*, away from the oppression of my parents.

"I've been thinking about what you said," I say.

"Yeah? About what?"

Now that I've started saying this, I'm afraid to finish the thought. To say it out loud. But it's the truth of my heart, and Riley has been nothing but a safe harbor in which to dock my feelings, so I continue.

"About leaving. About turning eighteen. And I'm in. I want to get out."

"Yeah?" She smiles. "Really?"

"Yeah," I breathe. "Really. I honestly can't wait to get out of here. I can't wait to start living."

"It'll be hard—like, so much work," Riley says. "Paying for a place to live and food and all that is expensive, but we can do it."

"We?" I ask, filled with warmth. "I mean, I don't really know, but I'm guessing my feelings have moved pretty fast with us. I just feel like I've waited forever to feel like this. Like I'm one of those sad spindly plants that grew in the dark, and I'm finally turning toward the sun, so I don't know if you mean *we*, as in—"

"We," she says again, firmly. Her confidence is so much, I feel it spread, warm and gentle through my chest. "I know this is ridiculously fast but . . ." She pauses. "I love you, Val. I don't know exactly what I'm doing but I know that whatever it is, I want to do it with you if you want to do it with me too."

"I love you, Riley," I reply, my breath shuddering but resolute. I pull our foreheads together, the space between us ringing with the conviction of our words in this sacred pine needle chapel. "I love you," I say again. "You, me—this is everything, right here. Let's figure it out."

"Let's figure it out," she breathes.

eighteen

. . .

It's Monday morning, and I'm in a terrible mood. I sat through morning devotional. I ate congee and did the dishes. I had my private devotional time where I did a page of sudoku I saved from the newspaper, discreetly hidden in the pages of my Bible. I sat with Mom and David and read a section of a Virtue Booklet. This one was about the authority of the Bible from the very first chapter, when God made Adam and Eve, showing that man and woman are the basis of marriage and on and on yada yada.

That's the funny thing about entwining literally everything we are supposed to believe with the Bible—when a pillar of it shakes, like me and all the not God-approved feelings I have for Riley, it shakes the entire Bible for me. Which is leading me to feel like maybe I should throw the whole thing out. I don't know. I really don't know what I think or believe anymore, I've just had a strong suspicion for a while that a lot of this is bull crap—*bullshit*, I think to myself smugly. Yeah, I can swear in my mind, and no one knows. God hasn't even started punishing me with lightning or mysterious illness like I've been told he would if I fell into sin. It's almost like that was something the adults made up to manipulate me.

I'm sitting at the computer in the office. The screen is turned toward the open doorway and my mom is walking by frequently. Internet rules have been extremely strict since David was caught looking at stuff online. I heard so much about how it was not "God honoring" and such a "grievous and shameful habit" that my parents kind of glossed over exactly what it was. All I know for sure is that they were furious. David had to get up earlier and stay up later for extra devotional time with my dad. They took him to talk to the pastor about it, they took the door to his room off its hinges for a while so he couldn't "hide his sin," and now I am watched like a hawk as I try to do my chemistry homework. My mom peeks her head in again.

"What, Mom? I swear I'm just doing my homework."

"Don't swear, Valerie. Let your yes be yes . . ."

"And your no be no," I complete the verse. "I know, it's not that I'm trying to hide anything. You're just making me anxious."

"And why would my presence make you anxious?" my mom asks, warning in her tone.

Dang it. *Damn it*, I correct in my mind, smiling slightly at the internal act of rebellion. Then I stop smiling as I realize I'm earning myself closer scrutiny.

"Actually, never mind, Mom. I'm glad you are keeping an eye on me, I appreciate the accountability."

"You are so welcome." Mom beams. "Thank you for your change of attitude."

I roll my eyes as I turn back to the screen. My parents are delusional. But it does make them easy to manipulate.

"You know you are lucky you even get to take these class-es," my mom calls over her shoulder as she turns to head back to the kitchen. "Your friend Hannah only studies Virtue Booklets.

You are lucky your father and I are willing to spend time and money letting you learn something as useless for a woman as chemistry."

"Useless?" I ask.

"Yes, useless," she says. "Most of the other parents expect their daughters to get married and raise godly children for the Lord." I roll my eyes at the screen as my mom continues. "And frankly, I worry about you and your interest in books and fantasy worlds."

I stay facing the computer. This is a familiar conversation—or rather *lecture*—I've endured many times. I mouth along as she continues.

"Why are you always reading fantasy books? Is there a reason you want to escape reality? You should really focus on your relationship with God and working to further His kingdom. Look at me when I'm speaking to you, Valerie."

I turn and glare. She gives me a look and I try to soften my gaze, but it's so hard to play this part.

"Focus on your work, Valerie." She turns and heads to the kitchen. I relax my face and throw my head back in frustration. I've been *trying* to focus on my school work. Who instigated this freaking conversation?

As I stare at the study guide on the screen, my vision blurs. What would it be like to relax from the lying? From the pretending? For just a day? And then I remember. Peach slices, dappled light through a weeping willow, the warmest smile on the kindest face I've ever known. I glance down at my ring—formerly my purity ring, now my Riley-wants-me-to-believe-in-myself ring—and I smile.

A notification pops up, a new email: "yourchemistry teacher496@gmail.com has shared a Google doc with you." I push a pen off the desk, bend down to pick it up, and casually glance behind me. My mom isn't there. It's sad how good at lying I have to be to survive around here. No wonder I'm so jumpy and high strung—my life is under a freaking microscope.

I open the email and head to the linked Google doc. The doc is confusing. It's a chemistry paper? But it looks more advanced than what we are covering in our online class. I wonder if this got sent to me by mistake, but it seems too great a coincidence since I am, in fact, taking an online chemistry class. I scroll down the document. I check the permissions. It appears I have editing permissions, but why? There is a weird amount of space between section headers. Like, a lot of space. I do a neck stretch to check behind me again—coast is still clear. I highlight the extra lines of blank space.

"I miss you every moment we are apart."

Oh my god. The profanity slips into my thoughts easily. It's from Riley. This whole ridiculous college chemistry paper is from *my Riley*. She's hidden her notes to me in the margins, in white, so I can't see it until I highlight the area. She is such a hot genius, and oh my god her *writing*. In real life, face to face, she's a little close with her words, she's cool, brief, and succinct. But here she's written me a goddamn love letter, and I'm melting into this old creaky office chair. I scroll through the document on a freaking treasure hunt, finding each delicious gift she's tucked away for me.

"I foraged some wild onions today, thought of you and our ramen date. I've never been happier than those days we had together."

"Remember that ridiculous sandwich I made? I put hot sauce on a hard-boiled egg today, like it would somehow take me back there. I dream of you and the way you taste like peach slices under the willow tree."

"I've been looking on Craigslist for a room for rent. I know we have months to go until you turn eighteen, but I'm already planning. I can't wait to fall asleep in your arms."

My eyes are flooded with tears and my heart is pounding in my chest. I check behind me discreetly, wipe my tears and sniff, check behind me again. Mom walks by.

"How much longer are you going to be?" she asks.

"This study guide is really kicking my butt. I don't understand half of it—UGH!" I groan performatively. "I'm so sick of staring at this screen, maybe I should just quit for the day."

"Your test is tomorrow, isn't it?" my mom asks in alarm. "Why didn't you get started on this sooner? Stay there and focus. Don't get up until dinner is ready."

I groan again for good measure, and then heave an enormous fake sigh. "Okay, you are right, I'll try to get another half an hour of study in."

Heart racing, fingers trembling, I quickly head to where Riley's messages ended. I glance behind me briefly again to ensure that Mom is still gone, and begin to add my own notes in the margins.

"My Dearest Riley, how I miss you. I look at my ring constantly"—I pause to roll it around my finger with my thumb —"and think of you, and me, and how beautiful the world is when we are together. Thank you for seeing me as I am, thank you for loving me without seeking to change me. I've spent so much of my lifetime trying to be saved, improved, made more virtuous or righteous or whatever, that it feels world-tilting to be loved as I am. And loved by someone like you."

I switch back to my study guide and rush through the end. Everything makes sense, I think. I'm honestly glowing with too much warmth to concentrate on chemical formulas and equations.

Switching back to our document, I add in another margin, "I adore that you are looking into a place for us. I love the thought that there is a place for us, somehow, somewhere.

Away from all this groveling and pretending and faking. I just want to simply be. With you. Your, Val."

I smile. I read a book once where lovers signed their letters "your" instead of "yours." A mistake at first glance, but removing that single letter somehow adds meaning. Belonging. And I do belong. Not here, not at church, not in this swirling vortex of judgment and Jesus. I belong with Riley.

nineteen

. . .

It's Halloween, and I'm filling plastic sandwich bags with candy. I suppose normal people stay at home to hand out treats, wear fun costumes, chat with their neighbors, even put up decorations. But not my family. Nope. My parents hate Halloween. It's the holiday celebrating death and evil, according to them, and even *seeing* children in fun little witch and vampire costumes is enough to pull our souls toward the dark side, or something. It's no surprise I've been pretty terrified of Halloween for most of my life, but this year, everything looks different.

Maybe these families out trick-or-treating are just . . . having fun. Maybe it doesn't have to be gloomy and weird; maybe *we* are the ones who have made it weird. I sigh as I put another mini Snickers into the bag with the Tootsie Pop and tract. Oh yeah—our family hands out not just candy, but salvation. Because that's what kids really want on Halloween. Not candy, but a little paper booklet that tells them how to save their souls. After all, what's spookier than telling kids they are going to hell?

I grab a handful of candy and shove it into another bag. My family is like this for every holiday. Easter? Heck no to the Easter Bunny and godless, non-religious celebrations. Christmas? Jesus is the reason for the season. Santa Claus is evil because he's stealing the focus. Giving those pathetic nonbelievers a reason to be happy without repenting.

The whole nonbelievers thing is incredibly othering. My parents and friends even call other Christian denominations nonbelievers. I guess that's another point in the cult column. We love to feel special, set apart, like we have all the answers and everyone else is lost and hopeless. The more I see people outside this bubble, the more I realize the script I've been fed just isn't true. I guess this is why our parents are instructed to never let us go to college or leave home or watch secular media or listen to secular music. The leadership is afraid we'll start meeting other people and thinking for ourselves.

"Valerie, pay attention to what you are doing!" my mom chides me. "You put four pieces of candy in this one! Three *only*."

"Oh. Yeah, sure, Mom." I remove the extra pieces, then tie ribbon around the opening to seal each bag. When I'm done, I pile them into a bowl and put them on the stoop outside with a handmade sign: PLEASE TAKE ONLY ONE.

"Why are you taking so long, Valerie? Come on, we have to get going! It's getting dark; people are going to start trick-or-treating, and I don't want to be here," my mom frets, gathering her purse and some bags of candy, and hurrying us out to the minivan. David is already in the van, dressed in overalls and a straw hat. I guess his costume is . . . *farmer*. I'm wearing a denim jumper with a plaid shirt underneath, my hair in long braided pigtails. I guess I'm a farmer too? Asian Raggedy Ann? We are heading to the Zellers' farm for a Harvest Party, and the mandate was absolutely no spooky costumes, so our options are limited. It's pretty funny how insistent the adults are that we are *not* celebrating Halloween. We get together and play games and eat candy annually, and the date just happens to fall on October 31. It definitely has nothing to do with Halloween.

"Bill? Bill?" my mom calls my dad. "Bill! We are all going to wait for you in the van!"

My dad finally appears at the door to the garage, slipping his shoes on, his reading glasses on his head. As he pulls the van out of the garage, he asks cheerily, "Are we ready for some Harvest Party?"

"Kind of old for it," David mumbles under his breath.

"What was that?" my mom asks.

"Yay!" David says with fake enthusiasm.

"What's the matter, son?" Dad asks, waiting for a few trick-or-treaters to cross the street in front of our van.

"I dunno, it'd be fun to go trick-or-treating just once. I was talking to DeAndre next door, and—"

"That's fine for them and their family," my dad says firmly, "but they aren't believers. We know better. And be careful of talking to him too much; I don't know that he's a good influence on you. As long as you are witnessing to him—telling him about Jesus, inviting him to church—then that's fine." David slouches down into his seat, staring out the window, pointedly not answering.

Children are pouring into the streets from the homes in our subdivision, decked out in costumes both colorful and dark. As we pass a tiny toddler in a ball gown with a tiara, her dad and his friend catch her before she walks straight into a telephone pole.

Wait. I whip my head around and look out the back window. Her *dads*. I don't know for sure, but now I wonder how many gay couples I've seen that my parents and upbringing have convinced me are just friends.

"So sad," my mom tuts from the front passenger seat. "Teaching children to celebrate darkness and evil."

We pass some older kids dressed as witches and super-heroes, laughing, unwrapping lollipops.

"Dear Lord God," my dad begins to pray aloud, "please bring these lost people to you. Help them see that you are the only way to peace and happiness." I snort softly in my seat. For being the people with all the peace and happiness, our household sure seems to have both in short supply.

"Yes, Lord God," my mom takes up fervently, praying with her eyes open, looking down (literally and figuratively) on the happy families. "Let them see the evil of their ways. Let them see that they desperately need you."

"Valerie?" my dad asks, "Would you like to pray?" The look in his eyes in the rearview mirror tells me it's not a suggestion.

"Yeah, sure. Heavenly Father," I start.

"Yes, Lord God. Yes, Lord God," my mom chants.

"Um, please let us have a good time at the Harvest Party tonight."

"Yes, Father," my dad picks up, "keep us safe, may you be glorified."

He keeps going, trading off with my mom. I press my face against the cool glass, watching the people blur past. I hate this. I've always been told it's my own problem, my own fault, my own bad attitude. But I wonder what it would be like to be normal. To not continually classify things as good or evil. To just feel feelings and do things for no other reason than fun? Joy? It must be nice.

We arrive at the Zellers' farm and head toward the brightly lit barn, where Christian hymns are playing loudly from speakers.

"Valerie!" Hannah attacks me in a hug. "Dude, you look so *cute!*" she squeals, while pulling back and smoothing her own costume, obviously waiting for me to compliment her.

"Thanks Hannah! Um, wow, you look amazing too!" She swishes her skirt back and forth. "What are you?" I ask.

"A vintage secretary!" She rolls her eyes like it was obvious. I guess I can see it, with her bun kept in place with two pencils, her high-collared shirt and vintage skirt. She looks . . . sexy. I'm surprised her parents let her wear this. But I guess since it's vintage, it feels like a tribute to "the good old days" the adults are always referencing. When men were men and women were women. I roll my eyes internally. I have got to get out of here.

"Have you seen Riley?" I ask.

"Riley who?" a familiar voice croons in my ear, and my heart skips a whole bunch of beats as I turn to see Riley. In a suit. Her curls are straightened and framing her face, and she's wearing a dark suit. Black collared shirt buttoned to the top. Black tie. It's an objectively modest outfit by Institute standards. Her wrists and ankles and neck are covered, and sure she's wearing pants (which are frowned upon), but they aren't tight—and good god does Riley look hot.

"What are you?" Hannah asks, more than a little snidely. "A secret service agent?"

"I'm John Wick," Riley says proudly.

"Who?" Hannah asks. I still haven't found my voice, still having the gayest of awakenings seeing Riley in this suit.

"John Wick—you know, from like, the John Wick movies?"

We stare back blankly. Stupidly. I'm surprised Riley is still surprised at how little we know of the outside world. My parents are vocally opposed to Disney movies, Star Wars, and other movies that must be popular but I just don't know about.

"Oh, well," Riley explains to our blank faces, "it's just a cool action movie series. Keanu Reeves, you know."

We obviously don't, but she's nice to act like it's no big deal.

"We'd better get to our stations." Hannah moves on from the awkwardness. "I'm in charge of bobbing for apples, and you are . . . ?"

"Horseshoes," I supply. "Riley and I are running it together."

"Let's get rolling!" Hannah chirps, and we head toward the barn.

Strings of lights warm the open space with a soft yellow glow. Hay bales are piled strategically, creating sections holding different games. Cornhole, ring toss, and some classic games that families have put a Christian spin on. I squint at a hand-painted church where I'm assuming you pin the cross onto the steeple? There's a craft station where kids can decorate a print of a Bible verse. There's a tractor being made ready for hay rides, and outside, a circle for pony rides.

People come from hours away for this every year; it's a big Institute family event. We used to invite "unsaved" friends as a way to witness to them and try to convert them, but after a family came with their kids dressed as a witch and a wizard, the parents quickly decided that the risk to the hearts and minds of their own children was just too great. Maybe that's what's wrong with me—seeing that little boy with a wizard wand was the start of my descent into debauchery. I chuckle quietly.

"What's so funny, Val?" Riley asks.

I glance with intention at Hannah and whisper, "Oh I'll tell you later. Let's go." I grab her hand and pull her outside, toward the Zellers' house.

The front of the Zellers' house is bright and busy in the twilight, moms bustling in and out with Bundt cakes, candied apples, and plates of cookies. I pull Riley down the hill to the back of the house, where it's growing dark, the area made private by huge shrubs. I push her against the brick wall, then throw my arms around her shoulders.

"Hey." She laughs, low and throaty. "I got your messages."

"YOU," I say, accusatory. I hold her shoulders and lean back to drink her in. "First, you in this suit are absolutely ruining my life. I mean, I just *cannot.*"

"You don't look so bad yourself." Riley smirks at me, fingering the end of my braided pigtail.

"Also. Your messages!" I lean in close, and she takes my chin in her hand. "You absolute evil hot genius," I whisper.

"Places, places! Harvest Party is starting! Time to celebrate the goodness of the Lord!" a booming voice calls over a megaphone from the direction of the barn.

"Do we have to?" I groan.

"I'm the newbie here, but I *do* feel like people would notice if our horseshoe station is unattended."

"One kiss. Please?" I lean in and kiss her. I feel her smile against my lips, and if it isn't the best feeling I've ever felt.

"I love you, Val, but we shouldn't be doing this here." Riley pushes me back gently. It hurts, but I know she's right. "Come on, cowgirl." She takes my hand and walks toward the barn, pulling me along. "Let's go have some definitely-not-Halloween fun."

Our horseshoe station is just outside the barn, I guess for safety. I mean, horseshoes are pretty heavy, so I guess throwing them around indoors where the crowd is wouldn't be safe. The great thing about being outside the barn, though, is that not everyone realizes this is even a game station. And we're a bit away from the crowd. So basically, we get to hang out while looking like we are doing our job.

"Alright, lil man!" Riley high-fives a little boy as he finishes throwing his last horseshoe.

"Pick a prize?" I offer him the bowl of candy.

"Thank you!" He looks greedily into the bowl, his eyes huge.

"You can take two," I say.

"What?!" he squeaks. He takes a minute, agonizing over Dum Dums suckers and Tootsie Rolls, finally taking one of each and heading back inside where most of the fun is happening.

"Geez, have these kids seen candy before?" Riley mutters to me once he's out of earshot. She offers me a bite of her candied apple. The candy coating is violently red and shiny, the apple crisp and tart. I wipe a dribble of apple juice from my chin.

"Not really?" I laugh. "A lot of the Institute families are super into natural living and all that, in addition to, you know, oppressing women. So candy is a big no no. In fact"—I lower my voice and nod discreetly toward the doorway where a severe-looking woman stands with her arms crossed—"that's Hannah's aunt, and she *definitely* does not approve of what's going on here."

"I don't think I'll ever get used to the constant judgment." Riley laughs. "Even the Institute people who are boring AF get judged by other Institute people. It's exhausting."

"Yes, it is." I sigh. "But I don't want to talk about that." I smile at her, wanting with all my heart to put my arms around her but fearing the consequences. "What have you been up to? Any word on . . . plans?"

Riley steps closer and lowers her voice. "So, it sounds like my mom is going to let me go to college."

"What?" I say way too loudly, then lower my voice and step even closer. "What?"

"Yeah, well, a lot of kids do go to college, you know." Riley shrugs.

"But not *here*," I whisper, looking around again. "I mean, that's amazing. I just . . . can hardly believe it."

"Yeah, well she's not super, you know, into the whole Institute thing. This was just supposed to get me graduated and keep me out of trouble. I know it hasn't been easy for her, raising me on her own. I think she really believes staying close to church people is better for me or something. Anyways, I've made it clear that I want to study art, and I guess she'd rather support me than cut me off."

"Wow, Riley, that's great! I'm so happy for you!"

"Yeah, I even have some money in a college fund from my grandparents." We stop as a few kids head our way, but they change their minds and turn toward the pony rides. "So, I'm applying to community college to get some prerequisites out of the way. I'm looking at applying to jobs—I can probably work as a cashier or maybe a barista part time—and I'm looking for a cheap room to rent close by."

"Wow, that's . . . Riley, that's awesome!" I feel myself forcing my enthusiasm. It's not that I'm not happy for Riley—I am. I'm just so sad for myself. I want so badly to have the support to plan for my future. And it hurts to see her making plans so freely, so confidently, when I don't even have the space to *breathe*, constantly worried about being found out, about my parents realizing the truth about me, about who I am.

"Hey, Val, where'd you go?" Riley looks me in my eyes, which I realize are filling with tears. "Don't leave me here by myself, I'm scared of these people." I snort a laugh, and she quickly brushes a tear from my cheek with her thumb. "I didn't mean to make you sad."

I take a deep breath. "I'm really happy for you. I just . . . I wish I could make plans for myself. Like, if I was stronger."

"Val. There has been nothing normal about your life so far.

I don't blame you for not having things figured out. You've just been surviving."

My eyes overflow with tears again. Laughter trickles from the crowd as a kid splashes around in the water barrel, bobbing for apples. I turn my back to the barn so prying eyes can't see.

"I guess I have been," I whisper through my tears. It's so true, and I love Riley for seeing it. For not judging me. "I'm sorry for reacting like this. I shouldn't be sad. I should be happy for you."

"I mean, I'd like that too."

"God, Riley, I *am*. It's just that . . . you don't need me to tag along and make your life a mess."

"Hey, who said anything about you making my life a mess? I want you with me. I want a shitty little room somewhere with you." She reaches out and rubs my arm gently, then pulls back.

It's painful standing here, trying to keep my posture up so I don't look sad to the people in the barn. Aching to hug Riley but not wanting to shatter everything. I see pain etched on her face, and I know she feels the strain too. I think about how bravely Riley is making plans, and why seeing that is so painful to me. And how I can explain that to her without taking away from the joy she deserves to feel.

"You said I've just been surviving," I start, "and that's so true? I remember one time, we had my Taiwanese grandparents over and my dad made all these conversation topics for us to talk to them about, and my mom was translating. And my dad kept asking them what their dreams were when they were young. What they dreamed about being. And they were just confused, because like, they were really poor, and they were just trying to survive, you know? And in a weird way I feel like I've just been trying to survive? Say the right things and look the right way and try to avoid pissing my parents off? I mean, I know my life hasn't been that bad, I really shouldn't even complain..."

"Val, we can know your life has been religious hell while also acknowledging that other kinds of struggle exist. It's okay to see that." I smile at her and push the tears off my cheeks with the back of my hand. "Let's just pretend for a minute that your parents aren't manipulative religious zealots who think women are baby-making machines," Riley says, and I look around instinctively to make sure no one is close enough to hear. "What would you want to do?"

"I... I mean, it's hard to think past what I know?"

"Of course, and that's okay." Riley squats down and pulls at a few strands of grass. "But pie in the sky, away from here, what's something you'd like to do?"

"Books," I say suddenly. "Books have been my only escape. I guess I'd like to see if I'm any good at writing, maybe. And I just want to be happy somewhere. I'd like to be with you."

"I want to be with you, Val." Riley stands and grins down at me.

"How's it going?" Hannah bursts from behind us, scaring the absolute crap out of me. I desperately wipe my hands over my face, thankful my eyes are mostly dry.

"Oh hey," Riley says, unflappable as always. "What's next on the schedule?"

"Pie-eating contest!" Hannah beams. "I made strawberry rhubarb, Seth's favorite."

"Oh yeah?" Riley asks, knowing Seth is an easy way to get Hannah excited and distracted.

"Yes, and I can't *wait* to see him try it. Everyone knows the way to a man's heart is through his stomach!" she sings. It's really strange seeing how weird this child-bride situation is, while also living in the middle of it.

"Help call everyone in!" she orders as she sweeps away.

"Hey." Riley grins at me. "Wanna check out the loft?"

We head to the corner of the barn and climb up the ladder to the loft. It's dark up in the rafters: dusty and chilly, hay covering the floor, farm tools hung on the wall. Down in the center of the barn, the lights are burning brightly, tables are being set up, and slices of pie are placed on plates in a row. Eager kids line up, blindfolds are tied, hands are placed behind their backs. I see my dad looking around for me, and I drop suddenly to the ground, pulling Riley down with me.

"Geez, give me a warning." Riley laughs softly.

"Sorry. I saw my dad looking for me."

"Oh yeah, there he is. Ha, he found your brother." We watch as my dad pulls David to the table. David clearly doesn't want to eat pie with no hands in front of this crowd, but my dad pushes him into a chair and ties his blindfold.

I reach out and take Riley's hand, and she holds mine back. We scoot back on the hay-covered floor so we can't see the crowd below, and they can't see us. We lean back against some hay bales, the straws poking into my back. I reach over and finger Riley's tie, something I've been itching to do all night.

"Nice suit," I whisper.

"You like it?"

"Um, *like* is not the right word for how you in this suit makes me feel."

"Shh." Riley puts a finger to my lips. I hear voices rise beneath us; two moms have stopped to chat directly under us.

"Well that's why we use a wide paddle for spankings instead of something narrower."

"Oh I see."

"Yeah, it makes the skin red, but over a wider area so it doesn't leave a welt."

"So sad we even have to be worried about that these days."

"I know, the state is incredibly overreaching. You heard

about that case where Child Protective Services took the children away from their parents? They were just exercising their God-given right!"

"Spare the rod, spoil the child, as we always say!"

"Amen. What is this world coming to." The voices grow dim as the women move away, and then they are lost in the hum of the crowd. We breathe a sigh of relief together.

"Come here." Riley pulls me to her, and we kiss. "I really didn't mean to make you sad by talking about college," she whispers, pushing wisps of my hair gently away from my face.

"No, no, I'm sorry for getting upset."

"You don't need to apologize." Riley smiles softly.

"Sorry. Ack, sorry." I chuckle, then continue, "I don't want you to feel like you can't tell me things. I really am happy for you. And I'm happy that you are asking me, like, what I want to do. It's nice to think about that."

"I hope whatever we do, we can do it together," Riley whispers.

"I'd like that," I breathe, and Riley leans over me, cushioning the back of my head with her hand, and kisses me. She tastes like candy and apple, and I feel her chest brush mine through her suit.

The sound of feet stomping up the ladder sends a shock through both of us. I can't pull away, trapped beneath her, but Riley jerks back and suddenly peels my eye wide with her fingers. "AH YES I SEE IT, HOLD STILL," she says loudly, clearly for the benefit of whoever is behind us. "If I can just . . ." She swipes at the outside of my eye. "How is that?! Did I get it?"

She leans back and I sit up to see Hannah staring at us from the ladder, her head peeking above the floor.

"Oh, yeah, yeah I think you got it," I say, rubbing my eye.

"You okay?" Hannah asks breathlessly.

"Oh yeah, yeah thanks, Riley, for getting that out." I scramble for words. "Hey Hannah, how did Seth like your pie?"

"Were you not watching?!" she asks incredulously. "He loved it! He won the pie-eating contest!"

"Ah," Riley says in her deadpan way. "Eating incredibly fast is a sure sign of enjoyment." I snort and cover it with a hacking cough.

"You should come down from here." Hannah looks at me with concern. "Maybe you are allergic to the hay or something. Anyways, time for us girls to clean up and do dishes!"

"Right behind you!" Riley says cheerfully. Hannah disappears down the ladder, and Riley leans forward for one last kiss.

twenty

. . .

I 'm sitting at the computer "studying" for chemistry, but really I'm passing notes with Riley through our shared document. I'm trying to look like I'm studying really hard, but inside I'm laughing and swooning and grinning.

Riley: Yeah, that's how I convinced my school to count ASL as a foreign language.

Me: I love watching people sign at church events, especially when they sign the songs.

Riley: I've never seen anyone signing at events?

Me: Oh, like Solutions in Genesis? They always have someone signing at big events, and I'd always watch them during the music.

Riley: Solutions in Genesis? Do I even want to know?

Me: Oh geez. Well, it's this group devoted to teaching Christians about Creation. Like how God created the world in six days, and evolution is a liberal lie, and the answer to all of life's questions are in Genesis.

Riley: And they had music at these events?

Me: Well, songs. About fossils and stuff.

Riley: Songs about fossils?

Me: YES. Songs about the fossil record, and how Noah had dinosaurs on the ark.

Riley: Dude. The more I learn about your childhood the wilder it gets.

Me: I feel the same way.

"Honey, you just about done?" My mom leans into the office. I jump a bit but try to keep my body still. I pull my face into the shape of a tired student's and turn.

"Yeah, just about." I sigh. "This unit is really kicking my butt."

"Valerie," my mom chides, "that's not very ladylike." It's really hard not to roll my eyes at times like this. Maybe I should say *ass*. Like a fucking lady.

"Okay, Mom, I'll finish up."

"Your brother wants to go for a bike ride, how about you go with him?"

I take a quiet breath, trying not to heave my shoulders in annoyance. "Sure, Mom," I say tightly.

"Great, you can deliver these books to Mrs. Miller."

"She wants to borrow books?" Mrs. Miller is a neighbor the next block over. She is not a churchgoer and didn't seem particularly interested in becoming one the last time we went door-to-door witnessing, trying to convert our neighbors.

"I saw her the other day and she said she'd like to read some books I suggested."

"She *said* she'd like to? Or you asked and she was too polite to say no?" I can't stop myself. The aggressive "witnessing" has always rubbed me so wrong. For years I thought it was my problem, that I just wasn't devout enough or something, but now I'm starting to wonder why my parents think it's okay to basically harass people into talking about religion all the time.

"She said she'd like to," my mom says firmly.

153

She's *definitely* lying, or maybe she's lied to herself so thoroughly she thinks it's the truth.

"I don't like what you are implying, Valerie," she continues. "Our neighbors are going to *hell*." Her voice is quivering with sincerity. "You'd be wise to start acting like you care about their salvation."

She sweeps out of the room, and I turn back to the computer with a sigh.

Hey, I gotta go. Love you, I type. I wait, but no message appears. I guess Riley had to step away from her computer too. With a sigh, I close all my tabs and head to the garage to get my bike.

It's hard to bike in a skirt, but my parents made sure to get me a girl bike, with a low-slanted crossbar. Who knew that bicycles had a gender? I roll my bike out of the garage. I spent one of my forbidden library internet sessions rage-reading about the history of bicycles and how the first women to ride bicycles in the 1880s were seen as independent, scandalous, and daring. And now, over a hundred years later, with all the progress that's been made, I'm still kept in a skirt—and made to ride a bike that accommodates it.

"David?" I call. "You coming or not?"

He comes outside, hops on his bike, and peels down the driveway. "Race you to the park!" he yells over his shoulder.

"Wait, we have to drop . . ." And he's already out of earshot. Boys. I throw on my backpack filled with Mom's books and jump on my bike to chase after him.

The air is crisp with the chill of late autumn, and most of the leaves have fallen. They crunch beneath my tires, the gears of my bike humming pleasantly beneath me as I pedal after David toward the park. I find him by the creek, his bike abandoned carelessly in the grass, throwing rocks into the lazy flow.

"David!" I jog up to him. "I have to deliver these books for Mom on the way home. I was going to do it on the way here, but you took off before I could tell you."

"Okay," he says absently.

"Why is it always my responsibility to handle things like this?" I gripe. "She could just as easily have asked you to do it."

"Because you're better at it?" he says, skipping a pebble on the water.

"I'm not better at it." I bristle. "I'm just *expected* to be. And you aren't. There's a difference." He shrugs. "Don't you see anything wrong with this?" I gesture vaguely at everything. "Endless random rules we are told come directly from God? With trying to revert to gender roles that the rest of society has moved on from? With the way we treat people who don't think exactly like we do?"

"I dunno." David shrugs. "I haven't always seen everything Mom and Dad's way, but I think that was my fault, you know? I just need to trust God more."

"But is it God?" I'm raising my voice, but I'm struggling so hard to maintain this act. Everything in me is pressurized to the point that entering my house makes me nauseous. My spirit is revolted by the oppression of this place. "Maybe." I blink back the tears crowding in my eyes. "Maybe it's not all God, you know? Maybe it's men making their own rules and saying they have the authority of God. Maybe we're being deceived."

David looks at me in surprise, just now seeming to notice how worked up I am. "Are you okay? You know Mom and Dad would freak if I told them what you are telling me right now."

"Don't you hear what I'm saying?" I'm desperate for a sliver of understanding. "Do you really think that this world we live in is it?"

"What brought this up?" David asks, his eyes a little wide.

Uuugh. I sniff and try to compose myself. I shouldn't be talking about this but . . . but David's a reasonable kid; he's got to understand on some level.

"Like, Mom putting the books in *my* backpack. Do you really think girls should handle things and take care of men?"

"If the men are working and providing, it makes sense, doesn't it?"

"But why is there that divide in the first place?"

He grabs a stick, breaks it over his knee, and throws the pieces into the water. The creek carries them away from us. I watch them go enviously.

"Because God created men and women differently. For different purposes. Equal but different, that's what Pastor always says."

"But it's not *equal* when women don't have a choice. And you don't have a choice either. What if . . . what if you don't want to be the breadwinner, what if you wanted to be a stay-at-home parent?"

"Why would I want to do that?" He chuckles. "That's not my job."

"There!" I yell. "You say that like it's beneath you. And all the men act like that. That's not equal, that's oppression!"

"I don't know, sis!" He throws his hands up. "I don't know where this came from, but you'd better get it figured out."

"You don't see it?! You really don't see it just because you end up on top here? You get to go to work and have a precious little wifey take care of everything, and you are the authority."

"Calm down, Valerie."

"Why would you care about me and how I'm being treated? Why would you try to see things from my perspective for one second."

"It's the Bible, sis! It's not just me! You are so far out of line with what you are saying—if you would just pray about it, spend some time reading your Bible, you would see."

"You really don't—" I break off, look up to blink the tears away, and take a breath. "You know what, you are right," I say harshly. "Thanks. I'll do that."

He eyes me skeptically. He looks like he wants to say something, but he turns away and heads toward his bike. "I'll see you at home."

"Yeah. See you there."

"And sis?"

"Yeah?"

"Don't bring me into this again. Or I'll have to tell Dad."

———

I compose myself for a minute, staring blearily at the creek. The breeze is cold as it winds through my hair and rustles the fallen leaves on the ground. I feel alone. There are no answers here. No empathy, no understanding. Just a cold hard line of Bible and rhetoric and endless exhortation to examine myself, to change myself to fit the shape of the cross. And I just can't. I've tried, I honestly have—I have believed with everything in me and offered myself to God with absolute faith, but the peace I was promised is hollow. The love and acceptance I crave have eluded me. I'm starting to see that I will never, never be able to make myself fit into the story my parents have written for me.

I sniff. My nose must be bright red from the cold and from almost crying. I miss Riley. When I'm with her, everything feels easy. Everything makes sense. The sermons on sin and repentance clang in my memory, but they wash away in the absolute wholesome deluge of good and love that I feel when I'm with her. I just can't take this madhouse any longer, or I am going to start screaming and never ever stop.

A squirrel startles me, leaping up from a pile of leaves and winding up a poplar tree, chittering giddily as it climbs. I turn and head toward my bike, pause by the tree, and punch it. It hurts my knuckles like fuck, but it feels good to feel *something*, and I hit it again.

"Uuuuuuuuuggh!" I scream at the sky. I storm away, grab my bike, and pedal hard toward Mrs. Miller's house.

The Millers' house looks almost exactly like ours, garage on the left instead of the right. I hear forbidden rock music blaring from upstairs as I approach the door. I've been taught, by white men in navy suits, that rock music is of the devil. That the African rhythms from whence these beats originated are inherently demonic and sinful. Sounds awfully racist, now that I think about it. I raise my hand to knock, but the front door opens.

"Oh, hi there . . ." Mr. Miller searches for my name as he ties off a trash bag.

"Valerie," I supply, smiling cheerfully.

"Valerie, that's right!" He steps to the side. "Come on in, I've got something on the stove I've got to get back to—hey honey, Valerie is here!" he calls back into the house. Then he steps past me and heads out with the garbage.

I hear stomping feet upstairs. The TV is on in the living room, some superhero movie, but there's no one in the room watching. I can't imagine being allowed to watch TV and looking away; our media consumption is so strictly limited, I'm greedy for every morsel I'm allowed. A pile of books sits on the floor—graphic novels I know I could never bring home—along with textbooks from public school classes. I bet they don't have a single Bible verse in them. I stand awkwardly in the foyer, and Mr. Miller sweeps back in, nearly running back to the kitchen.

"Oh, HONEY, DID YOU HEAR?" he calls. "Sorry, I've

got stuff on the stove!" he says apologetically as he disappears through the doorway. I hear the sounds of something sizzling, and smell oil and garlic wafting out.

Mrs. Miller comes down the stairs, looking surprised to see me. I look longingly at her sweatpants and scoop-neck T-shirt. I wish I could wear clothes like that.

"Hi, Valerie! Everything okay?"

"Oh, yeah," I say awkwardly. As I suspected, my mom was wrong, and Mrs. Miller did not ask to borrow the books in my backpack.

"My mom asked me to bring these to you." I swing my backpack off and pull the books out. "She said you wanted to borrow them," I offer apologetically.

"Oh, okay, well tell her thanks for me!"

"Yeah. Yeah, I will."

"We are about to sit down to dinner, do you want to stay? We have plenty."

I look longingly into the kitchen at the set table. Mr. Miller sings loudly along to the music as he bustles around the kitchen. "Could I maybe just have a glass of water? I've been biking."

"Of course, come on in!" She beckons me to follow her.

Within minutes, I'm sitting at their table between Jamie and Mari, the fourteen-year-old Miller twins. We used to hang out, years ago. Before we joined the Institute and my parents started telling me not to associate with nonbelievers. They pass around the dishes and soon my plate is full of chicken, pasta, and salad. The twins chat animatedly about their day. The rock music—there's got to be a better word for it, but "rock music" is all I've ever heard it called—plays softly from the speakers. I feel like I'm in a movie. Or a TV show. Everything feels amazingly easy and normal.

"I love your skirt, Valerie," Jamie says. "Did you thrift it? I love vintage finds."

"Oh um, yeah," I say, blushing.

"You can go ahead and dig in, Valerie!" Mr. Miller gestures toward me with this fork, and I realize I was waiting to say grace. To pray before eating like we always do at my house.

"Oh, yeah. Thanks!" I start spinning linguine around my fork.

"Chicken again?" complains Mari.

"Hey, if you want something different, feel free to make it." Mr. Miller laughs.

"At least it's not Mom's chili," says Jamie.

"Hey!" Mrs. Miller bursts out. I flinch and freeze. My heart starts racing. I take a shaky breath, looking around, and see that everyone is smiling. It's a joke. I try to smile and chuckle along with them.

"There's a reason your dad does the cooking around here." Mrs. Miller laughs.

"And a reason your mom handles the finances." Mr. Miller reaches over and squeezes Mrs. Miller's hand.

"How was lacrosse practice, Jamie?"

No one seems to have noticed my moment of confusion. It's all okay. Is this what families do? Do kids just talk to their parents like this? Is this how normal people talk to each other?

"It was fine. Hey Mom, can you take me and Jodie to the movies this weekend?"

"What, so you can make out?" Mari mutters, looking up from her phone.

"How dare you. But maybe."

"I'm going to pretend I didn't hear that!"

"Hey, no phones at the table!" Mrs. Miller chides, and Mari slips it back into her pocket.

I sit there, and eat, and soak up the casual normalcy of everything. The pure bliss of the ease with which Jamie and Mari talk to their parents. The freedom from gender roles. And I think to myself, for the one-hundred-and-first time this week: I've got to get out.

twenty-one

. . .

"Plenty of food in the fridge for lunch, sandwiches for dinner. Don't stay up too late. We are at the marriage conference all day and going out to dinner afterward; we should be back by ten. Don't forget that we have church early in the morning!" Mom lectures, slipping on her coat.

"They can take care of themselves—come on, we're going to be late," Dad says impatiently, halfway out the door to the garage.

"David, you are ushering with Dad in the morning—make sure you find your dress shoes before you go to bed tonight."

"He knows! In the van, now!" Dad yells as he climbs into the van. The garage door begins its rattling ascent.

"I'm coming! You don't need to raise your voice at me in front of the children," Mom retorts as she shuts the garage door. David and I avoid looking at each other as we hear the muted sounds of their squabbling.

"If you wouldn't spend so much time nagging, maybe I wouldn't need to raise my voice," Dad says. We hear the doors slam and the van back out of the garage.

"Geez. For people who spend so much time at marriage conferences, you'd think they'd have a better marriage," I remark.

"Dad's right, Mom can be such a nag." David shrugs, turning to head to his room.

"I mean, yeah, I find it annoying too, but you think it's all her fault?"

"Kind of, it is super annoying."

"Okay, it's not exactly fun, but it's not like Dad takes care of the house or helped take care of us, pretty much ever."

"Whatever," David huffs, heading to his room. Things have been a bit tense since our argument the other day.

"I'm going to the library!" I call up the stairs.

"Yeah, whatever, do you think I care?!" he calls back.

"I don't know, are you here to spy on me or not?" I mutter under my breath as I slip my shoes and coat on. It used to feel like David was on my side, but I don't know anymore. I might as well make the most of his current indifference.

I glance up and down the street to confirm the van is gone, and then peel out of the driveway on my bike. An entire afternoon at the library with no supervision—I almost can't believe my luck. But between meeting Riley and all our stolen moments since, I feel like God or Lady Luck or whoever is smiling on me. Definitely not my parents' God. But maybe a kinder, warmer God who wants me to be happy? Or something?

When the automatic doors to the library whoosh open, the faint vanilla smell of books pulls me in, and I head to my favorite spot in the very back. Logging in to the computer, I pull up Instagram and log in to my secret account. And then I search for Mira Patterson. I've been wanting to look her up for a while, and I'm not sure why it's taken me this long. Maybe I was a little scared? As much as I feel I've grown and stretched,

I'm nervous to see what her life is like. Maybe I'm afraid she'll seem happy, and her life beautiful, and I'll lose the thin tethers still binding me to my own home. Or maybe I'm afraid her life is hard and sad and I'll lose the hope of a better, kinder life. After searching through the profiles of a few Mira and Miranda Pattersons, I find her.

She looks so strong in her profile picture: hair short and styled, a calm look on her face. Mom always makes me smile in pictures, which usually ends up looking strained. I love the confidence in Mira's eyes. I scroll down to her grid and see her with her grandparents, pictures of food, hiking shoes on a trail, a cute corgi rolling in the grass—and then I see it. Her with another girl. I can't see the other girl's face entirely, but she's kissing the side of Mira's face, and Mira is smiling in this picture. Laughing, really. Head thrown back, mouth wide, a moment of joy and ease. I click the picture to see the caption— "She is everything to me. 🫶"

It takes a second for me to realize I've stopped breathing, and I pull in a shuddering breath. Mira is queer. Beautifully. Vibrantly. And she's found a place for herself in the world away from the Institute and her family and the greasy whirlpool of hurt and shame that is my daily existence.

I begin to type. "Hi Mira! It's Valerie, we met outside your parent's house?" I send the message and pause, not sure how to continue. I don't want to come across as too intense or anything, but I don't want to waste this chance.

"I'm sneaking time on the computer at the library and wanted to say hi, and you look so happy." I pause again.

"I think . . ." I erase that and try again: "I'm queer too, and I'm planning to leave home with my girlfriend"—my heart thrills as I type that—"when I turn eighteen, and I want to know how you did it, and if you have any tips for me." I wait for a minute, rereading my words, wishing I could delete them all and start over; then I force myself to log out and get up from the computer.

I pace through the library to the New Books shelf and scan aimlessly. I pull a few off the shelf and flip through, but I'm too distracted to really pay attention. I see the sweater-vested librarian who helped me that day I stole *One Last Stop*, and I duck behind the shelf. I don't even know why, really; he's been so kind and helpful. He let me take the book and turned off the alarm, saved me from getting caught by the library—and worse, by my mom. He recommended that queer book with the simple cover. But I'm so worried and anxious, the incriminating nature of the messages I just sent heavy and hot in my chest. And sometimes I feel that something must be wrong with me, that everyone is normal and *I'm* the problem—my hands are shaking. I rush back to the far corner of the library. I'll log in to Instagram and delete all my messages. Delete my account if I need to. I stated things too clearly, said too much—I'm too close to figuring this out. What if Mira's grandparents look at her accounts and they somehow warn the Pattersons or my parents?

I log back in and she's responded.

"Hi Valerie, nice to hear from you! I have so much sympathy for you and what you are going through, and I just want you to know—you are not alone."

A few days later, Mira and I meet at the library to talk. She offered to meet at a coffee shop close by, but I'm too nervous to go somewhere my parents haven't approved. I'm sitting on a bench by the front entrance, pretending to read but actually chewing on my fingernails, when I see her approaching through the glass.

"Valerie?"

"Hey! Hi!" I jump up from the bench. Mira hugs me warmly.

"I don't have a lot of time, I'm sorry. My mom expects me back at three," I say.

"Yeah, no problem. You want to head somewhere more quiet?"

"Yeah, there are some study rooms in the back, there's usually one open—this way."

She follows me past the circulation desk where my sweater-vested hero is absent today, to the quiet rear of the library. I peer in the windows until we find an empty room, and slip inside.

"Do you mind if we sit with our backs facing the window?" I ask. "I know I seem so paranoid, I just—this is the local library and I just don't want anything to get back to my parents."

"Yeah, no problem! I totally get it." Mira sits in one of the wheeled conference chairs, and I take the one next to her. "I remember before I left home, a friend asked to meet up for coffee—Allison Voeller, do you know her?"

"Oh um, no, I don't think so."

"Oh yeah, I think they moved to Ohio. Anyways, she was part of the the Institute, nice family, and I asked my dad if I could meet her for coffee, and he said no. Just straight up. Gave me the same crap about why did I need to see someone outside of the home, why didn't I understand that God gave him authority over me for protection, yada yada. Anyways, what I'm saying is, I really do understand the need for secrecy. And I'm honestly so impressed that you are asking questions and what—you have a girlfriend? Tell me everything!"

"Her name is Riley." I beam. "She's so great, I just—" I pause, overwhelmed, and Mira waits patiently. "I'm sorry, I'm just kind of stunned to be here talking to you. You are a real live person who has gone through a lot of what I have gone through, and you just represent like, hope to me? Is that too dramatic to say? I just didn't even know leaving was *possible*."

"That makes so much sense," she says. "I know when I was leaving, it meant everything to have my grandparents' support, but I know not everyone has that. That's why found family is such a huge deal to queer people. It's the people who *actually* come through for you that matter most. And I'm here for you. I'm your sister now, or your aunt, or whatever the hell it is you need, I'm here for you. How can I help?"

My eyes are brimming with tears. I wipe them away.

"Thank you. I really don't know what else to say, I just—thank you." She smiles and reaches out to squeeze my shoulder.

"I just don't know how to untangle everything in my mind, you know?" I say. "I feel like I cursed myself or something by starting to doubt. I think I was happier maybe before I started questioning everything? It's not like I want to actually go back to believing everything, or not being out to myself, but I just feel like I'm trying to . . . untangle a room full of Slinkies."

Mira nods, listening patiently. I wait for her to jump in and explain things, but she just waits.

"I guess I keep thinking in circles. I've read about how the word *homosexuality* didn't appear in translations of the Bible until it was added in 1946. And now a lot of Christians hate gay people. I don't think God hates me. But I'm also kind of mad at myself for *caring* what God thinks. Then again, I've literally spent my whole life doing nothing *but* worry about what God thinks. The only thing I *know* is that I will never figure this out at home. So I need to go. Does that make any sense at all? Did you go through this?"

"Yeah, for sure, that makes *so* much sense to me." Mira nods. "And I'm not here to tell you what to think or believe, I'm just here to support you and help you find the space to think through it. I'm like, in a different place than you with God and my childhood and everything, but I'm not going to try to convince you of anything. You've had *more* than enough of people telling you what to believe. But it sounds like you've kind of done the impossible. It feels like a damn miracle every time someone like you, or me, can see through the fog of our childhood and reach for the sun. And I'm proud of you."

twenty-two

. . .

The piped-in sermon is droning from the speaker while two moms nurse their babies in rocking chairs. I'm refilling the container of baby wipes on the changing table. Nursery duty is boring, but nice in a quiet sort of way. It's always a win to get credit for being at church, but not have to sit through the service. I'm thinking through my meeting with Mira yesterday, how quietly supportive she was. She didn't tell me what path to take, she just affirmed my journey. For all the sermons I've heard about the gay agenda, I'm finding queer people to have much *less* of an agenda than Christians.

"Hey!" a soft voice rasps behind me. I turn and see Riley, and my world brightens.

"Hey! What are you doing here?" I reach out to hug her, but pause and glance toward the nursing moms. They chat quietly with each other. I remind myself that to them, we are just two friends saying hi. Nothing suspicious going on here.

"What, I can't come say hi to my girlfriend?" She turns her back to them and gives me a ridiculous, open mouthed wink that only I can see. I chuckle softly. It's funny how *girlfriend* can mean different things depending on what you are expecting.

"The sermon is that good, huh?" I say quietly.

"Oh, *so* good. It was hard to tear myself away really. I was especially *convicted*"—she places a hand on her chest—"of the need to vote for whoever is for protecting life, regardless of their political affiliations."

"Ah yes, *absolutely*." I nod with mock solemnity. The conservative agenda indeed.

"Look at these guys." Riley points to the wall art, two lions climbing the ramp onto Noah's ark. "Get it, you two. Although I don't know that they'll be multiplying any time soon."

"What?" I stare at the lions, identical, with bushy brown manes. Two males. "*Oh!*" I snort.

"Do you want to, you know?" Riley gestures subtly toward the back of the church.

"Ugh, I can't. I'm signed up for both services today. Hey, but I've been wanting to tell you!" I lower my voice and lean in. "I met up with Mira yesterday. Remember I told you about Hannah's sister?"

"Yeah, she left home right?" Riley leans in to hear me, and I wish desperately I could reach out and touch her face.

"*Yes*, and she's—" I subtly gesture to a rainbow on the wall, arching over the Noah's ark tableau.

"Oh yeah?"

"Yeah! I'll have to tell you about it later. But I've been thinking about everything, and I feel more sure than ever. About our plans."

Riley's eyes are shining.

"I know it's about you and about us, but it's also about me, you know? I just know that I want this. That I'll never really . . . figure out what I want or believe until I get some space, you know?"

"*Yes*, Val!"

"It's also just nice to meet someone who made it out, you know? It gives me so much hope. That life can be good."

"I know exactly what you mean. I was reading this book, oh my god it's in *verse,* and it's so good—"

"Hold on," I interrupt. "I just want to acknowledge how hot that image is. Mmm. You reading. Yes. Okay, continue."

"Heh, you adorable dork. Anyways, so I was reading this book, *Ode to My First Car*, and the girl gets a job at a nursing home and meets this eighty-year-old"—her eyes flick meaningfully to the rainbow—"lady, and she's like, amazed you know? I think we forget that people have been"—a glance to the rainbow—"forever, you know? And it's not like Mira is old or anything, but it's just nice to have *hope.*"

"*Hope,* yes, exactly! It's like—" I pause as Hannah breezes into the nursery.

"Hope for what?" Hannah asks cheerfully. She smiles to acknowledge Riley.

"Oh, hope for the future!" Riley transitions seamlessly. "Where would any of us be without Christ, am I right?"

"Oh *absolutely.*" Hannah beams.

"How is Seth and the courtship and everything?" I ask, moving to her favorite topic.

"Oh, he's good." She says it cheerfully, like she says most things, but it seems extra thin today.

"Hey, I'm gonna head out, Mom's probably waiting for me," Riley says, reaching out and giving my hand a squeeze. I squeeze back and watch her leave. When I glance back at Hannah, she has a funny look on her face.

"You two have gotten pretty close, huh?" she asks.

"Oh, well, kind of, I mean." I'm floundering. "You were saying something about Seth?"

"Oh, yeah. Yeah. We actually just got engaged." She holds

her hand out, and I see a simple metal band with a tiny diamond.

"Oh my *gosh,* Hannah! Congrats!"

"Yeah! Thanks!" She smiles stiffly.

"Are you happy about it?"

"Oh yeah! Of course! I just feel super balanced? Like, I'm obviously excited, but not out-of-control excited, which is the way it should be, you know? I mean, obviously we are keeping pure, we haven't kissed or held hands or anything, and I'm just feeling really calm about it. I think that shows how healthy it is? We aren't in a hurry to do anything physical, and that's really good, right?"

"Oh um, yeah, I guess so? But you like, *want* to do stuff with him eventually, right?"

"Oh yeah, *totally.* I mean I don't feel anything *now,* but that's why we have all these rules, right? I'm sure I'll feel a pull or whatever when it's *allowed* once we are married. This is just super healthy. Super pure."

I think about me and Riley together. The magnetic pull I feel toward her, always. Her warm skin beneath my fingers. Her oh-so-soft lips on mine. I remember Hannah on the phone, saying that *everyone* knows girls are more attractive than boys, but we just can't *act* on it. I want to ask her if she feels an attraction to girls, but I know she would be horribly offended.

"Have you ever . . ." she starts, and stops. She's staring at me and I'm staring at her, and I know we both have questions we can't ask.

"Anyways." She shakes her head and continues, "Mom and Dad are *so* excited, and they get along so well with the Zellers. So I guess we'll be planning a wedding next year!"

"That's great, Hannah, I'm happy for you," I say, because I'm supposed to. Then a mom comes in to drop off her baby, and I'm listening to her instructions, and the moment is gone.

twenty-three

. . .

I'm doing the lunch dishes as fast as I can because Riley is coming over. Riley. Is. Coming. Over! My parents finally agreed to a sleepover, and holy crap have I been on my best behavior all week. I've picked my favorite verse first during devotional time, I nodded attentively while Dad droned on about respect and obedience, I volunteered to close in prayer twice. I cleaned the house yesterday and offered to make dinner tonight so there could be no parental objections, no nitpicky reasons to call Riley's mom to cancel.

As I wipe the last drops of water off the counter, Dad brings in a handful of mugs from his office and places them in the sink. Seriously? I grouch in my head, but I'm able to keep it locked in. I'm not going to blow this. Dad smiles broadly at me and I grimace back. He reaches out and strokes my cheek and, try as I might, I can't help but flinch. We don't get along—I am faking this whole obedient daughter thing—and the feel of his hand on my skin makes me cringe, body and soul.

"Daughter. We need to have a talk." Those words strike panic in me as the dread of it buzzes through my system. He turns and heads to the office, expecting—knowing—that I will follow. I take deep breaths as I obey, berating myself for making a mistake. Why did I flinch? Why couldn't I just take it? I swallow roughly. My throat hurts.

The walls of the office seem to close in as I enter. I breathe shallowly around the tightness in my chest as my heartbeat quickens. Dad sits and gestures to a chair. I want to stay standing so I can run out the moment he finishes his verbal lashing, but insisting on standing would only aggravate him. So I bend my knees, I push myself down into a chair, and I stare at his socks—the place I always stare so I am not accused of being too bold, too rebellious. Too opinionated.

"I know you are excited about having your friend over," he begins. *Riley*, I say in my head. Her name is Riley. But I keep it all inside, because to contradict would be to bruise his fragile ego. Truly, nothing is as pear-skin-delicate as my father's ego. "But you are not the parent. You are the child. My child. And you are to respect me as long as you are in this house. I see you becoming more bold, more confident, more worldly, and it concerns me. You know, I see some children, some adult children going off the deep end, leaving their faith, disrespecting their parents." I carefully glaze my eyes and nod in a steady rhythm, schooling my face into nothingness. Blank, unthinking devotion. Just how they like it. "Do you understand me, daughter?"

I nod stiffly. I try so hard to be convincingly obedient, but sometimes *not screaming* is the best I can do. I must have forced the right amount of nodding this time because he seems satisfied.

I stand and turn to leave the office, expecting one last punishment. Waiting for the final blow to fall. I did not pretend to be submissive enough, and now he'll remove the one scrap of joy from my life. But he doesn't. He doesn't even leave the room. I hear him turn in the creaky office chair and start using the computer. I run up the stairs to my room and take deep, cleansing breaths to recover. My room is clean, everything is ready. I have an air mattress inflated on the floor, made up with flannel sheets, one of my pillows, and a blanket.

So far, so good. Riley should be here any minute now and I've somehow dodged parental cancellation by a thread. "Cancel culture." I chuckle to myself as I smooth my comforter. My parents always complain about cancel culture, when really, no one is faster to cancel literally anything than they are. Disney, Starbucks . . . me. I pause as I straighten the stack of books by my bed. I've gotta be careful with Riley here. Gotta be smart. I hear the crunch of car tires in our driveway and skip to the window. She's here!

Riley gets out of the car, looking stunning as usual in dark jeans and a V-neck tee. She waves to her mom as she drives away before heading to the front door. I throw myself down the stairs, my feet trying to keep pace with the gravity of my body being pulled toward Riley. I throw open the front door just as Riley raises her hand to knock.

"Hi!" I gush breathlessly.

"Val," she says quietly, smiling at me and looking me up and down with obvious approval. I start to throw my arms around her, then pause as I realize where we are. We settle on a firm friendly hug. I'm doing my best to keep it cool, but it's hard when Riley is . . . *Riley*.

"Val. I missed y—"

"Hi, Riley!" my mom interrupts us. "Glad you could make it. Do you want to put your stuff in Valerie's room?"

"Hi, Mrs. Danners," Riley says politely. "Thanks so much for having me over!" I grab Riley's pillow and start heading up the steps when my mom clears her throat.

"Hey, Riley, you know we aren't really used to immodest

clothing here." Oh geez no, *please no*. I glare at my mom, hoping that I can stop her, but it's already too late. Why is she like this? *Why?!*

"I just really don't want David and Mr. Danners to struggle with their thoughts."

"Mom," I say aloud. I can't stop myself. "I'm sure it's fine."

"If you could just change into something that covers you a bit more, we'd appreciate it. If you need something else to wear, I'm sure Valerie can lend you a sweater."

"Mom," I start. I know contradicting her is a bad idea, but I can't let her shame Riley like this for no fucking reason.

"Oh yeah, no problem, Mrs. Danners," Riley says smoothly. "I was a bit chilly anyhow."

We head to my room, and as soon as the door closes I throw my arms around her. "Riley. I missed you."

"God, I missed you too, Val. Anyone ever told you that you hug like a hurricane?"

"It's only because I love you." I beam into her neck. "I'm so sorry about my mom," I whisper. "You don't have to . . ."

"Don't even worry about it. It *is* kind of cold in here."

"Yeah." I chuckle, pulling away. "She doesn't really believe in climate control. Gotta pinch the pennies."

"Now *that* I understand," Riley says, pulling on a baggy sweater from her bag. "Immigrant life, am I right? Americans sure are wasteful, but not on our moms' watch."

"Yeah! Exactly!" I throw myself on the bed and Riley lies next to me, staring at the ceiling, our hands clasped between us.

"You know, I had Hannah over one time and she couldn't believe my mom won't let me use all my lightbulbs."

"What, those?" Riley nods at my ceiling light.

"Yeah, Mom only lets me keep two screwed in, to save electricity, and Hannah made a big deal about it. Acted like she couldn't see anything in my third-world-country bedroom, it was so dim."

"That checks out." Riley chuckles. "Hannah is the hwhitest of hwhite."

We stare in silence at the ceiling for a bit. Reveling in our proximity. Breathing the same air, hands clasped warmly between us. I know we shouldn't be holding hands even in here —should be on our highest alert every second—but it's so hard to keep imagining the worst when the best is right here beside me.

"I missed you, Val."

"I missed you more."

"I love you," Riley says softly, turning her face toward mine.

"I love you," I whisper, leaning in for a kiss.

"Valerie?" my mom calls from downstairs, and we instinctively flinch apart. "If you two are going to make dinner, you'd better do it now!"

"So what are we having?" Riley asks as I hand her a kitchen apron and tie on my own.

"Muai," I say. "I guess most people call it congee? Muai is what my Taiwanese grandparents call it."

"It smells good," Riley says, stirring the pot gently.

"Yeah, it's maybe my favorite comfort food? It's a simple rice soup, but we eat it with yummy toppings," I say, pulling eggs out of the refrigerator. "How about you scramble eggs and I'll wash vegetables?"

"Sounds good," Riley says as she washes her hands, then starts to crack eggs into the bowl I hand her. I wash some Chinese chives and give them to Riley, who carefully slices them into thin slivers before scrambling them with the eggs. I wash some Taiwanese water spinach as Riley heats a pan.

"Just scramble them?"

"Yup, let's add some soy sauce too."

"Ooh, good idea." Riley knows her way around a kitchen, I note with pleasure, loving the confidence and ease with which she does everything. I reach above her for salt and she ducks under my arm; she reaches across to the sink and I lean back, an easy ballet of crisp green smells and sizzling pans.

"So these are Chinese chives?" she asks, tasting a forkful of fluffy scrambled eggs.

"Yeah, they are a bit less oniony than scallions, aren't they?"

"Hmm, yeah. A bit more tender too."

"Remember the wild onions in our ramen?" I smile as I dice garlic.

She lowers her voice. "Of course I do." We share a secret smile, remembering those blissful days at the hotel, our foraged green onions, those honeysuckle moments under the willow tree.

I sauté the water spinach with garlic, and we assemble the toppings on the table. Salty crumbles of crushed peanuts, a fluffy mound of sweet pork floss. Riley ladles congee into the bowls, and I call my family down for dinner.

"Hello there, Riley," my dad says with false enthusiasm. "So glad you could come visit."

"Thanks, Mr. Danners, glad to be here," says Riley.

"Really glad you could come. Any time at all, you are absolutely welcome. It's no trouble at all."

"Thank you!" Riley says politely. She gives me a quick glance as if to say, "Is it a problem that I'm here?"

I give her a tiny shake of my head. Don't worry about it. This is just how he is.

"Riley, your sweater looks lovely." My mom beams.

"Thanks *so much* for putting it on; I know David and Mr. Danners appreciate it." David and Mr. Danners are busy dishing up their food, but thanks for making it even more weird, Mom.

"Oh yeah, no problem." Riley smiles warmly. My dad fills his bowl with toppings. Like, *fills* it. He kind of hates congee and always makes sure we remember it's not his favorite.

"You know, Riley," he starts up. I wince internally, knowing where this is going. "Congee is really an acquired taste. Really not something most people like at first try."

"Dad. Lots of people love it. Like, literally millions of people."

"An *acquired taste*," he repeats assertively, giving me a glare that tells me to stand down. I sigh and slump in my chair. "I haven't quite acquired the taste for it yet, but I keep trying!" He stirs his bowl of peanuts and pork floss and takes a bite.

"What did you say this vegetable is?" Riley asks, carefully chewing a bit of the greens.

"It's ying tsai," my mom says. "I don't know how Americans call it."

"Water spinach," I say. "It's labeled that way at H Mart."

"It's delicious," Riley says, adding more to her bowl. I can't explain how pleased I am to see her eating one of my favorite meals with relish. I chose to make it tonight because I love it, but I also wanted to see how she would react. My childhood has been full of small slights by my white friends. Complaints about the smell of our house, or a church lady rambling about how gross soy milk is, and how it's a threat to American dairy farmers. Or my own dad insisting these treasured dishes are an acquired taste. Riley tucks in, eager to learn and try new things. It's really nice.

I lay toppings gently on top of my congee, carefully assemble the perfect bite on the oval bowl of my Chinese spoon, and gently slurp it into my mouth. The congee is silky, the egg salty, the pork floss sweet, the peanuts adding crunch at the end. I could eat this every day and never, ever tire of it.

David is already on his second bowl, quietly tucking away from his corner of the table. It's like he's invisible to my parents most of the time; I don't know how he does it. Goodness knows I've tried, I just can't seem to slip beneath their attention the way he does.

"Can I get some more?" Riley asks.

"Of course!" My mom beams. "Here, let me get it for you." Mom smiles at Riley approvingly, and I can't help but feel a little swell of pride that Mom likes her. Not that it means anything. Things would be different if she knew what we are to each other.

"So Riley," my dad asks, "how is school?"

"It's good. I'm applying to community college, hoping to get some gen ed classes out of the way before transferring. I'm planning to study graphic design."

"I see," Dad says. "You have to be careful. A lot of secular teachings at colleges. Professors trying to indoctrinate students, poison them against the Word of God."

"I'm pretty solid in my beliefs. I'll be alright," Riley replies.

"Well. I guess time will tell," my dad huffs. I squirm in my seat.

"How was men's group, Dad?" I flail, trying to change the subject. "Getting ready for the father/son campout?"

David looks up from shoveling congee into his mouth and glares at me. I know he doesn't appreciate being brought into the conversation, but I certainly deserve a break from the hot seat for a change.

"It's great, really great. You know the number one thing they say ensures an excellent men's retreat? It's not the location, not the accommodations." He pauses for dramatic effect. "It's the food. Lots of good, hearty, manly food."

"And what is manly food?" Riley asks. I can feel the under-current of snark, but my dad doesn't notice at all.

"Oh, good, hearty man food, you know! Sandwiches, burg-ers, bratwurst."

"Beer?" Riley asks.

"Oh no," Mom all but gasps. "Certainly not."

"I certainly wouldn't mind a cold one with the boys," my dad says. "But no," he concludes. My mom gives him a look. "No alcohol of any kind. My drinking days were before I met the Lord."

"That's right," my mom confirms. I squirm some more in my seat. Is there a single conversation topic that isn't embar-rassing around these people?

"I'll take care of the dishes," my mom says, gathering the empty bowls together. "Why don't you two go enjoy yourselves?"

"Really, Mom?" I ask, looking for the catch.

"Go ahead," she says. "David, you can help me."

David looks startled. "I've got to study."

"Oh okay then, you go ahead." She carries the stacked dishes to the sink. My dad and David leave to do their thing, like usual. Riley lingers, carrying the dishes to the sink, asking where to put the leftovers.

"Oh, aren't you helpful. I've got it, you go ahead," my mom insists again.

"Let's go for a walk?" I suggest.

twenty-four

. . .

W e pull on our jackets and head outside. The air is crisp with the smell of the coming winter, and I snuggle deeper into my coat. The cold air blows up my skirt and chills my legs—something I'm guessing doesn't happen when girls are allowed to wear pants, but I'm mostly used to it.

"Hey, wait up!" Riley laughs, running up beside me. I didn't realize how fast I'd been walking. "Geez, it's like you're in a hurry to get away from there or something. Where are we heading?"

"There's a park close by. We can find somewhere quiet." I smile. "But be warned. I'm probably going to steal a few kisses."

Riley's eyes spark; her grin is a hug. She lowers her voice to match mine. "Oh I hope so, Valerie Danners."

A few blocks away from my house, we hold hands. Her thumb glides across my skin, back and forth.

"Your hands are warm!" I smile at her.

"And yours are cold, Val—they weren't like this before!"

"That was because it's been warm." I laugh. "I'm actually an icicle for most of the year."

"And your nose is red!"

"It is not." I laugh.

She stops and pulls my face toward hers, feeling the cold of my nose against her cheek. "Cold nose!" She laughs too.

"Are you warm all the time? Even in the winter?"

"Pretty much. We complete each other." She smiles broadly, and if it isn't sunshine to my cold, tired heart.

We stand by the creek where I argued with David the other day, arms wrapped around each other, cold wind rustling our hair. Everything feels bleak this time of year. Empty. Everything except Riley, soft and real in my arms, her hands inexplicably warm and her smile the light of my life. She fingers my ring absently, and I smile, remembering what she told me what feels like a million years ago, on a different riverbank, beneath a different tree.

She breaks the stillness. "How's life in the cult?"

"Awful."

"I'm sorry, Val."

"It's not your fault."

"I know, but I still wish I could fix things for you."

"You make things more bearable."

"Nothing about this is bearable. You shouldn't have to bear it."

"Yeah." I sniff. I don't know if my nose is running from the cold or from my sadness, but it doesn't matter. Riley is a safe place to feel my feelings.

"I got a part-time job," she says.

I turn to her. "What? When did this happen?"

"Yesterday." She grins. "You're looking at the new barista-in-training at the Lakeview Coffee Shop. May I take your order?"

"That's amazing! Why didn't you tell me sooner?"

"Your parents were around. The whole *women shouldn't work* thing."

"Oh yeah, that. Well I'm so happy for you! When do you start?"

"Next week! They are training me for the holiday rush, but hopefully I can stay on afterward. I'm still looking for a room to rent in the area, hopefully close by so I can keep the job when I graduate."

"Gosh, Riley, that's so, so great." I smile up at her. "Will you make me a latte if I come visit?"

"Absolutely. What's your go-to drink?"

"I don't know!" I laugh. "We never go to coffee shops. One, a waste of money when we can make coffee or tea at home. Two, something about their goddess logo being of the devil? Something, something, gay people? I don't even know."

"Seriously?" Riley chuckles. "God, those people are mad about everything."

"Yeah. And . . . thanks for not saying 'you people.'"

"What? Oh yeah, of course. It's not you. Obviously."

"Yeah, I know." I blink away tears. "I know it's not me. But like, I'm still here. It's nice to remember it's not who I am. It's easy to feel lost in it sometimes."

"Oh I know. Like, I don't know-know like you do, but I see it, and I'm a part of it too. But we are almost graduated, I'm getting a job and moving out, and I hope you'll come with me."

"I'm in. I haven't figured out the details. I did some research at the library, and I can't legally leave without parental permission until I'm eighteen, and I think I need my parents to issue me my high school diploma. Well, I don't *have* to have it, but it would make life easier."

"Okay." She nods.

"It seems silly, like—the Virtue Booklets have not exactly

been a quality education, but in Virginia, homeschool parents issue a high school diploma and it's legit."

"That makes sense, I guess."

"I'll be eighteen in May, and I'll leave and get a job and we'll find a place together. We'll figure it out. Our secret document communication is working perfectly, so we'll keep talking there, and keep making plans."

She kisses me on the lips. "Let's do it."

"My parents can't suspect anything, or honestly, I don't know what they'd do."

"Do you know anyone who has left?"

"Actually, yes. Remember, I was telling you about Hannah's sister Mira?"

"Oh yeah, you said you were going to fill me in later. Tell me!"

"Well when she left, the Pattersons acted like she died or something. I hadn't seen her in years, but I was over there the day you came over for the first time, and she came back."

"Okay, so she got out! And things have smoothed over since? Enough that she can visit and get along with her family?"

"Not really. Mrs. Patterson lied and told her Mr. Patterson was going to apologize, but he expected her to repent and apologize for everything. It was a whole thing. It didn't end well at all, and it was hella awkward being there—I don't know that they'll be speaking to each other anytime soon. But the point is she did it, she left! She lives with Hannah's grandparents."

"That's obviously not ideal, but at least her grandparents are supportive?"

"Yeah, they really are! At least, that's what Mira said when I talked to her last week. Her grandparents accept and love her just the way she is! And she said if I need anything, to reach out, and that her grandparents have become allies I think she said? That they're supportive of queer kids, especially ones who need help or are in trouble."

"Val, that's amazing! I'll have to look her up myself!"

"You should! I'm just so"—I rub my hands down my face anxiously—"excited to know someone who has gotten out and that life can be *good*."

"This is such great news. And that'll be us soon. Your parents can't keep you here."

"Although they'd like to. Seriously, they want everyone to 'follow biblical law.'"

"Well, it's not actually the law. Not yet at least. We'll figure it out."

"Together?" I know the answer, but I can't help but ask. Maybe I'm weak, to be so dependent on Riley's love and reassurance, but it's all I've got. Somehow, her love feels like the safest, surest thing I've ever felt.

"Together," she says.

I wrap my arms tightly around her. A cold breeze rustles the dead leaves at our feet.

"You're shivering."

"No, I'm not."

"Come on, tough girl." Riley pulls my coat collar higher around my neck. "Let's get you ho—back. Let's get you back."

———

Later that night, we lie in our beds beside each other. I'd love to spoon, but I'm not allowed to lock my door.

"Riley?" I whisper into the silence.

"Yeah, Val?"

"What do normal people do?"

She chuckles softly.

"Like, for work?"

"Like, all the time I spend reading my Bible and praying and in church and listening to sermons and lectures, what do normal people do with that time?"

"Read. I guess you still do that though."

"Yeah, but it's risky."

"How do you get away with reading so much?"

I stare at the ceiling, its surface a gray shadow in the dim light. "Well, a lot of my friends' parents insist on pre-reading everything they read."

"Seems like you read a lot, so that's a lot for them to read."

"Exactly! I figured out early on I could pick a thick book, something super chunky and intimidating, and they'd maybe flip through the beginning and then get bored. Now they pretty much just check the cover, and if it has a crown or a spaceship or something, they let me read it. That's why I mainly read fantasy and sci-fi these days—the themes can be super queer, but my parents wouldn't know it based on the cover."

"Makes sense. You know, you're pretty sneaky."

"I have to be. It's the only way I've stayed . . . *myself* at all. I still feel pretty lost, honestly."

"Me too."

"You holding up okay?"

"Oh yeah. Yeah, I'm fine. It's been rough compared to Christian school, and I hated that too. But I'm almost done." She sits up from her air mattress on the floor and rests her chin on my bed. "And most importantly, I have you," she says. I reach out in the stillness and touch her face.

"I'm sorry you got thrown into all this," I breathe.

"I'd do it again." She leans in, kisses me softly.

"How is your mom with all of this? I mean, she's letting you go to college. Does she know you're gay?"

"I guess? I've come out to her a few times, and she's not thrilled about it. I think she doesn't really believe me. But she still loves me. So it's all good." Her body stiffens and she pulls away.

"Does it . . . feel good?"

"Maybe not *good*, but it's fine, you know?"

"I don't mean to pry, it just seems like that could still feel hurtful."

"I mean, it's not like she's disowning me or anything. It could be a lot worse? I just feel like I don't have anything to complain about." She flops down on the mattress.

"Riley, aren't you the one always telling me that my trauma matters? Even though worse scenarios exist?" She's quiet. I lean over the edge of my bed to see her face.

"I'm sorry if it's too sensitive or you don't want to—"

"I guess it does hurt a little." I wait for her to continue. "You know, Val, it's kind of hard for me to talk about this. Hypocritical of me, I know, always telling you it's okay to feel your feelings, but I feel like I've tried not to care about things, about my mom?"

"I totally get that. You've been protecting yourself."

"Yeah. And maybe it feels impossible? To hope for more than just being . . . not hated. So maybe I try not to think too much about what that would be like."

"Well, you don't *have* to talk about it. But if you want to, I'm here."

"Thanks, Val." The silence stretches, but it's a comfy kind of space.

"What else?" I ask.

"Hmm?"

"What else do normal people do?"

She plops back down on her back, arms behind her head. "TV. Lots of TV and movies."

"Sounds nice."

"Surely you've seen some movies—the classics?"

"You'd be amazed."

"*The Lion King?*"

"Watched the first half hour and stopped because it 'felt evil.'"

"Star Wars?"

"Watched Episode IV, but then stopped because our pastor gave a sermon about the force being part of the liberal agenda."

"*Wonder Woman?*"

"Strong woman in a skimpy outfit, no way."

She sits up. "Let me tell you about her as a bedtime story! It'll be so fun!"

"The story of Wonder Woman?" I laugh at her eagerness. "Okay, please tell me a story." She stretches, flexes her fingers like she's getting ready for an athletic event, pulls my blanket up high around my neck, and tucks it under me. "You're taking this so seriously."

"Gotta set the mood." She wraps a blanket around her shoulders and leans back against the bed. "You got a night light?"

"I have a candle on my shelf."

She lights the candle, and the warm scent of coffee and vanilla fills the space. "Okay. You ready?"

"Yes." I giggle and snuggle deeper into my blankets.

"Once upon a time, there was a mythical island named Themyscira, where there lived only women. Hot, buff women. They were warriors, and they were called the Amazons." The candle flickers gently on the floor, casting wavering shadows on my walls. Riley's voice is warm and deep, her presence steady and soothing, and my eyes drift shut as I listen.

"Their princess, the daughter of their queen, was named Diana. She was a warrior. She was tall, strong, and skilled in combat."

"Skilled in combat? I thought *I* was the storyteller," I say sleepily.

"Skilled in combat," Riley repeats, ignoring me. "She was kind, and beautiful. Every day, she'd walk the shores of her island and stare at the horizon, wondering what lay beyond it. Dreaming of the day she would sail the sea and find her destiny."

"Isn't that Moana?"

"I thought you said you hadn't seen Disney movies."

"We watched twenty minutes of *Moana* before my mom turned it off because Maui is a false god."

"*One day*"—Riley turns to glare at me—"an airplane crashed into the ocean off the shore of the island. And from the wreckage, Diana pulled a brave and beautiful pilot. Her name was Stevie Trevor."

"Wait, a girl pilot? I thought it was a boy?"

"Val, I swear to god, you need to let me tell it the way I want to tell it. It's the way it *should* be, and you haven't seen it, so it's my chance to make it perfect for you."

"Okay, okay!"

"No more interruptions?"

I giggle and mime zipping my lips, tucking my arm back under my blanket.

"A brave and beautiful pilot named Stevie Trevor."

I sigh contentedly as she continues, my mind drifting toward white-sand beaches and sky-blue waters. Toward an island of women who need no one but themselves. Who are proud, and noble, and sure of their own worth. I have no idea if the movie or comics or whatever are as beautiful as the story Riley is telling me, but I let myself be carried away in the current. Riley's voice is so beautiful. That's my last sleepy thought before I drift off to sleep.

twenty-five

...

I awake to a choir shrieking "It Is Well With My Soul." I cover my head with my blanket and groan. It's my dad, blasting hymns from the downstairs speakers, signaling it's time to get our butts in the kitchen for morning devotionals.

"Christ on a cracker," Riley moans, "what the ever-loving heck is happening?"

"It's my dad. I thought he'd skip devotionals today since it's the weekend and you're here, but apparently not."

"You usually get to skip weekends?"

"It depends on his mood. What time he woke up and how lecturey he's feeling."

"I guess we'd better get down there." Riley yawns. She pulls the baggy sweater over her sleep shirt.

"Sorry about my mom and the shirt situation."

"Not your fault." Riley is so beautiful in the morning. I'd almost forgotten, it's been so long since our magical days together at that hotel. Her hair is mussed, her face unguarded and relaxed from sleep. She catches me watching her and pulls me close in a warm embrace. We jump apart when my mom

191

throws the door open. I turn quickly to focus on tidying my bed.

"Good morning, you two! Rise and shine and give God the glory!"

"We're up, Mom," I grouch. "Morning devotional, I guess?"

"See you downstairs in five minutes. Do you want tea, Riley?"

"Sure, thanks."

Mom sweeps out of the room, leaving the door wide open.

We sit through devotional—which is a manageable amount of cringe—and drink our tea, which my mom made by carefully dipping and re-dipping tea bags into mugs of hot water to "stretch them." It's somehow both weak and bitter, and I'm not allowed to put sugar in it, but it warms my hands as I listen to Dad drone on, and sipping it gives me something to do.

We finish with a prayer, and I manage to produce a parent-placating amount of devotion. After the final "amen" is said, my mom gets up to start breakfast. "Riley, are scrambled eggs okay with you?" she asks.

"Oh, no thanks, Mrs. Danners, my mom is picking me up at eight thirty. We have some errands to run."

My mom looks disappointed. "Alright, sorry you couldn't have breakfast with us. We should have gotten up earlier."

"Oh, don't worry about it, I've had a great time. Thanks so much for your hospitality."

"We are *so glad* you came, Riley," my dad starts his weird excessive-welcoming-that-feels-unwelcoming spiel again. "It's not an inconvenience at all, I just want to make sure you know . . ." He pauses and makes oddly intense eye contact with her. "That you are welcome."

"Thanks, Mr. Danners. I . . . I appreciate that?"

"We'll go pack her stuff up, it's just about eight thirty now," I say, trying to get her up to my room so we have time for a goodbye before her mom gets here.

"You are welcome any time!" my dad calls after her as we head up the stairs.

The instant she closes my room door behind us, she rushes into me, pulling my face in for a kiss. "I wish we had more time together," she breathes, our foreheads resting together, her hands drifting down to hold mine.

"We will soon," I whisper. "I'm going to stay in line, get that diploma, turn eighteen, and then I'm out of here."

"You are so close." She leans back to look me in the eye. "We are so close. We got this."

"One more kiss." I lean into her and kiss her, her lips soft and full, the smell of her delicious and real. My fingers rake her short curls, her hands pull my waist even closer.

I hear a glass shatter and whip my head toward the doorway. David stands there, shock on his face, hand still on the doorknob. He dropped Riley's unfinished cup of tea. Mom must have sent him up here to ask her if she wanted to finish it.

"David, wait!" I step toward him, but he's already turning, running away. "It's not what you think!"

"*Dad!*" he screams as he throws himself down the staircase.

I look up at Riley. Her face is stricken. I hear her mom honk the car outside.

"Fuck it," she says, and kisses me again. Hard. Desperate.

"You go," I whisper tremulously. "I'll be okay."

"I'm not leaving you."

"Riley." The corners of my vision are watery with tears. I

hear voices rising downstairs. "I'll be fine, I promise. It'll be better for me if you go, I'll deal with them myself."

"No, I'm not."

"Listen to me." I grab her shoulders. "I need you to listen. Please. Go right now. I love you. Check the chemistry document. I'll be there. We'll figure it out."

Tears in her eyes, Riley grabs her bag, kisses me once more, and runs out of my room. I hear the front door slam and the car pull away, and I'm alone and trembling. The voices downstairs are rising. My stomach is acid, my head dizzy. I turn and sit on my bed. I used to sit right here all the time to wait for spankings. I'm still that child, face pale and hands shaking, as I hear my father's heavy footsteps on the stairs.

twenty-six

. . .

T he days are long and joyless. When David told my parents what he saw, my parents did what I knew they would. They combed through every inch of my room. They found my queer books and my sketches from Riley.

I'd been so freaking careful. I'd yearned, so many times, to write a love letter, to vent some of my thoughts into a journal, but I hadn't. And I was right to be paranoid. I learned long ago that privacy means nothing to parents who feel I belong to them. They take the door off my bedroom. My mom cries a lot, my dad yells and threatens. Every word cuts, and I am bleeding. I feel dead inside, my face schooled to stone, but tears still stream down my cheeks.

They already had access to my email account, but they comb through it, looking for more evidence. They analyze email conversations I had with Hannah, asking what every-thing means. They change my email password and ban me from the computer altogether. My dad locks my bike in the shed. I'm not allowed to go to the library anymore. They discuss burning my library books but decide to return them to avoid the fines. My secret stolen book they throw onto the grill and light on fire.

And then they start the campaign for my soul. I'm awakened earlier than the rest of the family for extra devotional time. I'm taken to church for counseling sessions with the pastor. I'm assigned endless extra Bible assignments. I write meaningless papers, the words flowing from my fingers into the keyboard while my mom hovers behind me, making sure I stay on task and away from the internet. I regurgitate every bit of rhetoric into essays and respectful replies, and when I can't anymore, I nod numbly and stare at my feet. I hate myself for it, but I hate them more. I just need to survive. I'll do whatever it takes to weather this storm and get to Riley.

Late at night, I lie in bed and think about her. And only then do I let myself weep. I cry tears of sadness, but mostly anger. My fists clenched and my tears hot, hating that I'm here, hating that I'm not legally allowed to leave, hating that no one is here to help me. Then in the morning, I dry my tears and get back to work. Flattering, bowing, pretending. The sooner my parents believe I'm obedient, the sooner they'll grow smug. And smugness leads to lenience.

On Sunday I see Riley from afar, but my mom is right next to me the whole time and I'm forbidden to speak to her. I wish that she would turn and we could share a look, a sign, but she doesn't. My mom signs me up for nursery duty and Riley leaves with her mom as soon as the service is over. Still, that glimpse keeps me going. I see Hannah in the hallway and try to say hi, but she ignores me. I know she sees me because she steps a little quicker, hurrying away from me. I don't know what I expected, but her coldness still stings. Like our years of friendship mean absolutely nothing. Like I'm some kind of disease she plans to keep her distance from.

My parents try to keep me busy, keep me out of what

they deem "trouble," so they sign me up for all kinds of volunteer work. I wash dishes in the church kitchen after fellowship hour, I jiggle babies on my hip in the nursery as the sermon blares over the tinny speakers, I fold church bulletins in the office for hours on Fridays. I play the part. I bide my time. And in my thoughts—the part of me that is still free—I plan.

"You about ready to go?" Mom peeks her head in the church nursery.

"Yeah, I'll take the diaper garbage to the dumpster and meet you by the van."

"Alright, don't dawdle!" Mom says, and turns to leave. I roll my eyes, knowing she'll stop to talk to five more people before she gets to the front door.

Hardly anyone talks to me anymore. I guess word has gotten around. The wet tang of the soiled diapers tickles my noise as I heft the garbage bag out, lug it down the hallway and out the back of the church. As I struggle to slide open the rusty door to the dumpster, I see white sneakers peeking out from the recycling receptacle. I'd know those shoes anywhere.

"Hannah?"

"Hey, Valerie." She steps out. She looks older. Tired.

"Were you waiting for me?"

"No, of course not," she says quickly.

"You were just hanging out . . . by the dumpster?"

"Maybe? I don't know." She pulls the dumpster door open for me, and I toss the garbage inside.

"I thought you were avoiding me," I say.

"I mean, I've been *really busy* Valerie. Not everything is about you."

"Oh, okay. Um, how is everything? How is the wedding planning?"

"It's great," she says flatly.

"You sound super excited."

"I know you are being sarcastic, but I am. It's going to be amazing."

"Okay, great! I just want you to be happy, Hannah."

"I *am*, Valerie."

"So, what. Is that it? My mom is waiting for me at the car, so—"

"I just don't get it, Valerie."

"Get what?"

"I *knew* it. I *saw* you and Riley touch hands in the nursery that day, and I *knew* something was going on. I mean, I tried to tell myself you were just close friends, but now that I've heard about you two . . . you know . . . you just can't *do* that, Valerie. We all have those thoughts and temptations and we just don't get to *do. That.*" Hannah's fists are clenched and her eyes are flashing. She's so angry.

"Hannah, you've said that before. That everyone has those feelings, but you know what? They *don't*! Some people really are straight! If you have those feelings, you have them, and maybe you could find a way to . . . be okay with them."

"How *dare* you," she says. "I am *not* like you."

"I'm not saying you are. But *if* you have those feelings, then—"

"Hate the sin, love the sinner," she says fiercely.

"Hannah, don't do this."

"*Hate the sin love the sinner,*" she repeats. "I can still love you as a friend, but I have to be clear about the sin in your life, Valerie. You need to repent and—"

"Hannah, that's such *bullshit!*" I think about Mira and what she said about love and control. "You, and everyone here"

—I gesture toward the church building—"you think that love means loving like God loves. That he made all the rules and then we break them and he kills his son for us and now we have to spend our lives serving him, but that's *fucked up*, Hannah. That's not love, that's control! It's abuse! So if *that's* the way that you are still willing to 'love' me? No thanks. Seriously, I'm done with being told I'm being *loved* when it feels an awful lot like hate."

"Well then," Hannah says, "if that's the way you feel, I guess we're done here."

"Okay." I shrug sadly.

"Okay?"

"Yeah, okay. Look, I've loved being friends with you. But I have to make friends with *myself*. And I can't keep . . ." I look up. Blink back the tears. "I can't keep inviting this hurt." We stare at the dirty concrete between us.

"I guess I'll see you around, Hannah. I hope you're happy."

"Oh I *am*," she says firmly. "Bye, Valerie."

"Please let me send Valerie over, she'd love to help you out. It's no trouble at all! You put her to work. She needs to be kept out of trouble."

I grimace as I rinse the soapy dishes. What fresh hell awaits me now? Water splashes up the edge of a bowl and soaks my shirt, but I don't care. I don't care about much at all these days.

"Valerie," my mom says, ending the call on her phone, "go help Mrs. Batra with some yard work when you finish those dishes." I nod stiffly. "Some good deeds will do you good. As the Bible says in James, 'Pure religion and undefiled before the Father is this!'"

"'To visit the fatherless and widows in their affliction, and to keep himself unspotted from the world.'" I complete the verse robotically.

"So you *do* know your Bible. Because you certainly have not been acting like it, young lady. Not in the least. You know I'm exhausted, working so hard to keep you out of trouble. Finish up and get over there."

Numbly, I place the last dish in the drying rack and head to the closet to put on my shoes and coat.

I sulk across the street. It's December now, and the wind is unkind. Trash cans line the street, but Mrs. Batra's are still next to her house. I climb the concrete steps to the front door and knock. I knock again and am about to head home when the door swings open.

"Oh Valerie, dear, thank you for coming."

"Sure thing, Mrs. Batra. Mom said I could do some yard work for you?"

"Yes, dear, yes." She grins up at me through her small round spectacles. "I could really use some help picking up the yard, if you don't mind. I'm having trouble getting around these days, and my son is away on business."

I spend two hours filling waste bins with sticks. As I'm lugging them to the curb, Mrs. Batra comes out wrapped in a shawl. "Valerie, dear, thank you so much for your time—here's something for your trouble." She places a crisp twenty-dollar bill in my hand.

"Oh, you don't need to—"

"Nonsense, dear, I have more money than I can shake a stick at. Please. Make an old lady happy."

"Okay, thank you."

"You know, I could really use a dependable hand around

here, if you have the time. I know you kids are so busy with extracurriculars these days."

"I'm not busy!" I say. "I could probably help you out."

"Oh lovely. Why don't you come over after school when you have time. Just odds and ends. My son usually stops by to check on me, but he's away on business for a few months. I'm happy to pay you."

"Oh you don't have to."

"Of course I'm going to pay you. You just come over after school tomorrow and I'll put you to work."

As I head back across the street, I glance at our front door. It's closed. I scan the windows. No one is watching. I tuck the twenty-dollar bill into my pocket. I'm sure I'm supposed to give the money to my parents. First tithe from it to the church, and then let my parents use it for my keep. But I don't want to. These people have betrayed me in every way. They have poured distrust into me and my anger has distilled it, turned it into a rebellion all my own. I'm keeping the money. And if Mrs. Batra is to be believed, there might be more. Over that grain of a thought forms the pearl of an idea. I can make money. I can save up. I can prepare to leave.

The rest of the afternoon, I wrack my brain for where to hide the money. My parents haven't ransacked my room since that first night, but I know from experience that losing trust causes them to be extra cautious. I should anticipate them going through my stuff every week or so. I should look for a hiding place outside of my room.

Before bed, as I'm writing another punishment essay, mindlessly typing rhetoric about the "sanctity of marriage" into a document, my mom leaves the room to talk to my dad. I'm alone. I stand quickly and move to the bookshelf. It's crammed full of books. Biblical lexicons on Hebrew and Greek, books from

Christian presses on parenting, discipline, apologetics, creation, godly character. And at the bottom of the shelf, an old set of encyclopedias. Most of my knowledge of the world comes from these vintage encyclopedias. Their smell reminds me of summer days of sheer boredom, begging my parents for knowledge but not being allowed to use the internet or go to a museum because of "dangerous liberal philosophies." They'd point me to the encyclopedias, where I'd read dated summaries of subjects that I was sure had far more to them than the musty books offered.

I reach for the one marked WXYZ, hesitate, and then take the one to the left marked U–V. It's a bit thinner. I'm taking a chance here, but fewer letters to a volume seems safer. I can't remember the last time I saw anyone open one of these. It should be safe for a while. And a simple bill, unaccompanied by any incriminating note, could have found its way there ages ago. I could easily deny all knowledge. Quickly, I slip the bill between the pages, tight up against the spine. I slide it back into its spot, and then notice the dust. My fingers have wiped the dust from the volume I removed, highlighting the fact that this book alone has been touched recently. Yanking my shirt sleeve over my wrist, I hurriedly dust the entire set, return to my seat, and resume typing.

twenty-seven

. . .

"Valerie, come help with dinner!" my mom yells as I enter the house.

"Can I take a shower first?" I call back. I'm dirty from hauling the musty contents of Mrs. Batra's attic to the curb for Goodwill to pick up in the morning.

"Wash your hands and help me first!" I head toward the bathroom but pause in the hallway and look around. I glance up the stairs. When I'm satisfied that no one is around, I duck into the office. Quickly, I pull the encyclopedia from the shelf, slip the two twenties I earned today into the pages, and slide the book back on the shelf. I've been helping Mrs. Batra after school every day for a few weeks now, and the money is adding up. My anxiety about it being found is also increasing, but it brings me comfort knowing it's there. My own silent little nest egg. My quiet act of rebellion.

After washing my hands, I head to the kitchen. I'm surprised to see my mom dressed up in one of her church outfits, a flower-patterned dress with a white lace collar. It looks like it's from a different century, but many of the outfits of families in our circles do. I remember Jamie calling my outfit "vintage." Huh. That's one way of putting it. I guess it might be fun to wear vintage clothes if you *choose* to wear them. I've never had the luxury of choosing my clothing for myself.

"Going somewhere?" I ask.

"Yes, just a meeting," Mom answers distractedly. She's got an apron on over her dress, and she's tossing some day-old rice in the wok.

"Meeting who?"

"Just some church friends."

"Like, *who*?" I know I'm pushing too hard, but it's so unusual for me not to know where they are going. My dad goes places all the time—work, lunch with friends, fishing with friends, men's retreats—but my mom hardly goes anywhere. Church, prayer meetings, and the grocery store.

"Just the Pattersons. Pass me the salt, will you?"

"What's the meeting about?"

"Valerie, let it go," my mom huffs, taking off her apron. "Fried rice for dinner. Your father changed the password for the wi-fi, so don't even try. Straight to bed after you do dishes and have your evening devotional. I'll expect a full report on your activity from David." Oh great, my traitorous brother is spying on me. That's totally normal and not at all weird.

"What?" my mom challenges me.

Did I say that out loud? No, but I forgot about my face—it must have betrayed my thoughts. Replacing my mask with care, I reply, "Nothing. Thank you for dinner."

"Hmm." Mom snorts as she heads to the front door to don her shoes and coat. "We've got to go or we'll be late!" she calls from the door.

I hear my dad head downstairs. I catch a glimpse of him through the kitchen doorway, clean-shaven and freshly showered. They gather their things and head out the door. A minute later, I hear the car start and roll out of the driveway.

David breezes into the kitchen as soon as they're gone. Things have been tense between us since the incident. To be honest, I'm pretty angry at him for everything I've been put through. I guess in a way he's a victim of our upbringing too, but I'm not ready to excuse him.

He heads straight for the stove and dishes himself up a bowl of fried rice, and then dishes up my bowl too. Grabbing the sriracha from the fridge, he squirts it in a crosshatch pattern over the top. I haven't been alone with him since he ratted me out, and just looking at his stupid fucking face, I can feel my simmering rage come to a full boil.

"You want some?" He holds it out to me and I just glare. "Listen, Valerie. I know you aren't happy with how things went down."

"*Happy?*" I fume. "Do you know the hell I've been living in? What your tattling has put me through?!"

"I was just doing what was right," he says defensively. "No need to get all pissy about it."

"*Pissy?!*"

"Hey, I have to report everything about tonight, so just stop. I'm sorry things turned out like this. I hope you can get the help you need and get back on the path."

"What path?"

"The path, you know. Just repent and God will forgive you."

"There's *nothing to forgive!*" My voice is shaking, but I am not backing down. "You've questioned so little, David. You haven't had to question things because all of *this*"—I gesture wildly around—"was set up for *you!*"

"Valerie, calm down."

"You've been told you are superior."

"Not superior. Separate but equal."

"Separate but equal, my *ass!*" I nearly scream. "You've been told you are the head of the family, the head of the church, the mouthpiece of God Almighty. Why would you doubt it? Why would you ever think of someone other than yourself for one second."

"I'm going to do you a favor and leave now," he says. I rub my face, knowing I've messed up. Knowing he could easily repeat all this to my parents.

He grabs his bowl and heads toward the stairs. "Just so you know, Valerie, I have questioned things. And I'm still processing them. I don't know. I just wish . . ." Without finishing, he heads up the stairs to his room and slams his door. I wish I could slam my door, but I can't because my parents took it off the fucking hinges.

I grab my bowl of rice and sit at the table by myself. I am so alone. I cannot believe I'm surrounded by such unending *madness*, and I'm the only one who seems to have a problem with it. Well, the only one except for Riley.

Riley. I miss her so much. I squeeze my eyes shut against the tears. I miss her warm gaze. I miss her beautiful smile. I miss the way I actually feel seen and heard around her. I wonder what she's doing right now. I wonder what my parents are doing right now. It's so unusual for them to go somewhere together and be so vague about it. Usually they announce it proudly: they're "doing the Lord's work" somewhere, picketing an abortion clinic, or going to a prayer meeting where they meet to gossip and shake their heads and feel quietly superior.

"David?" I yell toward the stairs, "do you know why Mom and Dad are meeting with the Pattersons?" No answer. Gossiping about me, no doubt. Maybe asking them how they raised a daughter as perfect as Hannah. Perhaps a bit more complaining about how I don't make enough of an effort to be friendly to Andrew.

I finish my rice and do the dishes. I glance at the floor. I'm supposed to sweep it, but it looks clean enough. I stomp up the stairs past David's closed door to my room.

I should be having an evening devotional, but I most definitely do not feel like it. I'm so bored and so, so lonely. I haven't been allowed back to the library, and this is the longest I've gone without a new book to read. Staring at my bookshelf, I glare at the awful books that I'm allowed. Missionary biographies glorifying white Christians who "save" people who had the poor sense to be born not white and not Christian. G.A. Henty books full of racist slurs and the glorification of British imperialism. I've heard our pastor praise these Henty books frequently, saying they "teach boys to be men." What a load of crock.

Sighing, I pull an Elsie Dinsmore book off the shelf, but I throw it to the floor in disgust after a few pages. The idealized South, the doting racist depiction of her mammy, the child abuse she goes through, the grooming by her father's friend whom she eventually marries. It's hard to stomach. These books are so awful and dated, and most of the world has moved on from them, but conservatives get them reprinted, praise them, stock their shelves with them. Why are these books considered canon in our circle? Do parents really want their kids to grow up racist pedophiles? Do parents truly believe that prejudice is something to be preserved and defended? I fall back on my bed, staring at the ceiling. I guess so. I guess none of this happens by accident. The leaders of this whole thing truly believe this shit.

I've never loved these books, but I read them for lack of anything else to read. I only realized how racist and awful they are once I started reading more widely, sneaking books from the library, googling the titles of conservative canon in secret, and reading articles unpacking how truly problematic they are. Once I started noticing, it was impossible to stop. And now I'm here. A teenager in a room without a door, counting the days until I can escape.

Eventually, I brush my teeth and turn out my light. I hear my parents return home strangely late, whispering in the foyer, heading to bed, and whispering more. I wonder what it's all about as I drift off to sleep.

In the morning, when I arrive at the table for morning devotional, its just Mom and Dad sitting there.

"Where's David?"

"Have a seat, Valerie," my dad says, a bit grimly.

"Where's David?" I ask again.

"Sit down, Valerie!" My mom is smiling and my dad seems somber. What the hell is going on here?

I sit down, placing my Bible in front of me on the table.

My mom begins, "We had dinner with the—"

"Sarah, let me tell her," my dad interrupts. He gives her a look of annoyance, and my mom lowers her head.

"I'm sorry, Bill," she apologizes. I hate it here.

"We met with the Pattersons last night, and we'd like you to seriously consider . . . to pray about . . ." I stare at the grooves on the worn wooden table as Dad goes on. "That is . . ." Why is it taking him so long to spit it out? "Andrew Patterson . . . would like to court you."

"*What?*" I look up in shock. I can't believe what I'm hearing.

"He asked his parents to discuss the possibility of a

courtship. Of our families getting to know each other better with the intention of you two getting married."

"*What?*" It seems to be the only thing I can say. Andrew is a strange young man who occasionally waves at me and says hi. We are acquainted only as a side note to my friendship with Hannah. We're basically children.

"Valerie, stop being dramatic," my mom chides. "Look at your father when he's speaking to you."

"Your mother and I feel that the Pattersons and our family are a great fit. You and Hannah have been friends for years, and we share a lot of the same values. It's incredibly important for your mother and I to get along with the parents of your future husband, and we do feel like we have a good rapport with the Pattersons. You are both young, so you have plenty of time to have a lot of children. Andrew does have some concerns about your interests, but we assured him that you will not be attending college or engaging in any worldly pursuits. That you understand your place in the world and will make a dutiful wife and mother."

"No," I say softly. I feel like my skin is sizzling.

"Excuse me? What did you say?" my mother challenges me.

"No," I say again, louder this time.

"Valerie, lower your voice," Dad says.

"*No*," I yell. "*No, no, no, no, NO!*" I stand from my seat, screaming now.

"Valerie. You will control yourself. Take a seat, child!"

Remaining standing, I take a deep breath. I can't see through the tears quivering in my vision. I am shaking with rage.

"We know you've been tempted by sinful thoughts and actions, but it's time to get back on track. To follow God's plan for you. You are just about done with your education, and we really believe that this is for the best."

"No," I whisper.

"Why not?"

"I don't like him."

"So you like him as a friend, but not as more yet?"

"I don't like him at all. As anything. *Ever.*"

"Why don't you take some time to pray about it."

"I *don't* . . ." I shout, then lower my voice. Swallow through the pain in my throat. I whisper tremulously, "I don't need to pray about it. I don't want to marry Andrew Patterson."

"Valerie, sit down," my mother orders.

"I will *never* marry Andrew Patterson."

"You will speak to us respectfully." My father is red with anger.

"*Respectfully?*" I shriek. "You treat me with nothing but *disrespect—*"

"You are the *child.* God has given us authority over you."

"*No!*" I turn and head toward the door.

"If you leave this house, you are never coming back!" my father bellows.

"Maybe I don't want to!" I keep moving toward the door.

"*Valerie!*" My mom's voice shakes. I hear a quality in it I've never heard before. Fear.

"Go to your room," she commands quietly.

With great effort, I turn from the door and run up the stairs to my room. I go to slam the door, but I remember once again that there is no door to slam. Screaming in frustration, I throw myself into my closet and pull the accordion door shut. And there, in the dark, without a single friendly book to comfort me, I cry.

twenty-eight

· · ·

"And did you get anything special for Christmas?" Mrs. Batra hands me a crystal glass. Balancing on a step ladder, I carefully add it to the top shelf of her cabinet with the others.

"Just books," I answer. I got books about being a godly wife and mother, while David got a laptop. But what's a little more bitterness on top of the bitter melon that is my life?

"Alright, that's the last one. Come into the kitchen for tea before you head home."

"Oh, that's okay."

"Nonsense, have some tea and a cookie before you go." I glance at the microwave clock. It's only four thirty. My mom isn't expecting me home until six.

"Mrs. Batra, I need to run to the library."

"Oh, all right dear."

"Would you mind if I go out the back? It's a straight shot to the library through the woods."

"Of course. Here's your money, and take a cookie with you."

Accepting the bills and a shortbread cookie, I grab my coat and shoes from their place by the front door, and head to the rear sliding door.

"Thanks, Mrs. Batra!"

"No, thank you, dear!"

Slipping out the back door into the crisp winter air, I walk briskly down the hill from her house, and head into the woods. There's a narrow trail that leads to the field behind the library. If I hurry, hopefully I can get there and back home before anyone misses me. A cold breeze winds through the naked trees, their soft and decaying leaves cushioning my steps. I had planned to leave, but I hadn't exactly gotten to the planning part. I thought I had plenty of time, but this unexpected proposal has made things more urgent.

I can't marry Andrew. I won't. I don't think my parents could force me to marry him, but I'm not sure. Thinking through the families in our circle, I can't think of anyone besides Mira who hasn't fallen in line. Who hasn't done what was expected of them. There are stories whispered in church hallways, shared as a gossipy request in a prayer meeting for a child who "fell away," but the details are kept quiet. I'm left guessing about who left and why and how. The wound left by their leaving is painted over, their prior existence quieted. Erased.

I've saved a few hundred dollars from working for Mrs. Batra, tucked in the forgotten encyclopedia. It's not a lot, but it's something. I just need to get in contact with Riley and make a plan. Except for a glimpse at church, I haven't seen or spoken a word to her in over a month. I hope she hasn't forgotten me. She wouldn't. Shaking my head to dislodge my fears, I push on down the path, sniffing against the tears threatening to gather.

I come out of the woods in the rear library parking lot and head inside, pushing straight to the computers at the back.

Even though I don't have my library card with me, I have the card number memorized, and that's all I need to log in to the computer and navigate to my email. But when I try to log in, I'm rejected. Of course, my parents changed the password. Raking my hands through my hair in frustration, I head back to the email login and create a new email account. I've got to hurry. I need to get home before anyone realizes I'm not at Mrs. Batra's. Reaching desperately through my mind, I recall Riley's email address, and I write.

Riley,

It's me. I have to leave. My parents want me to marry Andrew Patterson. I have some money saved and I'm ready to leave. I'll check this email one week from now. I love you.

Your,

Valerie.

I send it quickly, without reading it over, and log out of the computer. As much as I wish I could send a message to Mira, I'm trembling with worry that my parents are going to find me out.

It's growing dark outside, the light changing to a blue-gray. I see storm clouds gathering through the library's wall of windows. I rush through a book stack, skimming my fingers longingly across the book spines, and head out. The wind blows colder and harsher as I hurry, shivering, back through the woods. I jog to make up time, my long skirt pulling against my ankles, the sharp air burning my lungs and throat. I cut through Mrs. Batra's backyard, where I take a minute to calm my breaths and straighten my clothes and smooth my hair. Cold raindrops begin to fall as I cross the street and return home.

"I'm back," I call joylessly as I open the front door. I'd rather not say anything, but I need my time of return noted as soon as possible.

"Hey, honey, pull the door tight. It's cold out there," my mom calls from the kitchen.

"Okay, Mom." Shutting and bolting the door, I hang my coat in the closet. The bills from Mrs. Batra are heavy in my pocket, but I've got to make myself useful to divert suspicion. I head straight to the kitchen. It's warm and bright, the good smells of onions and meat hanging thick in the air.

"Can I help with dinner?"

"Set the table and get out any chili toppings you want," Mom says over her shoulder, stirring a pot on the stove.

"Okay." I put sour cream, shredded cheddar, and hot sauce on the table, along with soup spoons. Gathering bowls from the cabinet, I add a scoop of rice into each one, and Mom tops the rice with a ladleful of fragrant chili.

"I'm sorry I couldn't help you make dinner," I say as I carry the bowls to the table.

"Oh, no problem, you were helping Mrs. Batra. It's good of you to help her so much."

I feel guilty for a moment, knowing that I'm getting paid and have been hiding the cash, but I push away the thought. Guilt, I can live with. A life here with my parents, or—I shudder—with Andrew Patterson, I cannot.

"Call your father and brother, would you?" Mom asks as she dices white onions, swiping the perfectly minced pieces off the cleaver into a bowl.

I head to the bottom of the stairs and call out, "Dad, David, dinner's ready!"

David comes sliding into the kitchen on his socked feet a minute later, Dad lumbering heavily down the stairs soon after. We sit around the table, Dad prays, and we dig in. It feels cozy and familiar in a way that home sometimes feels, despite all the anger and strife.

Tears grow in my eyes as I look around at my family. My dad with his glasses perched on his balding head, resting on tufts of graying hair. David eating with gusto, in a race with himself to finish his first bowl of chili and dish up his second. My mom making sure everyone has what they need before herself, her hair having grown grayer in the last month. Is that my doing? Am I wrong for not trying harder to fit in here? For not believing? For not belonging?

I hear myself sniff just as Mom says, "Are you alright, Valerie?"

Brushing hastily at my eyes, I laugh. "Oh, just the onions."

"Aiya, you always were so sensitive to onions," Mom says, pushing them away from me.

As we eat, the conversation is light and easy for a change. David talks about the program he's writing on his computer. Dad asks questions and offers solutions. Mom is warm and kind tonight, and again I feel that pinch of guilt. I wish I could belong. And if things were always like they are right now, I think I would. I could be a part of this kind, chili-night family of friendly words and gentle smiles. I love my parents and my brother. Sometimes I even like them.

But this is only a piece of them. A bright, glowing corner. The rest of them is cold and piercing. A set of spikes in the shape of a cross. We've been taught that Christ is to be all. That Jesus Christ is to consume us, be every aspect of us; that we are to seek and burn and refine every speck of sin and discontent. The parts of my family that I love, that I feel closest to—most warmly received and tenderly nurtured by—are the non-Jesus parts. And if they strive to make Christ the whole, is there any love left, any space left, for me?

twenty-nine

. . .

The week passes colorlessly, each day the same gray blur. I get so bored that I read a few chapters of the Godly Marriage books I was given for Christmas. They read like something from the wrong century. I'm advised to rise before my husband to make myself presentable and prepare his breakfast. I'm supposed to do my evening hygiene after he's gone to bed to keep the "mystery" alive. I'm told to agree and submit and support, with no questioning of whether the husband is agreeable or correct or supportive. It sounds like a nightmare. Even more of a nightmare than my current reality.

I work for Mrs. Batra every chance I get. She has a lifetime of stuff in every room of her house, and together we organize and stack. I carry some boxes upstairs and others down. I haul magazines to the recycling bin and take the bin to the curb for collection. We assemble old lamps, books, and dishes in the garage for the next time the Goodwill truck makes its rounds. I suspect she could really do most of this herself, but she seems to like the company. Before she sends me home, she always has a cup of chai for me, strong and sweet, and she presses bills into my hand when I leave. I've never worked before, and I have no idea if she's paying me a fair rate, but I suspect it might be more than an inexperienced teenager like me deserves. I hear Dad grumbling about how much time I spend out of the house, but Mom assures him I'm doing good deeds, and it's keeping me out of trouble.

It's Friday again, and I'm carrying some old sports equipment from Mrs. Batra's basement to her garage. She doesn't seem like someone who plays golf, but I don't want to pry. I sense that these belonged to someone she lost somehow, and I move things quietly and respectfully.

"Mrs. Batra, do you mind if I take off early today? I need to stop by the library on the way home again."

"Sure, dear, not a problem. Come have some tea before you go?"

I glance at the clock. It's only four; I can still make it to the library and home in time. "Sure, that would be great, thank you!"

"Oh, you have the nicest manners. Your parents must be so proud of you." If only she knew. Funny thing is, my parents tell me they are proud of me all the time. They say they love me and support me, that they are proud of me and proud to be my parents, but it never feels real amid the constant tide of correction and shaming and belittling. I guess actions really do speak louder than words.

"Here we are." Mrs. Batra sets two steaming cups on the table. The tea swirls, rich and creamy in the clear glass, and I take a small sip. Delicious.

"How's school going? Here, take a cookie."

"Oh, it's good. I'm just about graduated."

"And what are your plans? Are you applying to colleges?"

"I'm not sure. I'd like to. But I'm not sure."

"I wasn't sure what I wanted to do with my life when I was your age either. What do your parents think you should study?"

"Oh um, I . . ." It's so hard to explain to people. I don't have much contact with people outside our close circle—our *cult* circle, I correct myself—but when I do, I recognize how weird my life sounds. It's not light conversation to say, "Oh, my parents believe women shouldn't go to college or have jobs. They don't want me to have any interests other than being a wife and mother." As normal as our group pretends this is, I can just feel that it's not right.

"Oh, they think I should take a gap year. Decide what I really want to do." I heard someone say something about a gap year once—that sounds like a normal person thing to do.

"What a great idea. You are lucky to have such supportive parents who want you to find your true passion." Hah. Yeah. So lucky.

"Thanks for the tea! I'm going to head out, if that's okay. I'll see you tomorrow?"

"Of course, dear, here's something for your trouble." She tucks some bills into my hand. "And wear something warm tomorrow. We'll be in the garage for a bit and it's cold in there."

"Will do, thanks!"

I slip out the back door and retrace my steps through the woods to the library. It's a bit warmer today, the edge of the January chill dulled by the clear sunlight in a cloudless sky. I lift my face to the hint of warmth, feeling the dappled light blinking through the bare branches as I walk on.

As I enter the library and head past the circulation desk, I'm startled to see the librarian who saved me that day, months ago, when I stole that queer book with the pretty pink cover. He smiles and nods at me, and I find myself cautiously smiling back, wondering if he has any more recommendations for queer books with discreet covers. He's wearing a sweater-vest, working through a stack of books piled on the counter. I think he'd be friendly if I talked to him more, but I am a walking bundle of nerves and suspicion.

I walk through the silent stacks, the smell of ink and paper light and lovely. It's dead silent in the back of the library, the kind of pin-drop peace that I long for every day. My house gets quiet, of course, but it's a bad quiet. An aggressive, scary silence that makes my heart beat fast and my head ache with tension. I breathe deeply and try to calm my racing heart. Did Riley get my message? Has she been denied access to her email like me? Has she responded? Are we still in this together, or am I truly, devastatingly, alone?

I slide into the chair and log in. I have an email. From Riley.

Valerie! I've got you. I'm making good money at the coffee shop, and they kept me on after the holiday rush. I reached out to Mira, and we are renting a room from her grandparents! It's a walk-out basement in Burke, in a townhouse close to the lake. It'll be tight, but it's all ours next month. I'll borrow Mom's car and come get you on the first of February, 7 a.m. I love you.

Riley.

I exhale a shaky breath. She's okay. She still wants me. We are going to be okay. I reach toward the keyboard, my hands trembling.

Riley,
I'll be ready. I love you.
Your,

Val

My mind is spinning with questions and possibilities, but I'll sit with them later. If Riley got a job, surely I can get one. I have to pack my things, get ready to leave. I've got to get back home. If our plan is discovered, I truly don't know what I'll do. My parents have discussed moving somewhere more remote before. Many of the families in our church live in the middle of nowhere, trying to keep their children isolated so they remain "untainted by the world's influence." In reality, these families spank and discipline—I suppose it might really be called abuse —their children so harshly that living in a rural area is a safety net against prying neighbors and Child Protective Services. If Mom and Dad find out, they won't let me leave the house. They'll keep me locked up until we move, or send me to stay with another family or at an Institute training center . . . I shudder at the possibilities. I've got to play by their rules for the next two weeks. I've got to be cautious and convincing. And when Riley comes, I'll be ready.

"Knock knock!" Mom says at the entrance to my room in lieu of knocking.

I'm sitting on the floor, leaning against my bed, my Bible open on my lap. I'm fully committed to operation be-the-perfect-daughter for the next two weeks. They can suspect nothing. I even have my prayer journal open next to me and am writing down verses and notes. My mom loves to snoop in my prayer journal, so this is a good way to play at being devout. I'm reading Psalms, and I especially like the verse "When my father and my mother forsake me, then the Lord will take me up."

It's hard to say how or what I feel about God and the Bible these days. As much as I want to trash the whole thing, it's hard to discard a lifetime of belief, to rip away something woven so tightly through my being. At the moment, I'm okay with questioning, with not knowing. It's better to not be sure than to be sure of something hateful, right?

"Ah, doing your devotional. I love to see it." Mom sits next to me on the floor. I stiffen. It's not unusual for her or Dad to come in to chat, but it's usually about something that I've done wrong, how I should improve my behavior. And I'm not in the mood to chat—spoiler: I rarely am—but I have to pretend to be happy anyhow, or else I'll have my attitude questioned. Many a friendly parental bedroom chat has ended in discipline because I haven't contained my feelings well enough.

"Yup! Second one today!" I fake cheerfully. It feels easier somehow, knowing there's an end in sight.

"I'm so glad to see you taking your Bible study more seriously." Mom tucks my hair behind my ear. She's warm and kind tonight, and I feel myself soften.

"You know, Valerie, when I left Taiwan with your ah-ma and ah-gong, we lived in such darkness. I was always home by myself while they worked at the restaurant, the TV was always on, we never talked to each other. We were all so lost. They are still lost, they haven't come to Christ. What I'm trying to say is —I don't know where I'd be without God. He gave my life purpose. Meaning. And if I can pass that on to you, that will be the greatest gift I could give you."

I think about my mom as a teenager in a dingy apartment, lit by the glow of an American sitcom. I wonder if American Christianity offered her structure. Safety. I wonder if she somehow believed that the surest way to the American dream was through the American God.

"Mom, do you . . ." I pause. I'm so close to asking if she'll still love me if I'm queer. But I mean love in the simple sense. Love that exists not as a rationalization for punishment, but a blooming feeling of acceptance and belonging. But I don't know how to explain this to her. And I'm afraid to ask, because I'm scared the answer is no.

"I know you've had a rough time lately, but I'm so proud of you for pulling yourself together and turning to God and the Word. Your dad and I are seeing a change in you, and we are sensing that God has great things planned for you."

"Thanks, Mom." I smile slightly at her. I don't love what she's saying, but somehow being told I'm doing good and being good has a firm tug on my heart. I despise that tug—I wish it wasn't there, that I didn't care what they thought or said. Maybe it's just part of being human, being a kid. I want her to love me so much. I want her to see me the way I am, the real me, and still love me and be proud of me. I've dreamed of it so much, it sounds so simple. Surely they can love their own kid? Surely that isn't too much to ask? But everything they've said and done shows me how impossible that dream is, and it hurts so much.

"We told the Pattersons *maybe* for now." I stiffen as she continues to stroke my hair. "We know you have strong feelings about it, but your father and I think you should at least be polite and consider the proposal. And if Andrew isn't the right one for you, there are other young men in the church who may be interested. Your father and I are here to help guide you to the marriage God has in store for you, and to start your new life as a godly wife and mother."

My skin crawls with the absolute ick of it all, but I squeeze the feelings tight and instruct my face to neutrality.

"Thanks for giving me some time to think it over," I say.

"And *pray* it over." Mom looks at me meaningfully. She taps my Bible. "See what God has to say about it." I'm so sick of being told that my parents' opinions are the will of God.

"I will, Mom."

She gets up and heads to the doorway, pausing to turn and say, "And don't take too long. Your most fruitful childbearing years are now!"

I bite the inside of my lip until I taste blood, willing myself to keep quiet while Mom leaves. Swiping at the tears brimming in my eyes, I snap my Bible closed and push it under my bed. I'm tired. So deeply weary of examining myself and magnifying and analyzing and criticizing every little piece of me.

I just want to feel my feelings, and trust that my feelings are okay. I want to let myself feel the way that I feel with Riley. Like I'm an okay person—even a good one. That I'm loved and lovely the way I am, and that it's not a sin to feel happy and to love without reservation. I'm not sure where God and I will end up, but I know that I only want to be friends with God if God is . . . different than I've been taught. If I come back to God after all this and find that God is a kinder, more loving presence than the one I've known, great. And if God is more loving than I've been taught, then I think God would be okay with me needing some time to untangle this. I think God would want me to feel a shred of happiness. That is the *impression* I'm getting from all this prayer and meditation. And for once, I'm going to trust myself and my feelings.

thirty

. . .

It's February first, 6 a.m., and I'm a mess. I'm trying desperately to play it cool, to keep it together just a little longer, but my emotions are a hurricane in my chest. I somehow make it through the family's morning devotional, I choke down a bowl of oatmeal, and now I'm in my room for my own morning devotional time—but I'm quietly gathering a few more things, tucking them into my backpack.

I'm not taking much. I couldn't find a way to pack without drawing attention, and I've waited until now to start. Last night, I removed every bill from the encyclopedia and tucked them inside the pages of my Bible—my best guess as to what would go untouched in my room between last night and today. I didn't take the time to count, but it's quite a bit—bless Mrs. Batra for her generosity.

It's go-time. There's no turning back from this. I have complete faith that Riley will come through—otherwise I'm thoroughly screwed. My backpack is crammed full of necessities: underwear, socks, a few shirts and skirts. I wish I could leave it all behind, every ankle length skirt a visual symbol of my oppression, but I have to wear something.

I slide a beautiful blank journal into my backpack. I've longed to write in it, to get some of these tangled thoughts out onto the clean, crisp pages, but I've known better than to give my parents evidence of how shaky my faith is. My faith is so shaky, I'm not sure it exists at all, and I know there is no space here—has *never* been space—for me to work through it.

I blink back tears. Stupid feelings. My chest hurts. With shaking hands, I grab my backpack and head down the stairs. Dad is putting his shoes on, heading out the door on his way to work. I freeze. I should have waited until he left, but some part of me—a stupid part, maybe—wanted to say this to his face.

"Where are you headed?" Dad asks kindly. I squeeze the rough woven handle of the backpack tightly. Why couldn't he be mean today? Why couldn't he be his normal level of hateful? It would make this so much easier.

"Well," I start, "I'm just about eighteen now."

"I'm running late," he interrupts me. "We can talk later."

"No, we can't." I'm a bit shocked at how strong I sound. Dad seems shocked too.

"What's going on?" Mom comes out of the kitchen, wiping her hands on a towel. "Your father has to get to work, stop bothering him. Let me help you with whatever it is."

"I'm leaving." Saying those words aloud feels like stepping into the sun. I feel the inevitability of what is happening growing, strengthening.

"Excuse me?" Mom asks.

"I really don't have time for this." Dad turns toward the door.

"I'm leaving," I repeat, with even more strength behind the words. "I'm almost eighteen, and I don't want to be here anymore. So I'm leaving."

"You can't just . . . Valerie, this is ridiculous, stop being so dramatic," Dad splutters.

"I'm not ridiculous. I'm not dramatic. But I am leaving."

"Where would you go? Who would possibly want to put up with you?"

"It's none of your concern."

"None of my concern?" Dad raises his voice. "None of my concern?! I raise you, shelter you, feed you, clothe you, and you have the audacity to disrespect me like this?"

"Respect? You have disrespected me every day of my damn life."

"Watch your language! Not in my house."

"I'm leaving your house."

"How *dare* you," Dad bellows as he takes a step toward me, drops his bag, and raises his hand. My heart is racing, adrenaline buzzing through my veins, trembling along my skin, but I stand my ground. Mom steps between us, puts her hands up to stop Dad from advancing.

"Bill," she says in her most soothing voice, but I see her hands are trembling. "I'll handle this," she continues. "Don't worry. Everything is fine."

"No it's not," I assert, but she cuts me a sharp look and I fall silent. I want to argue, to scream and make him *see* me for once, but her eyes beg me to shut up and let her handle him. And as much as I want to have it out right now, I want to leave more. And it will be easier to leave when he's gone.

"We can't let her become a . . . a *whore* who gets away with this kind of sinful, *disgraceful* behavior . . ."

"I'll handle it, you head out. We'll discuss it tonight. I'm sure, with your guidance, we'll get her back on the path." Mom is uncannily calm, carefully diffusing his anger like the dangerous explosive device it is.

Dad gives me a look so ugly and hateful I feel it in my gut, but Mom's words seem to soothe him enough that the red recedes from his face, and he turns to leave.

"We'll discuss this when I get back," he says. He always has to be convinced he's won. But he's not going to win this time. I'm not going to be here.

"Yes, of course, dear, we'll sort it when you get home tonight."

He leaves. We stand in silence as we hear the car door slam. The engine starts and we hear the quiet crunch of the wheels on asphalt as he drives away.

I break the silence. "Mom . . ."

"Valerie, are you sure?" she asks.

This isn't the response I was expecting. I struggle for new words, ones that I hadn't planned. "Yes, I'm sure."

"If you're sure, then go."

"You're okay with me going?"

Mom shushes me with a hand half raised. She glances for a fraction of a second up the stairs, toward David's room. She doesn't want him to hear.

"I know you've been putting on a brave face, but I see how miserable you are." Her voice is trembling. "And I'm afraid of what your father will do. If you are sure, if you have a plan, go. Let me know that you're safe."

I hear the sound of a car slowing to a stop in front of our house and glance through the small window in the door. It's Riley, driving her mom's car. I feel myself smile as I see *her,* my light at the end of this tunnel.

"It's Riley, isn't it?"

"Yeah, Mom. It is."

"Do you need anything? Is that all you packed? Here, take both of your coats." She grabs my coats from the closet, pushes them into my arms, sets my sneakers in front of me, and throws my boots and scarf into a bag.

"Mom . . . I—"

"Not now. You go before I change my mind." She sniffs as she hands me the bag, opens the door, and gives me a gentle push. "Aiya, you're letting the cold in!" she fusses, her nagging so familiar it makes my heart twinge as she slams the door behind me.

I step outside into the frigid February morning, barely noticing the cold as I hurry down the driveway, my arms and heart full of things and feelings. Riley opens the trunk for me, and I toss my stuff in. We are both smiling, but we know not to take our time.

We slide into the car. The doors close and we turn to each other, throwing our arms around each other in the small space, with the engine running noisily and the hot air blowing through the vents, scorching and relentless. We begin to pull apart, but I reach for her again and she reaches for me and we pause, foreheads resting together, hands held, breathing the same air again. Finally.

"God, I missed you," she breathes.

"I missed you."

"Let's go?"

"Let's."

She pulls away from the curb, and I turn to look back. I see Mom peering through the living room window, but she closes the curtain when she sees me looking.

"You have everything you need?" Riley asks.

I reach across the car and rest my hand on her thigh. A sense of peace settles over me like a heavy blanket.

"Yeah, I do."

thirty-one

· · ·

R iley pulls into the parking lot of a shopping center, and as soon as the car is in park, we are embracing. Hugging, kissing, warm breath and soft hair and the magnet pull of our hearts toward each other. I don't know if I'm laughing or crying —probably both—and Riley is kissing away my tears.

"We did it," she breathes.

"We did it. You did it. I don't know how you managed all of this."

"You did plenty yourself. How did they take it?"

"Not well. Dad stormed out. He thinks I'll still be there when he gets home. But Mom . . . well, she told me to go."

"She did?" Riley asks, incredulous.

"Yeah. I'm as shocked as you are. I guess she could see how unhappy I was, and . . . I don't know. I guess she understood a little."

"I'm glad. I'm so glad you did it, and I'm so glad you're here."

We rest our heads together, our breath warm between us.

"How did your mom take things?" I ask.

"Fine. She was planning on me moving out soon anyhow; she said she'd help a bit with community college tuition too. I think she's giving up on me in a good way? Like, I'm gonna make my own decisions and she can't keep controlling me."

"That's great, Riley." I trace my fingertips across her cheekbones, gently unravel a curl. "Is this real? Are we actually doing this?"

"So real, Val. This is the new normal. You and me. Together."

"Mmmm," I hum, breathing in her scent.

"You ready to see our place? It's not fancy, so don't get your hopes up too high."

"I'm so ready. I've been working for the neighbor, so I have a few hundred saved up."

"You keep that for now. I've got the first month taken care of. Between you and me, I think Mira's grandparents would let us stay for free if we needed to, but I insisted we could afford to pay them something."

"Okay. I'm gonna get a job and pitch in, though."

"Of course. Hey, were you able to bring any of your documents? Birth certificates and stuff?"

"Oh. No, my dad keeps them in a safe, I didn't know how to get them."

"Okay. You'll need ID to get a job, so we'll have to work on that, but don't worry. We'll figure it out."

"Okay," I breathe. "Thank you so much."

She rubs her thumb over my chin. "We've got this."

The townhouse is at the end of a row, cozy and sleepy with its burgundy shutters and rounded stoop. Through the gap between the houses, I see the lake glimmering under the gray

February sky. Hannah's grandfather, the elder Mr. Patterson, answers the door, his fluffy white hair mussed, his fisherman's sweater thick and cheerful.

"Well hello there, Riley! And you must be Valerie!" he says warmly as two furry corgis fling themselves at us through the open door. "Aw heck, I should have put them in their crates. Mr. and Mrs. Fluffy Butt, get inside, come on." He wrangles the dogs back inside, and we follow him and shut the door.

"Hi, Mr. Patterson, good to see you again!" Riley gives him a warm hug, and I'm not sure if I'm supposed to hug him too? But he offers me his hand and I shake it. His grip is warm, his palm rough.

"Nice to meet you," I say with a careful smile.

"Is Mira at school?" Riley asks.

"She sure is, but she should be back soon. Come on back to the kitchen. Let me give you the tour, show you to your room, and then you can carry everything else in around the back. I have a key to the back door so you don't have to come in through the front and see us old fogies every time!"

We follow him down a short hallway into the kitchen, greeted by scents of coffee and toast.

"This here is the missus." He gestures to a sweet white-haired lady seated at the table, newspaper spread out before her, her age-spotted hands curled around a mug.

"Forgive me for not getting up, dears. I'm still recovering from a knee replacement," she says warmly, smiling at each of us in turn. "Riley, good to see you again. Nice to meet you, Valerie! Please, sit down and have a cup of something with us, and then you two can get settled in."

"I've got coffee brewed—either of you coffee drinkers?" Mr. Patterson pulls mugs down from a cabinet as we take a seat at the table.

"That's great for me!" Riley says easily.

"Me too," I say, even though I don't know if I like coffee, really—but the last thing I want to do is make a bad first impression. I'm scratching Mr. Fluffy Butt behind the ear and he leans on me, moaning indecently.

"I understand you and my granddaughter Hannah are good friends," Mr. Patterson says cheerfully as he sets two steaming mugs in front of us. The dogs run over to the sliding glass door and whine.

"Oh yeah we have been, but . . ." I feel panic rising in my chest. Surely Riley told them about us. Surely this is a safe place. Mira said they support her, so they must be fine with everything, but panic still squeezes my throat.

"It's okay, dear." Mrs. Patterson reaches over and pats my hand gently with hers, her skin aged and silky-soft.

"I guess I'm just s—" I swallow and look to Riley. She smiles gently in encouragement. "Still processing everything."

"You take all the time you need," Mrs. Patterson says. "Goodness knows Mira is still healing from the things her family and that Institute put her through."

"I just want to apologize." Mr. Patterson sits holding his own mug, leaning forward. "For everything you girls have been through. I'm ashamed of the way my son has treated Mira, and I'm guessing your own parents haven't been much better. You know, I spent my life serving God and the church, but when Mira came to us for help, well, it made me reevaluate things. And I just want you girls to know we are sorry for the hurt that we've previously been a part of, but we are doing our darndest to make up for it now."

I glance at Riley, and there are tears in her eyes.

"Thank you," she says tearfully. I reach out and take her hand, and Mr. and Mrs. Patterson smile at us. Fully knowing that we are holding hands not in prayer, but in love. I feel my own eyes welling up.

"We want you to know that you are safe and loved here," Mrs. Patterson agrees. "Anything we can do to help, you just let us know."

Relief washes over my body. Something inside me loosening. Not completely, a quarter-turn of an over-tight lid. But if this kindness lasts, if this warmth is real, maybe I could eventually trust in that safety and love.

Riley clears her throat. Swipes at her eyes. "Thank you. I don't usually get choked up like this, but I guess . . ." I squeeze her hand. "You know, my mom is okay with me now, she's not rejecting me, so I feel like I have it pretty good, you know? Better than poor Val here."

"It's not a competition!" I chuckle.

"I guess what I'm saying is, it's just nice to have . . . more than crumbs."

"I'm just curious." I pause, doubting whether I should say anything, but wanting desperately to believe in the safety of this space. The Pattersons nod encouragingly. Mrs. Fluffy Butt comes over and licks my hand. "How come you two are so understanding? I mean, you are . . ."

"Old?" Mr. Patterson supplies with a laugh.

"I wasn't trying to—"

"It's quite alright, dear." He runs his hand through his wispy hair. "You know, when Mira came out to us, we knew her so well, trusted so much in her goodness as a person, that I realized the narrative I'd been given by the church did not fit at all. I really felt there was nothing I could do but keep loving and respecting her and grow and change myself to unlearn the harm I'd done. Never too old to grow and change, right, Marjorie?"

"Never." She smiles at him fondly. I take a small sip of my coffee. It's sour, but it warms me. It's beautiful that they loved Mira enough to grow and change, but it stings even more that my own family couldn't love me enough to do the same.

"But enough of this mushy stuff." He slaps his thighs. "Let's get you girls settled in!"

"You are welcome to use anything in the kitchen, and we've cleared a shelf for you to keep your things on." Mrs. Patterson gestures toward the open pantry. "We are puttering around here most days, but don't feel pressured to hang out with us; we know you are busy with work and whatnot."

"Oh, I don't have a job quite yet. There are some things I need to sort out." I glance at Riley, and then toward Mr. and Mrs. Fluffy Butt who are dancing in front of the sliding glass door, whining at something outside.

"Hush!" Mrs. Patterson shushes them. "You know, I've been looking for someone to take them on nice long walks around the lake. The yard isn't cutting it, and they don't understand why I've stopped since my surgery. Would you be interested?"

"Me?! Um, yeah, I'd love to!"

"We'd pay you, of course."

"You could just take it out of our rent? Or whatever works for you, but that would be great. Thank you!"

"Well, that works out perfectly." Mr. Patterson slaps his thighs again and stands. "Let's show you to your new digs." I hear the front door open, and the dogs go nuts.

"That'll be Mira now," Mr. Patterson says. "Come through to the kitchen, Mira! Look at this, the gang's all here!"

Mira appears in the doorway, grinning. "More like the *gays* are all here!"

We all laugh. And it feels so, *so* good.

thirty-two

. . .

The basement is small and bright. It has a twin bed and nothing else, and I've never seen anything so beautiful. When Mr. Patterson hands us each a key, I nearly weep from the beauty of it. Our place. All our own.

I help Riley carry some things around the corner of the townhouse and in through the sliding glass door: a lamp, a small dresser, some boxes. Riley has to return the car to her mom tonight, but the Pattersons have some old bikes on the back patio that they say we are welcome to use, and we are within easy biking distance of a shopping center and the local community college. I unpack my backpack, Riley arranges her things, and pretty soon we're done. It's tiny and cozy, and it's all ours.

We settle into a beautiful rhythm, and I've never been so happy. In the mornings, Riley and I wake up together in our little bed and then go for a walk around the lake. The morning sun glitters off the water, and Riley's smile is just as dazzling. I can't believe I'm here. That this is real. Riley heads to the coffee shop to work most days, and I walk Mr. and Mrs. Fluffy Butt, bike to the local library, read, and slowly begin to write a little bit. Angry rambles at first, scrawled on the backs of receipts and loose papers, and then Riley brings me home a beautiful writing journal and I just keep writing.

I'm trying on honest, genuine emotion like a coat. It's a bit scary, even disorienting to let myself feel my feelings. To simply let them happen and observe them, let them exist without judgment or violence. The voices of my parents in my head are loud and insistent, telling me that I'm bad, I'm sinful, that they alone can provide what I need. But I'm starting to untangle their thoughts from my own. I'm realizing that the biggest bullies in my life are behind me, and I can choose not to accept this counterfeit 'love' ever again.

I call my mom on Riley's phone when I know Dad will be at work, and let her know that I'm okay. She seems happy to hear from me, but even the familiar sound of her running the kitchen sink fills me with anxiety. I ask her about my birth certificate and social security card, and she says she'll work on getting the safe combination from my dad. I leave her my address, and she promises to mail them when she can.

When I get my documents, maybe I'll go to school with Riley. Apply for scholarships and work at a local coffee shop or grocery store or restaurant. Maybe I'll study writing or history or literature. Maybe I'll find something I love to do that doesn't need a degree, something surprising and interesting, and me. I don't know exactly what I'll do, and that alone feels wild and precious. For once, my future is not written for me; I'm not living to fulfill my parents' vision, or God's, but my own. I've read and recited the catechism "I am not my own" my whole life, but now I'm finally free. I belong to myself. I *am* my own.

And Riley and me? We are perfect together. She cooks us ramen and I top the bowls with green onions and soft-boiled eggs. She brings me a different drink every day after work, and I decide that the matcha latte—creamy, earthy, and baby-grass green—is my favorite. I lie in bed reading and she draws my profile, my hands, my shoulders. We walk around the lake, and every time I trip on a tree root and she catches me, I shriek, and she laughs so loud that birds startle in the trees and take off across the lake. We share chocolate and ourselves and frozen kisses on a bench by the reeds. We find a willow tree and kiss under it, our frosty breath rising and swirling under the frigid canopy. Riley makes a list of essential movies, and together we start the long journey of educating me on a lifetime of missed pop culture. We eat dinner with Mira and Mr. and Mrs. Patterson, and when they make jokes with references I don't understand, I laugh politely and then Riley explains them to me later. We take steaming showers together, we spoon in our little bed, we explore all the beautiful shapes and ways we fit together.

It's funny, I've always been told that peace comes through Christ. That leaving or letting go of my faith would lead only to guilt and sadness. But here I am, finding the truest joy I've ever known in all the places I was told not to look. Finding the deepest peace in "sin." Finding the purest belonging in leaving.

———

It's a dark February day, and I'm getting fresh water for Mr. and Mrs. Fluffy Butt when the doorbell rings. The dogs go nuts and I peek through the peephole to see my mom on the doorstep, several grocery bags at her feet. My anxiety spikes at the sight of her. What is she doing here? She'd said she'd mail my papers—was she unable to get them from my dad?

"I've got it!" I call, desperately hoping she's not here to make a scene as I slip outside and close the door on the yapping dogs.

"Hi, Mom." I'm trying to be strong, but my chest is tight and my hands are shaking. I shove them behind me.

"Hi, Valerie." She stares at me for a moment, waiting for me to hug her, and I finally lean in and pat her awkwardly on the back.

"You look good," she says. "Happy."

"Thanks, Mom. I am."

"Are you doing okay? Do you need anything?"

"Just that paperwork I called you about," I say. I wish there was more between us—that we could catch up with loving chatter—but seeing her, I feel the smoking tension of the home I've left behind.

"I've got it in here." She hands me a large envelope. As I open it and peer inside, she explains, "I've got your birth certificate and social security card, as well as your health insurance cards. You are still on our insurance for a few years, so make sure you use it if you need to. Any problems, just call me and I'll take care of it. Also, I graduated you from high school. Your diploma is in there too. I thought that might help you with getting a job, or whatever you plan to do."

"Mom, I . . ." I'm speechless. I didn't expect so much, and I especially didn't expect it to be given so freely. "Thank you. Is Dad okay with this?"

"I'll handle him, don't worry about it. You are so close to eighteen, I convinced him there's not much we can do. I'm sorry things turned out this way."

I'm stunned to hear her say she's sorry, even if she isn't actually apologizing, just expressing regret. "You and Riley are okay? You're taking care of each other?"

"Yeah, Mom."

"Here, I brought you some groceries. Make sure you are eating well. The bok choy needs to be cooked in the next few days. I've got garlic and ginger in here for you to cook it with. And the tofu bucket has winter melon soup in it, made with ham broth, the way you like it. There are clear noodles too. You can soak them and add them when you reheat the soup. It probably needs a little more salt, I know you like things a little saltier."

My eyes tear up at the familiar, gentle nagging in her voice. The good parts of home that I didn't know I missed.

"Thanks, Mom."

"Aiya, it's too cold for you to be out here without a coat, you'll get sick! Here, take it all and go inside. I have to get to prayer meeting."

"Bye, Mom." I gather up the bags, and she turns to head down the steps of the stoop. That was more than I could have hoped for. I'm a bit stunned at how simple and easy it felt.

"Valerie?" She turns back. I freeze.

"Yeah, Mom?"

"We're pra—" She pauses. I know what she's going to say. That they are praying for me. That God is going to convict my heart and bring me back. But she stops herself. And instead, she says, "I love you."

acknowledgments

SENDING this soft, vulnerable story out into the world is scary, but I'm so thankful to the people who have held my hand along the way.

Don, I love you. Mary Helen, thank you for believing in me and this book from the very start. Elishia, thank you for reading the first chapter I wrote and encouraging me to keep writing. Heath, Chelsea and Kelsey, you are the best friends a girl could ask for. Audrey, Evelyn, Abbie and Isabel, your support means the actual world to me. Thank you Jenny Bent for the time you gave me. Thank you to my editor Brenna Bailey-Davies, and my incredible illustrator Michelle Jing Chan for the cover of my dreams.

Thank you to all my ARC readers for your time and enthusiasm.

Thank you to everyone who has emailed or messaged me with your own story, I've never felt so seen and validated.

Thank you to all the Queer authors whose work I've narrated, your books have helped me find myself.

Thank you readers, with all my heart. I hope this story helps heal you the way it's helped heal me.

Made in United States
Troutdale, OR
12/17/2024

26747722R00152